Sole Brethren

☙ *If The Shoe Fits* ❧

Sole Brethren

⇐ *If The Shoe Fits* ⇒

B.A. Summer

First paperback edition January 2023

Book design: Louisa Fitch
Illustration: Alenarbuz

978-1-7396102-0-3 (paperback)
978-1-7396102-1-0 (e-book)

Elfado Island
www.ElfadoIsland.com

*Dedicated to the staff of
Britain's National Health Service.
We owe you everything.*

Contents

Chapter One

Everyone thinks of their dog as irresistible but in Cordelia's opinion, there was no question that Blanche was a canine cover girl: burnished copper silken coat with long floppy curly-haired ears, a feathered tail usually in motion, and a permanent smile. Blanche was a golden retriever and English springer spaniel mix. The common name for that hybrid is a 'spangold' but it made Cordelia picture something worn by an Iron Curtain gymnast for the floor exercises at the Montreal Olympics. Instead, she referred to Blanche as a 'retraniel' even though that sounded like the name of a drug used to treat hair loss.

Despite Blanche living in London, she was still a working dog, although unlike her country cousins who sniffed out dead game, Blanche had been trained by Cordelia to specialise in retrieving footwear. In particular, solitary shoes, never a pair, lying in the street. What had happened for the owner to lose just one? Something nefarious? Flitting in the night? Drunk?

Unlike the majority of people, Cordelia could discover the answers because of an extra-sensory power she possessed. It was similar to psychometry but her version had additional elements and she called it 'psychomatricks'. All she needed to do was hold the shoe, concentrate and her preternatural ability disclosed information about who owned it, what they looked like, their personality, thoughts, how they lived and episodes in their life. Cordelia could even hear conversations they'd had with other people. She was unable to interact with the shoe owner and was an observer only but it was still the most entertaining show in town.

Cordelia had discovered her unusual talent, when, as a teenager at an exhibition of vintage shoes, she picked up a purple snakeskin wedge formerly owned by Epiphany Montgomery, big band singer of the 1940s, and scenes of cocktails, cocaine and carousing flickered in her brain. Ever since, 'reading' shoes was her obsession and she went out early most days searching for abandoned footwear. Who needed to watch soap operas when you could stream one in your head?

That morning's walk took her through her favourite route: an overgrown nineteenth century cemetery that was part nature reserve, and part Gothic theme park, with grand mausoleums, crumbling funerary architecture and higgledy-piggledy gravestones as far as the eye could see.

For students of symbolism, as Cordelia was, Victorian graveyards were a bonanza where ferns, doves, pentagons and other imagery carved into stone all had meaning. Urns with flames indicated ever-lasting remembrance, and an angel holding a trumpet represented judgment day. Cemeteries like this were referred to as gardens of sleep where forgotten worthies lay for eternity, although not in peace because, as a popular location for music videos and fashion shoots, it sometimes felt like rush hour for the free bar at a product launch.

Blanche disappeared into a clump of trees shading the entrance to the catacombs and minutes later trotted out with a fawn canvas slingback sandal in her mouth, dropped it at Cordelia's feet and was rewarded with a tasty treat.

Cordelia picked up the shoe, closed her eyes and meditated. Prickling waves of energy pulsed through her body; a surge she thrived on. Images flickered in her mind's eye as information about its owner was revealed in moving pictures. *Poisonous Pauline Westwich, you saucy mare,* she thought, then opened her eyes and said conspiratorially to Blanche, 'This shoe belongs to one of the world's great hypocrites.'

The dog wagged her tail enthusiastically as if to say, 'Tell me more!'

'No, sweetheart, you'd be traumatised to hear about what's been going on. Westwich has been taking dogs' name in vain. If the tabs found out, she'd be ruined.'

Not that Cordelia would ever stoop as low as reporting someone to the tabloid newspapers. To her, anything went, so long as it was legal, or at least legal-adjacent.

Westwich, an apt surname for an individual who was a human black hole sucking jollity out of life, was the founder of 'Moral Universe: Society as It Should Be', a campaign to publicly shame those who did not behave according to her world view. Pauline was appalled at this, appalled at that, and positively appalled at the other, and she travelled the country booking village halls and small-town theatres to sermonise in, and used a bully-pulpit to whip up her multitude of followers into a permanent state of righteous indignation. Pharmacies could barely keep up with the prescriptions for high blood pressure medication that doctors routinely issued after one of her appearances.

'They'd be better off prescribing dog-stroking therapy to reduce stress levels, wouldn't they, my beautiful?' Cordelia said caressing Blanche's ears and singing one of the many nonsense songs she had made up especially for her pet before saying, 'Come on, Waggy, let's go home.'

++++++

Turning the corner into the side street off the main road, Cordelia stopped as she always did to admire the view. Her view. All eyes were drawn to an ornate pub, The Weasel: its façade covered by polychromatic ceramic tiles and a huge garden behind it, unusual in its scale for a private property in central London.

Next door was a nineteenth century Italian Renaissance Revival palace with columns, pilasters, high arched windows and a colonnade on the ground floor; its grandeur belying the fact it had originally been a millinery business which went by the splendidly monikered 'Plumage House', reflecting that century's craze for feathers.

Now it was 'House of Tanner', shoe purveyor of dreams. Not the feral footwear she chanced upon during strolls. No, we are talking Cordelia Tanner, designer of fashion for feet, high heels for high earners. It always thrilled her to walk into the majestic lobby, climb the imperial staircase with its polished marble balustrades, and feel the satisfaction of having worked for it all.

'Wish *my* home was a palazzo,' an associate had once commented, rather sniffily so Cordelia thought.

He thinks I live like a Medici. If only he knew, she thought giggling. Like many people, she lived above 'the shop'. In her case, on the roof. Good job it could not be seen from the street, because she did not have planning permission for an extension. 'Out of keeping with the architectural integrity of the building' was the lofty response from the authorities when plans were submitted for a penthouse in the shape of a platform boot.

Cordelia had gone ahead in any case because, ever since childhood, she had wanted to live in a shoe and could not wait until she was an old woman. So far, no one from the council had noticed. Living in footwear-shaped habitation was totally impractical but she spent little time there. She was not domesticated, usually ate out and used it only for sleeping in and to store her extensive clothing collection which was categorised by season on separate floors in the heel.

'Today, I shall be Rosalind Russell in *The Women*,' Cordelia declared as she rummaged through her rails and chose a purple cashmere top adorned with three surrealist seeing eyes outlined in bugle beads. She paired it with a slim-fitting violet coloured wool crêpe skirt to the knee and matching double-breasted jacket with such assertive shoulder pads it meant walking at an oblique angle through doorways.

Every now and again, Cordelia dressed up as a film star and challenged her staff to guess who she was channelling. Her shoulder-length mahogany coloured hair and the figure of a golden age of

Hollywood screen goddess made her a natural for Ava Gardner but with her vast collection of wigs, she could equally be Lana Turner or Lauren Bacall, you name it. No wig that day though, her own hair was pinned in a French pleat, upon which a hat that resembled a tiny salver trimmed with silk spring flowers rested at a jaunty angle.

'Lady Looking-Lush!' she said blowing herself a kiss in the mirror and mouthing 'Phwoordelia' as she did every time she saw her reflection, shop windows included, which, her being so stunning was hardly surprising. From anyone else that might have appeared vain, but Cordelia did everything with a light-hearted attitude so it was a joke.

'Good morning, my sole brethren. Is Rex around?' she called out in her mellifluous voice that always had a smile in it, popping her head through the door of the House of Tanner studio to wave at the design team.

'He's having breakfast at The Weasel, Sylvia,' Sebastian, her PA, replied, correctly identifying the film character being invoked by Cordelia, who grinned and flicked an invisible pocket of air at him, which meant, 'Correct, you're brilliant, and so am I for hiring you'.

Depending on who was looking, Sebastian, at six foot five with chunky muscles and long hair in an extraordinary shade of Titian rarely seen outside the fur of a red squirrel, resembled a wrestler, bodyguard, or a clean-shaven Neptune. Most people did not believe him when he told them about his job.

'You don't look like a personal assistant,' was the usual comment.

'And what is a PA supposed to look like?' he would respond.

'Don't know really, female?' they usually muttered, embarrassed at being called out for gender stereotyping.

Sebastian's main reason for choosing the profession was that he loved being around women, and never missed an Association of Personal Assistants' networking event where he stood out, not just for his impressive height, but because he was the only man.

'I'm off for brekkie too,' Cordelia said. 'Won't be long.'

She sauntered into the pub, sat down at the table where Rex was inhaling a plate of kedgeree, picked up a fork, speared a succulent lump of haddock and devoured it.

'How do you do?' he said shaking her hand.

'How do you do?' she replied. They often used the formal greeting, pretending not to know each other. Strangers observing them might think it a coincidence that two individuals who seemed to be meeting for the first time looked so similar. They could be twins. Which, actually, they were. Like Cordelia, Rex was tall, with dark wavy hair, and a happy face that lit up when he spoke. He too commanded a room, not least because he was so dapper; his passion for bespoke suits, that were so well cut they should have come with a safety warning, paid his tailor's mortgage.

'You're looking sharp, my man,' she said.

'Yes, I am, aren't I? Can I try on your titfer?' Rex replied, taking her hat and balancing it on his head.

'You'll never guess what I've discovered about WestBitch. She's been getting up to all sorts in a graveyard.'

'Urgh, don't give me details. Oh, go on then do, but none that will make me nauseous.'

'Two words: dogging den. Puts on a disguise, films the action on her phone, and livestreams it on a subscription site for voyeurs. That's how she's funding Moral Universe.'

'Who told you?' Rex asked greedily.

'Her slingback. Blanche found it this morning. WestBitch must have been disturbed and scarpered so quickly she lost it. Cheap and saggy. A few quid from down the market.'

'Wish I had a superpower like you,' he said sighing for dramatic effect. Several times over the years Cordelia had tested whether he ' psychometrise but his analytical brain was unable to let loose and succeed in the task.

'Effie darling, may I have a pot of Assam tea, and kippers with extra butter please?' Cordelia called out to the young woman behind the bar.

'Is she new?' Rex asked.

'Yes, she's fabulous. And she has one of the greatest first names ever bestowed upon a baby.'

When Effie brought the tea, Cordelia said, 'This is my brother. Would you tell him what you are called and its significance?'

'I was named Effortless because my birth was so quick.'

'I love a moniker with meaning. Mine is Rex, although I can be a bit of a Regina if the occasion demands.'

'That's a coincidence. My surname is Eze and it means king too in the Igbo language. You should meet my sister Tranquillity. She never cried as an infant, but now she's lead singer with a thrash metal band and not living up to the expectations ordained at birth.'

Effie worked days at The Weasel, and in the evenings performed her own comic songs accompanying herself on a harpsichord and building a reputation in comedy clubs because her act was so singular. She was a master at improvisation and could compose a ditty about any phrase the audience gave her, even if they tried to flummox her by suggesting seemingly unrhymable words, such as orange.

'Aren't you clever. Can I test you?' asked Rex.

His subject was London and the challenge was to include the phrase 'prime meridian'.

'She'll do it,' Cordelia assured him.

Effie did not disappoint. Ten minutes later, as she walked out of the kitchen with Cordelia's food, she sang:

'To the greatest city on Earth, give a cheer
Whether you're a pauper or a peer
And salute your cockney friend as they choose to recommend
The finest place to take you for a beer

Everyone en masse, raise a glass
To the place that is the top of its class
So, let's celebrate the city with a chorus of our ditty
And be proud of London Town.

'That's the first verse, and the next one, which I have not yet finished, will have the line: It's on the prime meridian and makes us all go giddy on our pride in London Town,' she said.

'Brava,' said Rex applauding. 'So talented!'

Cordelia tucked into her breakfast. 'This is majorly scrum. Food of marine goddesses. The oil keeps their scales supple.'

'What is the world's leading shoe designer up to today?' Rex enquired.

'Magazine interview, then lunch at the Audley Collection. After that, I have a meeting at the opera house to discuss the new production I'm designing shoes for,' she said reeling off her appointments.

'I'm ready to show you the final bit of Alibi,' he whispered even though only Blanche snoozing by the fireplace was near enough to overhear their conversation.

'How about this evening?' Cordelia replied, excited that their plot was developing to schedule.

'Date.'

Rex was rare amongst technology specialists in that he was erudite, sociable and looked a person in the eye when conversing. Which he did a lot, being the loquacious type. He worshipped art and beauty but unlike Cordelia who genuflected to Rococo styling with her mantra 'too much is never enough', minimalism dictated his domestic and work surroundings. Symmetry made him happy, hence living in a pared down mid-eighteenth century Huguenot silk weaver's house. His brain wiring made him an ace at implementation, computer coding and — whisper it — hacking. Order ruled his life and he had a spreadsheet for everything, including his clothes so he could refer to what he had worn when and did not repeat an outfit too quickly. His favourite musicians were Handel and Bach because of the mathematical precision of their compositions.

'Music and maths are both dominated by patterns and are predictable,' he explained.

Rex named his office 'House of Hypatia' in honour of the Greek astronomer and philosopher murdered by Christian zealots in 415 CE. He was determined to celebrate history's overlooked female mathematicians so on the walls he had portraits of Marie-Sophie Germain, who in the eighteenth century was forced to assume a male identity to study at Paris's École Polytechnique where women were not permitted to enrol, and Ada Lovelace, mid-nineteenth century computer pioneer who collaborated with Charles Babbage on the first programmable computers. Her work was so ahead of its time the practical application was not fully understood until a century after her death.

'Not everyone's brother is a feminist,' Cordelia said proudly of Rex. 'And not everyone's brother has dead mathematicians as pin-ups.'

Like Cordelia, he never ate at home. She had numerous excuses for not doing so including: 1) she lived in a shoe without a kitchen; 2) she could not cook and anything with more than two ingredients was beyond her; and 3) life was too short to chop vegetables.

Rex's main reasons were that cooking was so messy and made his flawless show-home smell. Besides, his dirty little secret was greasy spoon cafés and he was a ticker when it came to their traditional menus. Liver and bacon, tick; steak and kidney pie, tick; spotted dick pudding, tick. He had even built an app to help him keep track of where his top-rated dishes were to be eaten. He lived in hope that one day he would sit for breakfast inside one of London's nineteenth century green wooden cabmen's shelters but unless he spent several years studying 'the Knowledge' and passed his exams to become a licensed Hackney cab driver, that would not happen.

While Cordelia was the creative director and public face of House of Tanner, a bona fide shoe-lebrity who described herself as having a duty to spread beauty, Rex worked with no fanfare behind the scenes, the non-glamorous aspect of the business. Seven years previously, he had developed supply chain software that companies the world over licensed annually which was so lucrative it sustained the financial foundation of their brand.

In the shoemaker's Hall of Fame, Cordelia and Rex deserved their own floor because they created footwear like no others. Roger Vivier invented the stiletto heel, Christian Laboutin made red soles a visual motif of luxury. House of Tanner, or HoT as people who worked there often referred to it, had not one but two unique selling points — one enchantingly whimsical and the other practical — reflecting the different personalities and sensibilities of Cordelia and Rex.

Wearers of House of Tanner shoes were accompanied by birdsong as their feet struck the ground and trills were transmitted from tiny speakers hidden in the heels. The song could be switched off if desired, except that rarely happened because the whole point was for others to hear it and be impressed that the wearer could not only afford House of Tanner shoes but was deemed worthy to be a client. There was even a collective noun for the clientele — a dawn chorus.

During the fashion couture collections, it was deafening as dozens of guests shod in House of Tanner took their seat, but designers craved it because the songs were the soundtrack of exclusivity, and like the couturiers' impeccable clothes, the shoes were handmade and limited edition. Each design was named after a songbird. The Painted Bunting had been exceptionally popular, a suede wedge sandal consisting of vivid lime green, fuchsia and periwinkle blue striped bands, an homage to the bird's multi-coloured plumage. Nightingale too was a hit, its ethereal song a love letter to a prospective mate. The undisputed biggest seller was the Northern Red Bishop, not for the simple ode it sang, but because the heels of the black and yellow velvet ankle boots were covered in mirrored panels which, in the absence of a looking glass, the wearer could use to reapply their lipstick.

The song shoes had made House of Tanner a household name, thanks in part to Glaswegian comedian Marie McReedy who had a recurring joke in her primetime Saturday evening TV sketch show. Each week, she wore different footwear from House of Tannoy, as she called it, such as wellies that complained about rainy weather through a public address system hooked on the boot top, and brothel creepers that sounded an emergency siren in traffic jams prompting other vehicles to pull over and let her car through unimpeded so she could get home in time to watch the football.

Rex's innovative idea had been to insert a smartphone battery charger and USB socket in the shoe heel, both concealed, and with each footstep the charger was topped up. Flat batteries begone! That concept and Cordelia's birdsong were trademarked which deterred most footwear companies apart from one in China that had stolen the charger idea and was marketing inferior mass-produced shoes under the brand name House of T'Anna. It was maddening, and impossible to stop because the lawyer's warning letters were ignored.

Potential clients of House of Tanner were vetted on how considerately they treated others. Their background was investigated and, if they scored highly on the scale of nasty-piece-of-workery, their custom was declined. Terms and conditions of being a fit and proper person to be afforded the privilege of wearing the shoes were clarified beforehand. Customers signed a contract and were warned of the consequences of breaking any clauses of conduct. If they did, then the punishment protocol was activated. The birdsong loop was suspended and changed instead to a recording that sounded like the owner's own voice saying repeatedly, 'I am so horrible that even my mum hates me.' It could not be switched off so the owner's options were to bury the shoes deep underground in a soundproof box, or destroy them.

Whichever humiliating choice was made, they were never allowed back to House of Tanner. There were no public complaints about this action because that would be admitting they had lost access to the world's most desirable brand of shoes. Social suicide.

Like shoes, birds were a fascination of Cordelia's, and she had chosen the Wilson's bird of paradise for the House of Tanner logo. The spectacular feathers of that exotic avian resembled a Mondrian painting: emerald breast shield, iridescent aquamarine crown, yellow neck mantle, scarlet cape, electric blue feet, and violet curlicue tail. To attract the female's attention, the male puts on a show with a courtship dance. He is a picky perfectionist fastidiously clearing the stage, discarding leaves, twigs and anything from the forest floor that would distract his intended from appreciating the full works. If any debris gets in the way, he is discombobulated. Just like Rex when anything was out of place in his office. Which is why the Wilson's bird of paradise was such an apt emblem for a business partnership between the diva of display and spick and span man.

'Fancy a quick game of Snappy Families?' Rex asked as they finished breakfast, pulling from his bag a pack of cards.

'Botticelli!' replied Cordelia which was their nonsensical answer to any rhetorical question. It came from primary school days and their class teacher Mr Bottomley, whose surname naturally caused much mirth. The other children called him Botty but because Cordelia and Rex had been brought up to appreciate art, they nicknamed their teacher after the Renaissance painter. In one lesson, he had interrupted their chat to ask whether they were going to concentrate on learning or continue to talk.

'Talk,' Rex had replied with a pronounced 'dur' in his response and even more so in the expression on his face.

Snappy Families, a game Rex had devised, was based on Snap and Happy Families. The cards were printed with portraits of distinguished historic figures, all snappily dressed in their finery. The aim was to collect groups in similar outfits, such as cloth-of-gold gowns, bejewelled doublets and soaring wigs, to make a stylish fashion family with an imaginative group name.

That day, Rex played like a demon and won three games in a row, creating the Codpiece Wars with King Henry VIII and male members of the families of wives he had discarded; assembled the Sisterhood of the Fontage, named after the towering hairpiece consisting of a wire frame covered in tiers of lace, ribbon and linen ruffles, popular with aristocratic European women in the seventeenth century; and Frock and Awe, exquisite evening gowns including the one worn by Madame X in a painting by John Singer Sargent which had scandalised the Paris Salon in 1884 because her dress was considered to be indecently revealing.

'You're on form today,' Cordelia said, throwing down her cards in concession and jumping up. 'I'm latey matey. Mustache!'

As she did, her phone rang. It was Sebastian to say Tommy Leung, the journalist from Hand Crafted, was in the House of Tanner lobby.

'One minute, Basti. I'm going to meet him now,' Cordelia replied, walking out of the pub. 'Cordelia Tanner, how do you do? Welcome to House of Tanner. I'm so happy that you want to feature the venerable profession of cordwaining in your magazine. Let's go upstairs and I'll explain the procedure,' she said to the young man who, rather than being on-message with the theme of the publication he worked for, was wearing trainers. They climbed the stairs and sat down in the workshop.

'First, we measure a client's feet and note all its dimensions. We do a drawing of the shape of it including any lumps and bumps so a hand-carved beechwood model of each foot can be made. These are called lasts and the shoes are built around them and made to fit perfectly. Here, I'll do yours. Don't be shy, I've seen thousands of feet.'

Tommy started squealing, 'I'm ticklish!' as soon as she touched his right foot, forcefully pulling it away. She tried again, with the same reaction. 'So sorry, Cordelia. It's daft but it always happens.'

'Don't worry, I'll stop and you can just imagine this stage. One of our clients is a senior member of the royal family. We're forced to tie her legs to the chair, and a lady-in-waiting sits on her lap to prevent the writhing.'

Cordelia continued, introducing him to the clickers, closers and finishers she employed who were all busy on their specific function in the teamwork of bespoke footwear. 'It takes weeks to months to complete a pair of shoes. During that period, clients come in for fittings. Every stage is meticulously attended to, and perfection is the only acceptable result. Time is not a luxury at House of Tanner, it is a necessity.'

'I had no idea it was such an intricate process. What about cheap factory-made shoes? I suppose they are just churned out.'

'Actually, even that type of shoe passes through several stages, although high volume off-the-shelf is largely mechanised, whereas we are one pair at once and, as you see, there is no automation. We have a large team because of our worldwide demand. I'm determined to maintain the skills required to create handmade shoes, that's why we have apprentices, and take students as interns. They are the future of this exceptional craft.'

'Tommy, your photographer Lucy is here,' Sebastian said, walking into the studio. 'Cordelia, you have twenty minutes before you need to leave for your next appointment.'

'Thanks, Basti. Tommy, if Lucy could do me first, I'd be grateful, then I can leave you both to take the other photos you need.'

When you are chatelaine of a palace, it would be a waste not to use it as a backdrop, so the portrait was a wide shot of Cordelia in the imposing lobby holding a shoe from the latest collection. It was the Royal Flycatcher model, a high-heeled mule festooned with yellow and blue feathers reminiscent of the bird's vivid crest and also a nod to the original name of the building, home to another consummate craft: millinery.

Precisely twenty minutes later, Cordelia was on her way to the Audley Collection, Marylebone, housed in the grandest of buildings, a splendid Georgian pile designed by Robert Adam and now Grade 1 listed. It had been commissioned in 1773 as a pavilion of entertainment by the Duchess of Audley, one of London's most avid party hosts. Outside, it looked like an understated townhouse but inside was a warren of reception spaces used for different purposes — parade rooms, banqueting parlour, music salon and a vast ballroom with walls bearing murals of Roman life inspired by (at the time) the recent excavations of Pompeii.

Central to the house was a stunning marble staircase that rose through the four-storey height of the building to a glass dome which flooded light to the interior. The duchess had bequeathed the house and its contents to the nation with the proviso that it would become an art museum with free access to the public.

It was now run by Juliet Ponsatrain, an enlightened director on a mission to introduce never-before-seen works from little known artists. Juliet also encouraged primary school outings, especially from deprived areas so the pupils would see paintings, sculptures and decorative arts. Her dream was for nascent creative talent to be inspired there.

The new exhibition was 'Libertas: Freedom to Create'. At the heart of the show was a visionary named Minerva Cicciano who, in 1930, had created a utopia on her private island in the Bay of Naples. Its grand hotel and casino had contributed to her fortune and she wanted a legacy other than having accrued wealth. As a fervent patron of the arts, it had always bothered her that the valuable collection she had amassed contained few works by women. Most dealers did not rate them, so finding and buying their pieces was all but impossible.

One day, she woke up and decided change was needed and took a decision that her business advisers warned would be catastrophic. She renamed the island Libertas and announced it was to be a colony for female artists, musicians, writers, photographers and filmmakers, all of whom struggled to make a mark in their male-dominated sectors.

When art-loving holidaymakers arrived on the island, they were greeted with a sign at the jetty that read 'Bliss' in multiple languages. Travellers on a five-star budget tended to stay in the hotel, others who preferred simple accommodation had a choice of rustic lodges, and those for whom lack of funds meant they could not afford it at all applied for sponsorship to cover travel and accommodation costs.

Men were welcome as day-trippers, providing their intention was to buy or commission artworks. And they did. Without Libertas, the world would be ignorant to the oeuvre of ceramicist Hiranur Aygün, portraitist Liesl Behringer, jeweller Aminata Momoh and dozens of furniture designers, printmakers and others working in every art discipline imaginable.

Cordelia had stayed on the island as an art school student, courtesy of a Libertas grant. Meeting so many dynamic women had reinforced her belief that she could make a career using her creativity.

'I was so taken with this work when I first saw it. It was on the wall of the lodge I stayed in.' She was standing in front of a vibrantly coloured landscape of the island and talking to Isabella Cicciano, Minerva's great-granddaughter. 'If I ever came downstairs bleary eyed, I sometimes forgot that it was a mosaic and not the view from a window. It made me so happy. It still does.'

Over lunch, Isabella and Cordelia talked about the soon to be launched annual art award.

'As my great-grandmother was named after the Roman goddess of poetry, crafts and inspiration, it will be known as the Minerva Prize,' Isabella revealed.

'I owe so much to Libertas. If I had not visited it, my business probably would not exist. Did you know I studied sculpture for my first degree? During my stay, I met an Iraqi architect and she told me how sculpture informed all her work. It made me realise I could apply what I was studying and create art for the feet. So, after my bachelor's degree, I studied footwear design at Cordwainers' College.

'Is there anything I can do to support Libertas' aims? How about me endowing a sponsorship fund for students from countries under-represented in global arts? Would that help?'

'That is so generous, Cordelia. Thank you. I shall think of how your offer can be of the most benefit. And you must return soon and see how the island has not changed since you were last there.'

'Please don't ever change.'

+++++++

Cordelia was early for her next appointment so she walked to Covent Garden taking a meandering route through Fitzrovia to Fitzroy Square where she liked to give a little wave to the blue plaques on buildings that had housed notable writers and artists, including Virginia Woolf and Roger Fry, then down into Soho for a coffee at Maison Gaston, the oldest patisserie in the area. It was known as Going-Going Gaston for the fact it was in a topsy-turvy eighteenth century building that threatened every day to collapse.

She sat at a table outside, opposite the restaurant where, in her student days, she had once tried to do a runner with Wilbur Brannigan, a friend from art school, now costume designer at the opera house. Thinking they were invisible, they had sneaked out of the fire escape without paying but were caught by the maître d' and forced to do the walk of shame through the dining room back to their table where the bill was presented with a fanfare so other diners could witness their embarrassment.

Why don't I see Wilbur more often? He's adorable, Cordelia thought as she strolled to meet him. They had been close pals years before and he was that dependable friend who passed the 'who would help, no questions asked, if you were in trouble and called them at 3 a.m.' test.

With an unusually constructed face where all the features were arranged so he resembled a work by Picasso in his surrealist period, Wilbur often attracted sneers, and at college Cordelia and him were known as 'Beauty and the Beast'.

'I assume you mean that I am the beast because Wilbur is the most beautiful human I know,' was her answer when he was insulted that way.

Wilbur was funny, kind and thoughtful and always had gorgeous girlfriends. Now he was married to Shantina, the megastar singer-songwriter. They had met when he designed costumes for the video that accompanied her first Grammy-winning song 'Alright Me Luvver' which, as a Bristolian, was her standard greeting. She went on to become Britain's first black self-made billionaire; her wealth accrued from her own royalties, songs she wrote for countless other leading performers, tours, films and her own line of cosmetics.

When Cordelia arrived at the opera house, Wilbur was waiting in the foyer. He had landed a coup by commissioning her to create the footwear for the new production of *Orpheus in the Underworld*.

'Come here, you. It's been too long,' she said fondly, kissing him on both cheeks.

'Hon, is it possible you could be anymore fabulous?'

'Probably not,' Cordelia responded with a laugh, 'But I still try. Anyway, talking of fabulous, your *Orpheus* costumes are beyond, and they inspired the glitter goddess to come out and play!'

In this new production, Orpheus was an uptight administrator and Underworld was a rakish nightclub in 1970s New York — the type of place where a coke spoon was issued on entry, stepping onto the dancefloor meant passing through a dank curtain of poppers and, if anyone fancied an anonymous encounter, they had a choice of dark, rubber-lined side rooms.

Eurydice was jaded with her marriage to Orpheus and longed to change her distinctly ordinary existence with something *outré*. Pole dancing was her fantasy but she made the mistake of revealing that desire to her husband. He was repulsed. This impelled her to leave him and apply for a job at Underworld and she revelled in the happy-go-lucky attitude of her colleagues and customers. Who would want to return to life with boring Orpheus? Not Eurydice, so when he turned up at Underworld and informed her they were going back to suburban life in New Jersey, she refused, opting instead to remain for non-stop revelry in the fun palace.

What a juicy proposition for Cordelia! As to be expected, the temperature was so warm in Underworld, the costumes were scanty so she had plenty of leg to work with and came up with a plethora of thigh-high boots with platforms soles, decorated with lurex, lamé, crystals and flashing light bulbs, all in fiery colours. They were particularly eye-catching for the Infernal Gallop finale, better known as the music to the Can-Can.

Cordelia had always longed to go-go dance in a cage on top of the bar in a racy club but by the time she was old enough, venues like Underworld no longer existed, so as a consolation, the opera's producers gave her a non-singing role as the club's doyenne of dance, groove-mistress-in-chief. It was a dream come true and she would be appearing for ten performances in the autumn.

++++++

By the time Cordelia returned to House of Tanner after her busy day of appointments, all the staff had left for the evening meaning her and Rex could discuss Project Alibi in his office without being overheard.

'Meet Jill Mitchell,' said Rex pointing at his computer screen and the photo of a woman in her forties, neither ugly nor pretty, hair in a shade of mouse.

'Hard to identify in a police line-up — just what we need,' replied Cordelia.

'Exactly. It's a composite of four females, purposely non-descript. She now has a presence on the net with a website, business page profiles and a Connect With account.'

Cordelia typed Jill Mitchell's name into the search engine and learnt that she'd studied economics at a red brick university in the Midlands, had worked lucratively in merchant banking, was now an angel investor, had a low social profile and, apart from being wealthy, was completely unremarkable.

'Perfect, she's ordinary. Doubtful if anybody would remember having met her. But imagine being so unmemorable. I feel quite sad that no one would ever want to boast about knowing her.'

Jill Mitchell was the virtual progeny of Rex, born to be the cover story behind a notion that, although not anticipated when it was devised, would have a profound impact on human habits and purchasing decisions. They had decided that this secret project should not be openly connected with House of Tanner because it was contradictory to the exclusivity of their brand. As far as the public was concerned, Jill Mitchell's offshore millions made it possible. Rex had found it surprisingly straightforward to seed the Internet with webpages featuring fictitious Ms Mitchell, many of them so dull, that the three-second rule of surfing, whereby a person moves quickly to another page unless there is a good reason to stay and browse, became the nano-second rule.

'We can unveil it as soon as we want,' Rex said.

'You are the top digi-dog,' Cordelia exclaimed, then looked down at her much-maligned feet and said to them, 'Not long now, girls. Get used to my admiring rather than pitying glances. Let's do some dressing up. Footward ho!'

After a couple of years of clandestine development, 'Footloose' was ready to launch and feet would never be the same again. It was an ingenious holographic technology where customers purchased a proprietary ankle bracelet, downloaded a smart phone app and were then able to access an extensive database of footwear designs. With one click whichever shoe, boot or sandal they browsed was transformed into a hologram that was projected from the anklet. It was so convincing that the user could be in their old slippers but to everyone else it looked as though they were striding out in footwear fantasies.

Premium subscribers had unlimited daily downloads so they could change their gear as often as they wanted, and, most popular, was VirtShoe Signalling a service that permitted them to create exclusive personalised designs.

Footloose had been conceived because of Cordelia's regret at being unable to wear the masterpieces produced by House of Tanner. She was fortunate, however, because unlike most others with a similar foot condition, she could design shoes and boots handmade to fit the surrealistic terrain of her feet but even so, this restricted her to wearing enclosed footwear and whatever she wore was understated so as not to draw attention. Each time she inserted her orthotic inner soles, she scowled and swore at them even though they meant walking without pain.

Cordelia shimmied around the room seemingly in transparent PVC peep-toes with ultra-high heels shaped like the Eiffel Tower.

'So last minute, bored with them already,' she said then scrolled her phone and clicked. 'Well, hello,' she whooped as knee-length macramé weave boots trimmed with dangling swishy beaded braids materialised at her feet.

Meanwhile, Rex sashayed up and down his office, one minute sporting pimp daddy buck-skin platforms in a fetching shade of mint green, the next, a pair of rainbow coloured golf shoes dripping in rhinestones.

The hologram idea was sparked after Cordelia passed an off-license and, as usual, admired her reflection in the window. Inside the shop, she noticed the holographic image of a bottle of well-known lager suspended in the air. *We should use a hologram for marketing our brand*, she thought and made a mental note to discuss it with Rex. Over a pint in The Weasel's garden, Rex had enlightened her on how the technology worked.

'It looked so realistic,' Cordelia replied, sipping her beer. The best ideas are always born in the pub and a few drinks later, the blueprint of Footloose had been conceived.

'I'll be known as the saviour of soles,' she proclaimed. 'As a member of the society of sore feet, this will mean that me and my comrades-in-pain can still wear our orthopaedic shoes but now we'll look magnificent! No one can know about my dodgy plates of meat though. Too embarrassing. As a peddler of opulence, I can't admit to not being perfect.'

So, without telling anyone, they developed the project in between their day-to-day work. Cordelia sketched hundreds of designs that Rex's newly assembled team of tech-wizards in India transformed into computerised 3D images. She had no limits on shape, materials or structure because this footwear was not to be manufactured. Every creative but impractical thought she'd ever had to abandon when designing House of Tanner collections could now be digitally rendered. What a gift for people with problem feet who were forced by lack of any stylish options to wear clumsy and ugly footwear.

To maintain secrecy, the programmers worked individually and had no idea about the final product. As for the ankle bracelets, they were sourced in Taiwan from a business that also produced electronic tags for monitoring felons on home detention. Contractors and suppliers were paid through a company ostensibly owned by Jill Mitchell and registered in Zurich so it could not be connected with House of Tanner. Rex was confident that all roads led to Switzerland but just to be sure, another layer of obfuscation was planned as an insurance policy. Two days before Footloose was scheduled to launch, an astonishing new shoe-related experience conceived by Cordelia was to be unveiled. She would be ubiquitous in TV and radio studios, the concept trending on social media, and eager queues down the street.

Cordelia's phone dinged. 'It's Celestine asking if we can we go in to see her tomorrow. She's ready for us to sign-off on Shoeseum.'

Chapter Two

'My precious jewels,' said Celestine as she crossed her office at House of Tanner and kissed Cordelia and Rex warmly. Stately was the word often used to describe Celestine. Magisterial another. Chic for sure with her platinum quiff. Today, she was sporting a fuchsia velvet riding jacket, black satin jodhpurs, silk scarf patterned with bridles and other horsey motifs and knee-length black riding boots.

'Did the lads on the building site say "giddy-up" on your way in this morning?' asked Cordelia.

'Yes, and they all neighed in unison.'

'I hope you flashed them the two-fingered Kit-Kat.'

When Cordelia and Rex were three years old, their orchidologist parents disappeared with no trace during an expedition in Madagascar. The Tanners had asked close friend Celestine to look after the twins for the period they intended to be away and jokingly said that if anything happened then her baby-sitting service would last for the next fifteen years. As a precaution, with no other family members to nominate, they updated their wills stipulating her for the legal guardianship.

'It's just a formality, nothing bad will happen to us, and besides, we must be back on time otherwise our library books will be overdue.'

It was a huge shock when her friends failed to return, and especially the realisation that she now had responsibility for not one but two young lives. Celestine had never wanted children of her own and had no parental instincts so she treated them like adults and raised them in an unconventional manner which for any confident and daring child, as Cordelia and Rex were, was heaven.

'Go and explore, have adventures, then come back and tell me all about them,' she had said. 'And remember, no junk food, always sit down in a café or restaurant for proper meals, tip the staff well, and never fail to have tea and cake in the afternoon.' She then handed them spending money to cover travel, victuals and treats.

After school and during the holidays, they roamed their city and beyond, exploring back streets, grand public structures, derelict buildings and anything that intrigued them.

Cordelia made drawings of what they had seen, and Rex, with his photographic memory, could relate in detail their escapades. One day, they ended up on national TV news with a group of eco-protestors who lived in trees in an ancient woodland to protect it from being felled to make way for a new road. Cordelia had taken chocolate bars as gifts because the campaigners would have little chance to go to the shop during their bid to save the natural landscape.

'You're a bit young to be protesting, aren't you?' the reporter had said patronisingly.

To which she replied, 'Even more reason if our youth draws attention to what we care about. Where will birds live and nest if there aren't any trees?'

This led the Association for Protecting Birdlife to issue a special certificate to her and Rex for highlighting the issue.

One of their favourite activities was searching for unexpected architectural features above eye-level. By looking up instead of at the pavement, they discovered another realm; one populated by mythical creatures, giants, goddesses and cherubs, all waiting to be admired, and illustrating an alternative story of the city missed by pedestrians who rushed along and never raised their gaze.

Celestine loved Cordelia and Rex right from the beginning and it was a testament to her that they were not precocious and certainly never bratty, being well-mannered with a default position to find fun in everything they did. That was apparent from their cheeky facial expressions and attitude which endured into adulthood.

Each year on their birthday until the age of eighteen, she took them on a tour around portraits, statues and sites associated with outstanding individuals who had been a positive influence on society, and at each location reminded her wards of the clauses in Celestine's Womanifesto for Living. It was like the beating of the bounds in the medieval era where youths were inculcated in the location of the parish borders, except in the case of the Womanifesto, instead of boundary stones these were wayfarer's stops in the journey of life. Her philosophy, which both of them adopted, was:

▶ Be kind and generous of spirit
▶ Be courageous
▶ Be dashing
▶ Be extraordinary
▶ Be playful
▶ Be curious
▶ Seize opportunities
▶ If you pass by an unfamiliar alleyway, investigate it
▶ Share your good fortune
▶ Always sit on the top front seat on a double decker bus
▶ Choose honey over vinegar (apart from on chips) when interacting with others
▶ Don't be a saint, not on Earth anyway

She had insisted they took unglamorous employment as teenagers to learn the value of money and realise how lucky they were. Cordelia worked in a clothing factory which had to be fumigated when the stock was infested with fleas. The owners slashed the price and sold it as seconds and her task was to comb through the garments and pick out the dead fleas with a pair of tweezers. As with everything, she found the humour and, along with her adult colleague Joan, giggled through each day. They told daft jokes and sang along to pop radio as they undertook the gruesome task. At the end of the shift, the supervisor demanded to see the pile of corpses to prove they had been working and not just laughing.

'Good job we're not on commission like the country folk who are paid to kill moles and then tie them to field gates to prove to the farmer how many they caught,' Joan said.

Rex was hired as dogsbody at a bacon butty kiosk where the early morning rush of workmen was relentless. He thought it wise to learn about the local professional football team and genned up on the players and fixtures, so he had something in common with his customers. They thought him a bit fey with his insistence on yellow rubber gloves for washing up the greasy utensils, but appreciated his allegiance to their team, and the way he crisped bacon like no other.

'Bunsen burner, borrowed from the school chemistry lab,' he explained.

Celestine was the reason they lived for beauty. Growing up, they accompanied her to the opera, galleries and museums where decorative arts were treated as a religion. All three revered the Victoria & Albert, in particular the Costume Court where Cordelia and Rex pressed their faces against the glass in the display cases and longed to play dressing up with the spectacular collection of suits, evening gowns, cocktail dresses and, for Cordelia in particular, the shoes.

Other adults might have bought toys or books as Christmas presents for youngsters, but not Celestine. Instead, she took them on architecture tours to venerate Art Nouveau in Brussels and Riga, and to Asmara, an African city of entirely unexpected Art Deco magnificence. For Rex, who felt a bit 'liver-y' with too much ornamentation, the pared down modernism of Eritrea's capital was his preferred style. Wherever they went, Celestine always took them to non-touristy restaurants and bars for refreshment.

'You can understand much about the culture of a country through its food and drink. Mmm, try this,' she said, letting them have a sip of the local hooch wherever they went and waving cheerily to anyone who frowned at her for letting youths have alcohol.

Celestine was also the reason Cordelia had a passion for films because at the start of her working life in the 1960s, she had acted in motion pictures. Towering over the leading men, she was never considered for starring roles but made an impact with every supporting character she played. Her soul was not in acting, however, so instead she made a career in set design, first as the assistant, then as one of few women in that era to be the boss. In the end credits for numerous British and Hollywood films, Celestine's name was there; three Academy Awards being the ultimate acknowledgement for her stellar work, and now those golden statuettes displayed in her office at House of Tanner acted as a paper weight, a door stopper and as a target for throwing screwed up pages from the sketch pad.

Her latest project, Shoeseum, was unlike anything she had worked on before. For years, Cordelia had been collecting footwear that belonged to noteworthy figures of history, purchasing it at auction and from private dealers. Amongst her collection were sandals owned by Nzingha Mlongo, queen of the Atamba kingdom, superb military tactician of the sixteenth century; boots worn by eighteenth century poet and adventurer Lord Byron; and shoes that had belonged to Maude Sanderson, American comic actress and the first woman to own her own TV studio.

Museum and amusement park in one remarkable venture, Cordelia had said of Shoeseum, 'I want customers to be transported from a city street into an ethereal landscape and feel as though they are hallucinating.'

'A phantasmagoria, what a treat!' Celestine replied, opening her notepad. She never disappointed and now, after a year of development, it was ready.

'Let's walk through and pretend we are seeing it for the first time,' she suggested.

Rex and Cordelia linked arms with her and she led them downstairs where Shoeseum took up the entire second floor. Strolling through the doors, they entered a woodland of gilt-painted trees, flickering light percolating through the leaves, soft green spongey moss underfoot impregnated with mind-altering essential oils that were released when stepped on, and a glee club of forest birds joyfully trilling; their enchanting arias piped through speakers in the boughs. Fleeting apparitions of shoes appeared to be promenading unaided through the trees and the idea was to follow them into a glade and, once inside, the show began.

Soft lights focused on a pair of shoes, sandals or boots exhibited on a waist-high plinth topping a Corinthian column, from which a voice emanated detailing the purpose or symbolism of the footwear, who had owned it and an insight into their life. Cordelia had plundered her Master of Arts thesis for research so people would leave Shoeseum knowing footwear was not just for protecting the feet, it was also an indicator of identity, gender, eminence and taste.

Eroticism played a role too: the bound foot in tiny lotus shoes that some Chinese men in past centuries found alluring but were so torturous for the female victims of the barbaric fashion, and the stiletto heel said to be an expression of sexuality, also used by some males to transform themselves to resemble women. Visitors learnt that footwear was a motif in numerous fairy tales, sometimes symbolising freedom, dancing, transportation to divine realms, or other times punishment as in the fable of the *Red Shoes*.

What someone wears on their feet projects a message about them, their economic position, profession, outlook and aspirations. The material used for footwear is symbolic too. In the past, rustic wooden clogs for outdoor workers signified poverty, whereas the affluent who stayed inside and were waited on by servants wore soft fabrics. This was illustrated in Cordelia's collection by a pair of sumptuous, embroidered silk slip-ons encrusted with rubies, diamonds and emeralds with improbably lengthy corkscrew-curled toes curving over the foot. They had belonged to an eighteenth century Indian sultan, known as the Tiger of Hyderabad. Their impracticality indicated his rank — this man did not need to work — and the value of the jewels proclaimed his considerable fortune. He owned no hard-soled shoes because he never walked outside, carried instead in an opulent palanquin borne by eight barefoot bearers.

'Where are the Sun King shoes?' Rex asked Celestine.

She led them past the exhibits dedicated to Zenobia, Warrior Queen of Palmyra, and Molly Deganwadonti, Native American Mohawk leader, diplomat and spy, and there they were: the status shoes that had once belonged to Louis XIV of France. White kid leather embellished with diamond-studded buckles and pink satin ribbons around the ankle. They had scarlet heels because that colour communicated vigour, courage and religious fervour.

In 1673, Louis ordained that all aristocrats with a suitable genealogy must wear scarlet heels as a sumptuary privilege when at court. Those who wore them were known as *les talons rouges* with footwear being a visual indicator of who was in and out of favour with the monarch. On a whim, he could remove the privileges, and no one wanted the shame of being relegated to dark coloured heels. Footwear failure.

And there was more. Cordelia was determined to find practical applications for her psychic gift and she used it at Shoeseum to reveal the backstory, foibles and secrets of the shoe owners for a glimpse into their lives in a format called 'If the Shoe Fits'. Augmented reality, video game technology and kinaesthetic communication applying motion, touch and smell, created a dream-like dominion in which users became immersed so their brain persuaded them that what they saw, heard, felt and smelt was real. What people were actually seeing were character actors on sets designed by Celestine, in vignettes directed by leading filmmaker Astrid Stayler. Rather than don the usual clumsy virtual reality headset to access this fantasy world, they stepped into a pod with a screen wrapped around the interior. When the action started, all the stimuli made it feel as though they were in the scene too.

Cordelia had delighted in auditioning the historic characters for 'If the Shoe Fits' and was searching for a particular personality and lifestyle — bon vivants with unbridled enthusiasm and a 'go there if you dare' attitude.

She had two favourites. First, the Countess of Bennington (named Charlotte but friends called her Charlie) whose thigh-skimming brown suede wide-topped cavalry boots were a clue that this was no ordinary seventeenth century woman. Heels were originally worn by men for securing their feet in stirrups when riding a horse, and only later were they used to increase the wearer's height. For Charlie, heels were useful for both reasons, and the length of the boots protected her legs. She relished not having to ride side-saddle, which society dictated for her sex, and the freedom of movement that men's boots gave her was empowering, unlike the impractical and delicate footwear designed to keep women passive that she was expected to wear.

Few people were aware that the Countess of Bennington was the mysterious 'Fletcher', a highwayman with a difference. Fletcher rode England's coaching routes straddling a white horse named Albion accompanied by a troop of seven lieutenants known as the Arrows, also females masquerading as men.

When they came across a carriage, Charlie would stop it with the command, 'Stand and I'll deliver', then jump off Albion, smiling, arms outstretched as she strode towards the fearful passengers. They expected to be robbed, violated or worse if they failed to hand over their valuables. But that was not Charlie's intention. No, she would announce herself saying, 'Good day, ladies and gentlemen. Do not be afraid for I am Fletcher and this is my quiver of Arrows. Who is hungry or thirsty?'

And with that, hampers of cheese, ham, bread and ale were distributed and the travellers sat down for a picnic before Fletcher and the Arrows escorted them to the next coaching inn ensuring they were secure from violent thieves who terrorised the roads. When the coach arrived safely, Fletcher handed out tiny portraits of the Arrows as souvenirs and off they trotted leaving the grateful beneficiaries excitedly discussing their encounter.

How did a woman of Charlie's social standing manage to live that type of life? She was married to Edward, Earl of Bennington, but it was a lavender marriage and he agreed to fund her enterprise so long as she did not bring disgrace on the family name and turned a blind eye to his proclivities. What an offer! She had never fancied him in the first place because the match had been forced upon her the way that aristocratic alliances often were. It was a union without issue leaving her free to pursue adventures that otherwise would have been forbidden.

Charlie took young working-class women who were destined for a life of graft and trained them in equine skills, poise, manners and self-defence. She also gave them elocution lessons and taught them how to lower their voice to sound masculine when in character. They were sworn to secrecy about their work and none ever broke the confidence. Not a soul suspected they were in disguise because, during that period, men often wore fulsome wigs so with the Arrows' long locks under Cavalier hats trimmed with plumes, faces hidden behind silk scarves so only their eyes showed, and figures concealed under black cloaks, they did not look like women.

Fletcher and her Arrows became sex symbols throughout the land. Collecting their miniatures became the fashionable thing to do and it was commonplace to see people in coaching inns offering to swap duplicates to have the complete set.

The adulation heaped on Fletcher's Arrows made the brigands who prowled the highways jealous and Charlie received overtures from outlaws who sought freelance work. They had heard of the generous wages, employment benefits and the pension paid after retirement. For men like them, the threat of the noose was ever present so an easy life with a band of brothers was seductive.

Instead of refusing and causing more resentment, Charlie encouraged them to franchise her operation, and in the absence of a wealthy benefactor as she had, suggested they fund it by charging passengers a modest fee for the picnic and bodyguard duties. This was not the equivalent of gangsters extorting protection money, because they were offering a necessary public service.

The idea worked for a time until the laughter and comments about them being worse than girls became so loud from their bandit peers that they returned to their criminal ways. It seemed that even the unequivocal fate of a death sentence if they were caught and prosecuted was preferable to having their masculinity impugned.

Meanwhile, in the regions where Fletcher and the Arrows operated, streets were thronged with fans hoping for a glimpse of them each time a coach drove into town. People stood, ready to throw flowers, and hearts beat madly as women and men gazed admiringly at their handsome folk heroes.

Cordelia would have been friends with the vivacious Charlie Bennington in real life, and as for Lancelot 'Beau' George, her other favourite, he was her perfect male fantasy — mischievous, witty and cultured. Anyone who aspired to be anyone in late eighteenth century English society needed his approval. As Master of Ceremonies responsible for all social entertainments, making introductions and keeping enemies apart in London — and then in Brighton after high society followed the Prince of Wales to his seaside retreat — he was the most powerful person in town.

Lancelot was physically beautiful in his looks and stylish in his wardrobe which is how he earnt his nickname. He wore his own hair tied back in a pigtail in an era when powdered perukes were still the fashion, and in doing so helped consign wigs for men to essential wear for judges and other court officials only.

Cordelia owned a pair of his shoes, ultramarine velvet slip-ons with pointed toes, the buckles ornamented with carnelians. His signature motif was to wear buckles in the shape of hearts, diamonds, clubs or spades depending on which playing card he had randomly picked before dressing. Lancelot had worn the shoes for the Night of a Thousand Dreams, a spectacle that had gone down in social history as the greatest party of the century and which cemented his reputation as Voluptuary-in-Chief.

The Night of a Thousand Dreams had taken place in Brighton at his purposely built temple of amusements which went by the name 'Elysium'. Inside it was a thrill for the senses where lighting, music, aromatics and multifarious décor that took inspiration from Persian and Chinese interiors dazzled everyone. Shades of red dominated the colour scheme with the intention for it slightly to increase blood pressure and excitability. Refreshments included a choice of punches served from capacious bowls and those people daring enough to take a cup of the one named Hocus Pocus, laced with magic mushrooms, would be loosened up for a satisfying buzz that was gentle enough not to inspire them to climb onto the chandeliers and dive into the throng below.

Every member of the Ton, as the upper crust was known in that era, claimed to have been at the Night of a Thousand Dreams which was mostly untrue because Lancelot found the majority of them too stuffy and, when he was hosting at Elysium, chose naughtiness over haughtiness. Hence the attendees included notables who had achieved something or who did not conform to what society dictated. Cross-dressers, dowagers with their much younger paramours and female composers who refused to accept that their place was in the home working on their embroidery were priority invitees. Luminaries such as Vivienne de Valois added sheen to the already glittering goings on. Vivienne was the first woman aeronaut and inspiration for the Mile High Club — although it was more like the Six-Hundred-Metre High Club because, in 1788, hot air balloons were limited in achievable altitude.

Rooms large and small offered a panoply of entertainments — tableaux vivant, card tables and international opera singers, including Maximilien von Dieskau the celebrated tenor, who took requests and even performed duets with guests, whether they could sing or not, which most could not. In one room, solo dancers swayed to a new style of music devised by Lancelot where a drummer and a double bass played repetitive rhythmic tunes that encouraged a trance-like state. In the ballroom, traditional marches and reels were banned and instead couples, same and opposite sex, held each other as they danced, long before the waltz scandalised the world decades later.

Lancelot ensured, as he always did, that a production 'By George', the label he attached to all his professional works, and source of the exclamation used to this day, was unforgettable. His personal touch made all the difference; he greeted everyone individually, solicitous they had enough to eat and drink, making sure they found a diversion to entertain them. His amiable attention made almost everybody who met him swoon, including Cordelia watching from the twenty-first century, unable to interact with him but wishing she could meet him in real life. She was besotted.

+++++

'More tea, darlings?' Celestine asked when they were back in her office, pouring Lapsang Souchong into their cups. 'If you're happy with it all, I am too. We're ready for a grand opening.'

Cordelia was overwhelmed at how breath-taking Shoeseum was but inside felt sorrowful that she and Rex were hiding what they were about to do with Footloose. Keeping quiet about their involvement after it launched would be agony.

'I couldn't love it more. Thank you, dearest Celestine. Let's not just have a grand opening, but let's have a grand party too!'

Chapter Three

House of Tanner parties were always hosted at The Weasel and, without fail, they were the best shindigs ever. That was down to a combination of the venue, and brilliance of the MC: Oscar Rivington. Oscar, witty and playful, transmitted a promise of devilment. He was Cordelia's ex-husband and they were still the closest of friends, having only divorced because they never spent enough time together; him being nocturnal, starting his day post-meridian, and she up with the sunrise. Whenever Cordelia saw Oscar's lovable face and breathed in the bergamot cologne he wore, she wished their body clocks coincided. He felt the same. They both loved the idea of each other but the reality of maintaining a marriage was too complicated.

The Weasel's nineteenth century makeover had transformed an eighteenth century coaching inn into a magnificent gin palace with mosaic décor, marble classical columns, glazed windows, brass fittings, carved mahogany bar servery and soft lighting to beckon in passers-by. An indoor theatre, the Minoan Lair, where leading music hall stars of the Victorian era had entertained, was all gilt trims, red velvet drapery, swags, swirls, and plaster-cast friezes of Greek and Roman mythological scenes depicting frolicking putti, and Dionysus surrounded by ecstatic acolytes. Oscar changed little of the interiors when him and Cordelia bought the place, and instead focused his efforts on turning the extensive outdoor area into a latter-day pleasure garden.

In the eighteenth and nineteenth centuries, London's pleasure gardens were the scintillating centre of nightlife presenting a smorgasbord of opera, art, fireworks, dancing, musical debuts from illustrious composers, gaming rooms, and such entertainment that nobody wanted to leave and return to normal life. They were formally laid out with classical temples, water features, tree-lined walkways and shrubberies. It was there, beyond the lights, that shenanigans, paid and unpaid, flourished and gave the gardens their louche reputation. Aristocrats mingled with artists, merchants with musicians, and politicians with playwrights. Members of society in the thousands flocked to them because if you weren't there, you were square.

At the centre of The Weasel's twenty-first century pleasure gardens stood a rotunda in a melange of Moorish and Indo-Gothic styles with an onion dome, minarets, and horseshoe arches: the architectural lovechild of Mughal and Ottoman emperors. Inside was a central floor for mingling. Saloons along its perimeter hosted activities including Masterpiece, an interactive entertainment that involved reenacting the subjects of well-known paintings on sets designed by Celestine, in costumes (or lack of) similar to those worn in the artwork. Titian's *Bacchus and Ariadne*, and Caravaggio's *Cardsharps* were the most popular. A number of dance rooms catering to a variety of high energy styles, a piano bar, and a Hall of Mirrors promenade kept all regaled.

If guests were hungry, they had a choice of food made by star chefs-in-residence, served in a Baroque dining room lit by dozens of beeswax candles where everybody looked fetching in the low light. For refreshment, there was the pale ale infinity pool, an enclosed transparent tank of beer that never ran out; a fountain dispensing spa water from an underground chalybeate spring running beneath the pub; a ziggurat of dusty wooden boxes containing rare wines; a beehive from which mead poured through a tap; and vintage cider and perry served at tables beneath the trees in an apple and pear orchard.

Flaming torches illuminated the setting and the air was perfumed by flowers along an avenue that led to a grove of trees where hanging fronds created a hidden den. Here, anyone needing a rest could relax on divans and puff on coloured cocktail cigarettes that contained a blend of hops, valerian root and lavender for their soporific effects.

+++++

'Blimey, let's think of a theme for the party,' Oscar said to Cordelia late one afternoon as he ate breakfast in The Weasel.

Their nicknames, which only they used, were Vulpy, from Vulpini, on account of Oscar being so foxy and because of Cordelia's mental comment of disbelief, 'Foxtrot Oscar', when she first saw him even though that was absolutely not what she wanted him to do. Tall, kind eyes, luscious mouth, thick dark hair, pleasing countenance, and naughty spirit, he was the physical embodiment of her first crush, eighteenth century naturalist Joseph Banks whose portrait by Joshua Reynolds she had seen in her teenage years. Joseph's looks were the template for the fanciability factor of any man she subsequently dated.

Oscar's name for her was Blimey. As in 'Cor Blimey' which he had uttered when she walked into the room on their first date.

'Suggest anything and I'll say yes,' she replied.

'Which exhibit in Shoeseum would you run into a burning building to save?'

Cordelia mused for a while. *I won't mention Lancelot. He might think I am bonkers to be infatuated with a dead stranger.* So she said, 'All of them! But sculptor Gabriella d'Este is very special. She was a sixteenth century Venetian heiress who refused to marry because any future husband would take all her money and independence. Gabriella wore ornately jewelled fifty-centimetre-high wooden overshoes known as chopines to protect her feet and dress from the dirty streets.

'She looked down on everyone, literally in a physical sense and figuratively to the gold-diggers who came a-wooing, and needed an attendant to lean on and help keep her balance while she walked. And when not precariously negotiating the passageways of Venice, she was busy in her studio sculpting exquisite young women and memorialising them in marble. I have one in the HoT lobby.'

'Perfect. Masquerades were big in Venice. How about "The Garden of Good and Evil" as a theme with guests dressing up as allegories of virtues and sins? We won't have a clue who they are because they'll all be disguised behind a mask. I might end up snogging Rex,' he replied chortling.

'So might I!' Cordelia shot back.

Engraved invitations were sent out and everyone RSVP'd almost immediately. All the rental costumiers ran out of outfits that represented the heavenly virtues, although unsurprisingly, there was no demand for temperance or chastity.

Cordelia chose to dress as Archangel Gabriella d'Este with feathered wings adorning her back and a white velvet gown cinched at the waist. On her feet were reproductions of the signora's very own chopines created by the House of Tanner production team.

'I like the view from up here but Gabriella must have only been able to shuffle along,' she said to Sebastian as he leant against her lower back to keep her upright.

'You won't be able to dance,' he said.

'I have these,' she replied, showing him ballet slippers in her mother-of-pearl evening pouch. 'After I've made my entrance, we'll have a meander round and then I'll dismount.'

Oscar went as Dorian Gray, angelic from the front, and from behind his frock coat was ripped and bloodied; an image of the devilish portrait in the attic printed on a mask worn round the back of his head.

'Who are the young men with Celestine?' he asked Rex, admiring his ex-guardian-in-law's eye-catching Joan of Arc attire.

'Bart and Juan, Cel's walkers. She wants to add another to the roster in case she wears them out but mostly it's to make a fourth for bridge,' he replied distractedly looking for a drink.

'Contract?' Oscar queried.

'No, they're free to come and go when they please,' Rex chuckled.

A waiter resembling a faun, bare chested and resplendent in a headdress of fresh flowers, walked by carrying a tray of cocktails served in chalices. 'Would you like Inferno, or Paradise?'

'Tell me more!'

'Inferno contains whisky with a hint of chilli, and a cherry soaked in bitters. Paradise is navy-strength gin flavoured with rose petals.'

'Both please. I'll double park.'

Over in the pub-piano singing salon, not one, but three of the global superstar vocalists in that exclusive club of being known by their first name alone, came as a crew, decked out as malevolent characters in fairy tales. They were recognised only when they blasted out a medley of their greatest hits accompanied at speed by Mrs Tillicent, popular honky-tonk pianist whose TV house parties were essential Saturday evening family viewing.

Meanwhile, Cordelia was kicking up her heels in the Charleston room, exhilarated as she jumped, stomped and skiddly-do'd. The moves were exaggerated, and subtlety was forbidden so it was impossible not to laugh which made it ideal for any jollification.

'How about a snifter?' she said to her dance partner Percy Atterwill, the box office film favourite, attired in a tight black pullover and ski pants. He was wearing a mask fashioned in the shape of a double O.

'Thought you'd never ask!' he replied following her to the Shoes & Booze bar where the drinks, named after House of Tanner creations, were mixed in bejewelled shakers by bar staff dressed as priestesses of Bast, the Egyptian goddess of pleasure.

'Quetzal Martini please,' Cordelia said.

'One for me too thanks. Shaken,' Percy added.

Cordelia cheersed him and said, 'Glad to see that you drink them in real life.'

'Shush, don't tell. I actually prefer shandy but I have a sponsorship deal with a distillery so need to be seen drinking spirits,' he whispered, leaning towards Cordelia.

'Does it stipulate that you must also wear figure hugging duds and dress like a secret agent on assignment?' she giggled.

'If you worked out the way I have to for that film franchise, you'd be showing off your muscle definition every chance you had. Want to see more?' he asked flirtily.

'So tempting but I'm needed for a Highland fling. I can't resist a shake and turn. How about another evening when there aren't as many distractions? Promise me you'll wear the mask,' she replied with a cheeky raise of an eyebrow.

What a splendid do, Cordelia thought as she ambled through the party, peeking into the different rooms. There was Celestine cleaning up at the newmarket table; Rex surrounded by a small group of people doubled over with hilarity about an anecdote he related, with the punchline: 'I see you've been polishing your sequins again'; Sebastian being cheered on as he succeeded in repeatedly ringing the bull in the eponymous game; and Antonio from the local greasy spoon café, whose bubble and squeak was manna particularly the morning after, was having a tap-dancing lesson from Verity Redlake. *I didn't know the Prime Minister was a hoofer,* Cordelia thought as she watched her demonstrating the ball change.

And there was Agnieszka, House of Tanner's inestimable office manager, playing 'shoepla', which was like hoopla but with replicas of Shoeseum's exhibits as targets. She turned out to be a hotshot and managed to flip the hoop over the fire-engine red winklepickers once owned by rock and roll legend Big Jerry Cuthbert, and the simple lavender silk dancing shoes worn by Jane Austen.

Mrs Gupta, who supplied luxury fabrics to House of Tanner, looked fierce in a cerise sari and was chatting with Nicholai Gigli, a principal dancer at the Royal Ballet, who had come in his Don Quixote costume.

He was very proud of his shapely calves and often wore ballet tights that obscured very little of his lower regions when he was out and about. He told her that whenever cat-called in the street, which often happened, he would respond by performing a *tour en l'air* and that usually shut them up. Then he demonstrated what he meant and Mrs Gupta applauded enthusiastically.

At the other side of the rotunda, Cordelia saw Oscar moving from group to group, flirting with guests and ensuring they were enjoying themselves. Then it struck her. *No wonder I fancy Lancelot. He's like Oscar in profession, looks and charm.*

Rex wandered by and handed her a cocktail.

'Mmm, what is it?' she asked.

'A Lovebird. The orange blossom flavour is divine.'

They clinked glasses and stood in contented silence, sipping their drinks and watching the party. The place was rocking. Smiles, laughter, dallying.

'Impeccable,' Cordelia sighed. 'We're so lucky.'

'Gorgeousness is always rewarded,' Rex replied.

++++++

It was no surprise, given the starry invitation list, that photos and reports of The Garden of Good and Evil were everywhere on social media, in gossip columns, and video clips on news feeds at train stations. This served two useful purposes: it unveiled Shoeseum which almost immediately became London's most popular attraction, and it also put the spotlight on Cordelia for her incredible flair in conceiving a new way to appreciate shoes. When Footloose was launched simultaneously worldwide, nobody would ever think of connecting it with House of Tanner.

Footloose was a case study in marketing ingenuity. Cordelia had said to Rex, 'Have you ever seen orthopaedic shoes? Zero glam. In design terms, us ortho-shoe-sters have as much choice as a vegan in a steak house. Onion rings, that's about it. We deserve something shiny and sparkly so let's go big on a launch and make a huge splash. It's about time we of the disadvantaged feet should be able to walk proud.'

The campaign began weeks before the launch when the slogans 'Free Range Feet' and 'No More Podal Purgatory' written in chalk started to appear on urban pavements with high footfall. They were also projected by lasers into the night sky, onto landmarks including the White Cliffs of Dover, and small planes flew over cities trailing banners on which they were displayed. What they meant was a mystery as there was no website and nothing online to explain them. Naturally, this intrigued the media, inspired speculation and generated countless memes that went viral on social media.

Only when a frenzy had built was Footloose unveiled. Adverts were shown in Times Square, Piccadilly Circus and Shibuya, on the sides of buses and taxis, and on subway and railway platforms across the world depicting mountaineers making the final ascent on Everest, a footballer scoring the winning goal at the World Cup, and a squad of soldiers on manoeuvres; all of them shod in wildly impractical Footloose designs. Cyclists were hired to ride along roads with a device that beamed impressions of colourful shoes where pedestrians would see them. In Las Vegas, where lights compete with lights, Footloose was presented as a fireworks extravaganza with representations of shoes illuminating the sky, and in the casinos, slot machines were repurposed to spin footwear instead of fruit.

Cordelia and Rex, still naively thinking only people with podiatric problems would be interested, were astounded that only days after its release, Footloose became the number one selling app and maintained its position in the top ten for months. Sales went stratospheric when the editor of American Mode admitted that the Footloose post she had liked on the Visuality social media platform was not an accidental slip of her finger; she hated high heels because they made her walk like a praying mantis in pain and only did so because fashion dictated it. To say Mode magazine's shoe advertisers were vexed was an understatement but their anger was futile because within a fortnight of the surprise revelation, twenty million downloads in the USA alone almost broke the Footloose server. 'We the People' were voting with their feet.

Several well-known fashion models spoke off the record to say that, given the chance, they would always wear flatties but supermodel Rem Taigita was open about it and said heels gave her backache and it felt as though she was balancing on stilts when wearing them. Designer shoe brands tried to have her black-balled and threatened to pull advertising from the publications that hired her, but editors refused to be bullied and her face continued to adorn covers of the glossies. Podiatry International announced her as Person of the Year and increased their social media presence with factoids about how heels and poorly fitting footwear caused posture and skeletal problems. And the biggest beneficiary of this focus on shoes and feet? Footloose.

Rex was stunned as he looked at the numbers and saw there were users on every continent, Antarctica included, where scientists at New Zealand's Scott Base research station were personalising their Loosies, as downloads became universally known, with the silver fern, national emblem of their homeland. It symbolised stubborn resistance and strength which, for humans working in such an inhospitable climate, was most appropriate.

Footloose was everywhere, not only on feet, but on lips too because it was chosen as the Oxbridge English Dictionary's word of the year. A clip of the world's fastest woman winning Olympic gold in a digital pair of platforms with her country's flag and sponsor's logo outlined in sequins went viral, so did the TV news interview with a head teacher explaining how Footloose was banned at his school because it violated strict uniform policies where flat lace-ups were the only permitted shoes, unaware that, in the background, a parade of youngsters resplendent in boots that resembled space hoppers meandered past the camera.

There was no typical user because almost everyone with a smartphone was a customer. Female cabin attendants, required by their airline to work in heels despite the discomfort of their feet swelling at altitude making their shoes rub, loved Footloose because underneath the black court shoes they appeared to be wearing, they sported comfy trainers. Women at the French Film Festival who were not welcome to attend premieres unless they wore heels, no longer had to totter along the red carpet and could instead wear flip-flops concealed by whichever glamorous evening shoe they chose from the app. Those with feet that made them struggle to find footwear to fit and often had to resort to expensive custom-made shoes saved a fortune. All these groups had reason to revere the geniuses who had invented such a mind-boggling notion.

No one took more joy from Footloose than Cordelia. After a lifetime of never purposely looking towards her peculiarly shaped feet, now she couldn't stop. Throughout the day, she would click her phone, choose a design, blissfully admire it, then move on to another. One minute she was clad in Perspex mules with Statue of Liberty shaped heels, the next a pair of vertiginous wedges that made it look as though she was levitating barefoot over a field of sunflowers. She was euphoric.

One morning, Celestine popped into Cordelia's studio and handed her a newspaper. 'Darling, have a look at this feature. It's about that shoe app.'

Cordelia took it and read the report. Researchers who analysed body posture had noticed a change in how females walked. Now so few wore real heels because of Footloose, they no longer resembled wading birds picking their way through the mud, no more buttocks and breasts forced forward, no more hips swaying as they slowly ambulated. Instead, they stomped along at top-speed, reached their destination quicker and were more productive.

'Fascinating,' she replied, and was relieved when her phone rang and did not have to discuss it further and give anything away. The assistant producer for 'It's Breakfast' TV show was on the line inviting her to come and chat about how Footloose was changing the physical stance of women.

'Why you and not the businesswoman behind the app?' Celestine asked after Cordelia finished the call.

'Apparently they couldn't track her down but the producers know me and can trust that I'll be able to string a sentence together about the subject,' she replied avoiding Celestine's gaze.

The next morning, Cordelia sat waiting in the familiar green room at the studio. She was not a fan of co-host Vance Dorkin because he was arrogant, unpleasant and bound to make an insulting or crass comment. He always did. That day was no exception and after she settled in on the sofa, his first question was, 'You're supposed to be the world's leading shoe designer, how come you missed the trick with Footloose?'

Cordelia replied she was a big fan of the app and used it daily herself, then adroitly turned the conversation to Shoeseum, her passion project, describing the exhibits, Celestine's sets, how the virtual reality worked, and offering free tickets to one hundred viewers. This took up so much of her allotted time that any further talk of Footloose was abandoned.

'Deftly side-stepped, sissy,' Rex said when he called her later.

Cordelia sighed. She didn't like the deception and she dared not admit to being thunderously envious of fictitious Jill Mitchell for receiving all the kudos for the flabbergastingly successful concept.

++++++++

'Look at this nincompoop,' Sebastian said to Cordelia pointing to the front page photo on a news website. It was a scruffy young man with a long straggly beard that made it hard to work out whether he was a wizard, gonk or craft beer brewer. Around his head dangled a string of sun-shaped fairy lights, and his garb was camouflage army fatigues, unexpectedly decorated with a large embroidered rising sun image containing the letter M which covered his private parts. He was pouring petrol on a pile of shoes.

'There's a video,' he said, clicking the play button. They watched as flames gorged on the footwear and Gandalf Junior shouted, 'Free your feet, give them a treat.'

A tiny crowd whistled and cheered in approval. Cordelia looked closely and saw they were all wearing Jesus sandals.

'Who is this hirsute Messiah?' she asked.

Sebastian read the accompanying report. 'Seems to be a cult, led by sunny boy.'

'Wonder what his gripe is with shoes?'

'Here's a manifesto,' Sebastian replied and read aloud the meandering creed of the leader, Melchizedek.

'Bet his real name is something like Nigel,' Cordelia said, rolling her eyes.

It turned out that 'Free Your Feet' was the latest in a litany of single-issue and unrealisable campaigns dreamt up by Melchizedek, each with its own portentous name. He led a motley bunch of gullible hangers-on with good intentions and a desire for a simple life off the grid. They lived in benders in woodland outside Bath, shared resources, and because their leader said that money corrupted, worked on a barter system. They ate communally, usually slop that could only be described as indeterminate vegetables in a pan. Before they were allowed to start their repast, Melchizedek closed his eyes, and with arms outstretched, meditated over the food before declaring it cleansed. After they had eaten, he began a rant about whatever got his goat that day.

'We will outlaw mobile phones. I don't like ringtones,' he commanded. Another time it was, 'Antibiotics are guilty of mass murder, they kill bacteria.'

When he finished his histrionics, he disappeared from the camp. The disciples assumed it was to a shelter deeper into the woods where he had privacy.

To describe Melchizedek's tribe as brain-washed would be to suggest they actually washed anything. His raggle taggle of believers went along with the ramblings because they had little else to do after they had gathered wood, water, and returned from scouring the bins behind supermarkets in search of discarded food.

But in the weeks after the bonfire of footwear, they were busy acting on his instructions and made themselves very unpopular by standing silently outside shoe shops holding signs that read, 'Don't Treat Your Feet Like Meat' with crude illustrations of veal calves in small boxes. They attempted to shame people who wore real shoes, following them down the street and moo-ing loudly. When police officers took to discreetly walking by the shops to monitor activity, protestors grunted like pigs. Then a group of teenagers started turning up and singing, 'Old MacDonald Had a Farm', with a moo moo here and an oink oink there, and all but the bender brigade cackled at how silly it all was.

While Melchizedek did not succeed in closing Bath's shoe shops, he did attract international media attention, which for a demagogue is catnip. As it turned out, despite him not being taken seriously, his Free Your Feet ideology was, and it made many people rethink packaging their feet and choose instead to let them go commando. It was particularly popular with the politically active who adopted the cause and understood how to amplify it. School children did assemblies, university students formed special interest groups, and petitions were circulated demanding health warnings be printed on shoes with heels, equating them with the risk from cigarette smoking. This direct action vastly increased the sales of flat sandals and it benefitted Footloose as millions more downloaded the app.

'If I didn't know better, I'd think we'd paid the Free Your Feeters,' Rex commented gleefully, 'Jill Mitchell's bankers will be planning an extension to their Swiss counting house!'

'Well, in that case, I'm off to LA to spend some of her lolly. There are shoes in an auction that I can't live without and if they are not in Shoeseum by next week I will take to my bed with an attack of the vapours.'

'What *are* the vapours? I've often wondered that.'

'Similar to the collywobbles, but not as bad as the heebie-jeebies.'

'That's clear. Thank you.'

Chapter Four

Los Angeles was a treasure trove for Cordelia to expand her silver screen shoe collection and she regularly travelled to the City of Angels for Hollywood memorabilia auctions. Top of her target list for this trip were the black satin evening pumps embellished with a silver chrysanthemum of crystals worn by Bette Davis for a cocktail party as the character Margo Channing in the film *All About Eve*. Margo's friends knew trouble was brewing when she uttered the immortal line about fastening seat belts and bumpy nights.

As usual, the auction room on Sunset Strip was busy, mostly with film fans who were curious to see the starry artefacts going under the hammer but who had no intention of bidding. Cordelia was in a spending mood and had won the bid for a pair of red patent leather Mary Jane's worn by silent movie star Constance Tiverton, nicknamed The Indestructible because she had survived two ship sinkings: once as a Red Cross nurse on an allied troop carrier that had gone down in 1916 as it transported wounded soldiers from Turkey, and then in 1922 on a transatlantic liner she was emigrating to the USA on.

When it came to Bette's shoes, Cordelia was ready to triumph and had decided where in Shoeseum to display them. Rex worshipped *All About Eve* and they planned to celebrate the shoe coup by throwing a little cocktail party with her as Margo and him as Addison de Witt, drinking Gibsons as they did in the film. The bidding started with nine individuals, seven of whom dropped out until it was just Cordelia and one other. Both were determined and the bids quickly increased.

'Keep calm,' Cordelia said to herself, 'You've wanted these shoes forever.'

She was just about to raise her paddle again when the auctioneer made an unexpected announcement.

'Sorry, ladies and gentlemen, this lot has just been withdrawn from sale.'

An audible ripple of disappointment filled the room, led by Cordelia who loudly uttered an English vulgarism that Americans did not realise was crude.

Wonder who the other bidder is, she thought, standing up, rearranging her jacket and heading to the exit. Suddenly, she was oblivious to anything else apart from a tall, slim woman with honey blonde wavy hair, surrounded by a dazzling aura of golden light and walking towards her as though in slow motion.

'We were robbed of our reward!' the woman said with the hint of a French accent and beaming a smile of enough wattage to power a city. 'And we wanted them so much. But I had a plan — we would share: one shoe each. Then meet annually to reunite the pair and drink cocktails. Gibsons, of course! Elodie l'Archambeau,' she said offering a handshake.

Cordelia had a profound sense of familiarity as they shook hands and a warm rush of endorphins raced through her arteries making her momentarily breathless. She looked into Elodie's lively eyes and saw something she recognised — mischief.

'Cordelia Tanner. How do you do? But I feel as though I already know you. Have we met before?'

'In a previous life maybe. And now we've met in this one, let us make up for the lost time,' Elodie replied. 'Lunch?'

Strolling along the Strip with her new friend was like being with the girl from Ipanema in that everybody turned to stare and most went 'aaah'. *What an extraordinary effect she has. Charisma superpower and her weapon is a meteor shower that spreads loveliness. Glorious,* Cordelia thought.

Unsurprisingly for a restaurant headed by one of LA's top chefs, it was full, but the way the maître d' reacted to Elodie when she asked for a table was as if he was bewitched.

'I will set up a place for you in the owner's private roof garden. It has superb views over the city,' he said, and when she clasped his hand and thanked him to say how happy that made her, he visibly quivered.

One long lunch later, Cordelia and Elodie had compared scars — both in the eyebrow, both acquired in their teenage years. Elodie's by being whacked with a racquet playing doubles at tennis, and Cordelia's when a woman on a hen party stumbled and knocked her over on the down escalator at Leicester Square tube station, then accidentally stepped on her head. It was not the necessity of a visit to Accident and Emergency for a tetanus injection that bothered her, but the fact her skin had been punctured and scarred for life by a white plastic stiletto heel.

In addition to scars, they had much else in common: same height, shared the same age and birth date, and had a mutual passion for collecting shoes. In Elodie's case, it was through her work as an academic, with a PhD in the symbolism of footwear.

'I am engrossed by that subject,' Cordelia exclaimed, and then went on to describe Shoeseum and how she was able to tell the story of the shoes' owners through her special power.

'Psychomatricks? Please tell me more,' Elodie begged, 'And will you do a session with me?' she asked, pointing to her knee-length mustard coloured boots.

'Such soft leather — gorgeous. I'm a shoe designer,' said Cordelia leaning down and stroking one of the square toed, Cuban heeled biker-cowboy hybrids. 'Are they bespoke?'

'Yes. I have many pairs, different colours and materials. I like to wear them with all my outfits, formal and casual.'

'Here, lay your left leg across my lap,' Cordelia said placing her hands on the boot. She concentrated for a couple of minutes then said laughing, 'So, these aren't for show, you do drive a motorcycle. And break the speed limit too.'

She then returned to her meditation and gave a commentary on the activities she was 'seeing'. 'A trip around downtown LA's movie palaces yesterday evening with Clyde Mackintosh riding pillion.' He was the oh-so-fine-looking and enduringly popular king of the box office. 'Up onto Mulholland Drive to gaze at the glimmering lights of the Valley. Then there's a gap of several hours that I can't read. If you had your boots off, that's why.' Elodie smiled at that particular memory. Cordelia continued, 'Breakfast tacos with Clyde at a street stand on Pico. He looks good in biker leathers. So do you!'

'*Formidable.* You've recounted everything just as it happened. Now, do you have things booked for the rest of the day? No? Good. I have a plan. Should I reveal it or maintain a surprise?'

'I love a surprise, so please don't tell.'

'Let's go then,' Elodie said, and linked arms with Cordelia as they left the restaurant, leading her to a high-performance motorbike parked down the street.

'Does it have a name?'

'Yes, Nike — no relation to the shoe company — goddess of speed and strength.'

'I've always wondered why you never see anyone riding side saddle on these beasts.'

'Try it!'

Cordelia climbed on and sat at a precarious angle, but feeling unbalanced as Elodie set off slowly, she tapped her on the shoulder and said, 'Now I know why they don't,' and manoeuvred into a safer position.

'Let's take the scenic route along Sunset. Hold tight,' Elodie shouted as she set off at pace.

After fifty minutes of cutting through LA's interminable traffic, they arrived at the airport and approached a private jet parked near the perimeter.

'We have a short flight. Nike is coming with us for the other end.'

It seemed that no sooner were they in the air, they were landing again. What Elodie referred to as 'the other end' was the Mojave Desert, an unearthly landscape of rocky outcrops, low-lying scrub and Joshua trees standing sentinel as the motorbike sped past until it reached the end of the road at which a wooden nineteenth century Wild West saloon stood; the sole built structure in sight. This was The Blue Moon, not only a purveyor of refreshments, but also the area's post office, general store, church, and with its two-lane indoor bowling alley, sporting venue.

'Drink?' Elodie said.

'Botticelli!'

They looked out of place in the saloon. The regulars who lived in ramshackle properties dotted around the area were gruff, hardy and suspicious of strangers. Cordelia pictured the scene from the film *An American Werewolf in London* when the two hapless central characters accidentally banged the door as they walked into a rural pub and distracted a local who was aiming a dart and missed the board. He gave them a murderous look.

Not only were they the only women in the place, but they were the only ones dressed in a copper and saffron plaid blazer matched with cocoa coloured slim-fit trousers (Elodie), and a purple linen suit printed with double helixes in a vibrant shade of lime (Cordelia). Cordelia was determined to right the wrong whereby Rosalind Franklin's role in the understanding of the molecular structure of DNA was overlooked when it came to Nobel Prize recognition. So, whenever she wore the suit, she always explained the significance of the print whether people asked her to or not.

Nobody was immune to Elodie's Love Potion Number 9 and after buying everyone a drink, she and Cordelia were surrounded by men begging them to try on *their* cowboy hat, playing pool with all-comers, line dancing, and the two of them up on the tiny stage singing along to

Loretta Lynn blasting from the jukebox.

'What would life be without a song or a dance?' Elodie said happily between tunes.

After more than a few bourbons, the duo staggered out of the bar, keeping each other upright, and singing the song 'Walking After Midnight'.

'Where to now?' Cordelia asked.

'Follow me,' Elodie stage whispered, leading them down the road in the dark for ten minutes and up a track to a wooden fence. 'We can climb it,' she said, and they shinned up and fell over the other side in a heap, shushing each other from laughing too loudly — sound carried in the desert.

Cordelia peered around in the gloom. They were by a mineral hot spring and the steam rose from the water like a wraith.

'I need to be horizontal in the middle of that pool,' she said removing her clothes.

And that was how Cordelia spent the night: floating on a Lilo under the endless sky where the absence of light pollution meant the heavens revealed the Milky Way in detail she had never seen before. Every now and again, her Lilo gently banged up against Elodie's, who was quietly reciting the names of constellations she recognised. It was magical.

Next morning, they were up with the light and over coffee and carbs at a diner in the nearest town, Elodie asked, 'When are you returning to London and do you have any plans in LA before you go?'

'I'm on the late afternoon flight tomorrow and was planning to see an exhibition at the Getty Museum before I leave.'

'Can I give you a lift instead and tempt you to have lunch with me in Paris? You can see my shoe collection. It's so much more convenient than you rushing to LAX and going through departures with hundreds of others.'

It was impossible to say no to Elodie. Not that Cordelia wanted to.

Her rule of life was that she yielded to all temptation and needed no persuasion to join Elodie on the jet.

'I'm so pleased. That gives us more time for adventures. If you want to freshen up, I have booked us into Oasis Palms spa. We can have one of their famous mud baths and then go on to our next quest.'

A few minutes of swift riding on Nike and they were at the deluxe Oasis Palms, opened in the 1930s as a retreat for rich Angelenos. After ninety minutes of being enveloped in mineral rich clay, followed by a shower, they felt revived.

'Do you want to go prospecting for gold?' Elodie said. 'There's a ghost town down the road, and I am feeling lucky!'

++++++++

The Mojave Desert was dotted with several forsaken settlements whose sole purpose had been to support gold, silver and mineral prospectors during the nineteenth century rush for riches. Riches were rare and most miners left disappointed or could not survive such brutal working and living conditions.

Elodie pulled up in a place called Gold Top where skeletons of mining equipment and ruined buildings presented a post-apocalypse sight that in science fiction novels would have been caused by cyborgs intent on scorching the earth in a bid to eradicate humans. There was no sign of life in the silent vista until they heard, 'Howdy y'all,' as a man's voice called out from a wooden hut by the town's dilapidated sign. 'Wanna look round Gold Top? I can take ya. Ten bucks each.'

This was Quinn Manniton, the sole resident, who had been camping out there for three years chasing his fantasy of finding gold so he could afford a trailer home at the Salton Sea, a landlocked body of water further south. So far, gold had eluded him and he scraped a living showing tourists round the former mining centre. Everything about Quinn was beaten up: his scruffy baseball cap, blue jeans, denim shirt, and chiefly his spirit. It was hard to guess his age because he'd neglected to wear factor forty-five and his skin was so wrinkled and freckled that he could have been eighty but judging by the lack of grey in his sun-bleached brown hair tied back in a ponytail, he was probably in his mid-fifties. His only permanent company was a coyote called Tooth that had habituated to him as a puppy. Cordelia noticed Quinn's scuffed cowboy boots made of an animal skin that resembled, but was not, the scales of a pangolin and made a mental note to do an animal armour collection for Footloose.

'I can show ya everywhere apart from inside the derelict mine. Too many dreamers died down there in a fire and it's haunted so don't go anywhere near,' Quinn said.

'What a shame, because I have a good instinct about this,' said Elodie turning to him with a smile. 'As we have travelled so far, can you make an exception and show us where it is? If you are intrigued to know what it's like inside, we'll take photographs so you can show future sightseers without going in.'

How could he resist? He couldn't.

Ten minutes later, Cordelia and Elodie had ignored a metal sign printed with skull and crossbones and the warning 'Abandoned Mine — Stay Out — Stay Alive' hanging skewwhiff from a post and clambered through wooden slats blocking the entrance into a tunnel which, with blackened walls, showed evidence of a fire that had closed the mine decades earlier. By the light on their phones, they gingerly picked a pathway along a slope towards a shaft and looked down. Nothing but forbidding black.

'Wonder how deep it is. I'll throw a stone and test,' Cordelia said picking up a fragment and dropping it into the void. Seconds elapsed before they heard a clunk as it hit the ground metres below.

'If we had proper lights, we could investigate. Do you think that was used to attach a rope to winch miners up and down?' Elodie said pointing to a hook attached to the wall. 'What a horrible job this was. And all for the obsession with gold that only has value because humans say it does. The worth depends on a shared belief in the said value of the commodity.'

'Fascinating, isn't it? It's like diamonds — just bits of crystalised carbon. And how about the stone currency of the Yap Islands? Limestone discs with holes in the centre. The largest one has a diameter of over three metres. Try putting that in your purse!' Cordelia jumped suddenly. 'Something just flew by my ear. We're in the Batcave. That must be what we can smell. Want to go?' she said with an 'urgh' in her voice.

'Can we look in that side tunnel on the way out? I have a feeling.'

They walked along it and came upon the charred remains of a wooden ore shoot. On the ground below, there was a pile of iron oxide quartz abandoned after the fire.

'Quartz is the most likely source of gold in this part of the desert. Let's take a piece outside and have a look,' Elodie said pointing to the largest one. 'I think I can manage to carry it outside if you lead with your light.'

'Doctor l'Archambeau, you make a very convincing geologist! You will be my "call an expert" if I'm ever in a general knowledge quiz and the jackpot depends on me knowing about minerals.'

'I am obsessed with natural crystals, in the form they come out of the ground, unworked and unpolished. Red beryl is my favourite. Such a rich fuchsia colour. She's remarkable and very rare, found only in a few places.'

Back in the fresh air, they examined the mineral with its veins of red-brown haematite and metallic seam.

Quinn was waiting for them. 'Whatcha got there, ladies?' he asked, bending down to look at it. He shaded his eyes in the early afternoon sun and said, 'Well, I never. I think this is gold. And it's a mighty weight. You darn well succeeded where I failed.'

'Beginner's luck,' Cordelia said, trying to stay cool even though inside her excitement was that of a boisterous puppy.

'It's a gift for you, Quinn,' said Elodie, smiling at his dumbfounded expression.

His bottom lip trembled and tears came into his eyes. 'Ya mean it, ma'am? This changes everything.'

'Yes, and there might be more where we found this one. Only the three of us know it is there. It's our secret. We'll go back in and retrieve it all for you.'

Cordelia felt rather emotional for him. He had been so animated telling them how he longed to return to the Salton Sea where, as a child, he and his family took their holidays at the Bombay Beach resort and swam, fished and played on the sand.

'Folks think I'm loco because it's not exactly Miami Beach, but I like the unusual landscape.'

Unusual was an understatement, more like dystopian. Describing it was inadequate and seeing was disbelieving. With its sulphurous smell and the macabre sight of thousands of dead fish and birds rotting on the shores attracting plagues of flies, it was a vision of hell that not even Hieronymus Bosch could have imagined. That's how it was now, but it did not start that way.

It formed by accident when a canal carrying water from the Colorado River flooded an area called the Salton Sink and created an artificial lake which, when seeded with fish, led to the growth of recreational tourism infrastructure. This miraculous source of irrigation in a desert encouraged widespread agriculture in the area which voraciously took the water and generously gave back dense fertiliser and pesticide run-off. With no inlet and outlet, over decades the lake became increasingly saline, killing the fish. Water evaporated in the heat increasing salinity even further and the concentration of nitrates and chemicals from farming made it even more toxic.

Naturally, tourists ceased visiting and the infrastructure decayed. Quinn knew all this but did not care. His existence in Gold Top was hardly Eden, and he was looking forward to joining the misfits who chose to inhabit a place that mainstream society never ventured into and where the American Dream was a parallel universe.

'What a good hour of work. You are a wellspring of kind-heartedness. Now he won't just be able to buy a trailer but the whole park too!' said Cordelia as they walked back to the motorbike.

Elodie was like one of the reality TV shows where millionaires change lives, but she did it with no fanfare or expectation of glory. *She lives life according to Celestine's Womanifesto. That's why we were instant friends. That and her boots.*

Elodie looked at her watch. 'What do you think of an evening at the Hollywood Bowl? Maureen Merridon is headlining, and I adore her voice. If we rush back to LA, we might get there before the support act finishes. We can buy tickets for the top rear — it's rarely full up there and we can enter discreetly.'

'Botticelli!'

++++++

Cordelia settled into the roomy black leather armchair in the cabin of the jet and laughed when Elodie announced, 'Welcome to Elodelia Airlines, official carrier for adventures and escapades.'

The plane started speeding towards lift-off and when they were at cruising altitude, she heard, 'The captain has turned off the seat belt sign and invites the VIP guest into the flight deck.'

'I like the idea of pretending to fly a plane,' Cordelia said sliding down into the co-pilot's seat. 'Crikey, look at all these screens and switches. Complicated! How long have you had a pilot's license?'

'Eight years. I thought it would be a useful skill to have because my work sometimes takes me to remote places. It also means I'm the back-up on long journeys for Colette, my permanent pilot.'

She handed Cordelia an aviation headset. 'I'll give you lessons another time if you want me to but now, I must concentrate and get us back without delay. I will be talking to air traffic control, and you can listen too through the headphones.'

Elodie was not only fluent in French, English and Italian, but also in the language of flight. Most of the conversation with air traffic control happened in the approach to the airport when Elodie said, 'Los Angeles Tower, Tidal-Jet Foxtrot Delta Oscar Alpha Mike, over Chula Hills inbound.'

'Tidal-Jet Foxtrot Delta Oscar Alpha Mike make left 360 for spacing.'

'Roger.'

A few minutes passed then the controller said, 'Tidal-Jet Foxtrot Delta Oscar Alpha Mike make short approach runway 24L, cleared to land.'

'Roger.'

I'd be so tempted to reply 'Rabbit' if I was an air traffic controller, Cordelia thought as she watched Elodie being so grown up and in charge.

After a quick flight from the desert over the relentless conurbation of San Bernadino and Los Angeles counties, Elodie landed the plane and taxied to a corner of the airport. Ground crew assisted with unloading the bike, for which they were generously tipped. Elodie and Cordelia mounted it then accelerated north, taking the fastest route past the incongruous sight of nodding donkeys pumping oil in the middle of Ladera Heights.

It was a rush to reach the Hollywood Bowl before the interval but Elodie rode Nike as though she was in a video game and her task was to score points by manoeuvring between four wheeled vehicles to get ahead of traffic. If the other drivers had known this might possibly be one of the final concerts from Maureen Merridon, last of the singers of the ilk of Peggy Lee and Rosemary Clooney, they would have pulled over and let the bike through as though it was an emergency vehicle, but as they didn't, it was up to Elodie to be assertive.

When they arrived at the Bowl, there was nobody in the rows at the back so they bought tickets and made their way up, up and even further up to the top and entered the amphitheatre without distracting anyone. Warm-up act Nate Finkel, Broadway stalwart, was in the middle of 'Blow Gabriel Blow' from the musical *Anything Goes*, winking suggestively as he sang the lines about being a sinner and scamp and trimming his lamp. The crowd was enraptured.

After the applause had quietened, Nate said, 'Can you believe there are unfilled seats right in the front of the stage when we are about to see one of the world's greatest entertainers? I'll wager five bucks they are allocated to corporate season ticket holders who could not be bothered to come tonight. It's so disrespectful to Miss Merridon. We can't let her see any empty places so I invite those in the back row to come down during the interval and fill them.'

Cordelia, languidly zoning out, did not hear the announcement but Elodie did and nudged her. 'He means us. We're going down there in the break so Maureen will see friendly faces gazing up at her.'

It took around ten minutes to shuffle through the interval crowds and find the route towards the front of the stage. They walked past a steward into the enclosure, giggling that he had not stopped them, and Elodie said, 'These seats look good,' and they sat down.

A couple sitting just behind glared and the man said, 'Are you supposed to be here?'

'Yes,' Cordelia replied.

As there was no response to that, he fired eye-daggers at the interlopers. More so when the head usher came over to check tickets.

'Sorry, you're in the wrong place, these are for the back. Hurry or you'll miss the start of the main act.'

Elodie beamed at him and said, 'Nate invited us down just before the interval. We're here to smile at Maureen Merridon and show her some love.'

The usher, who only seconds before had been polite but insistent, gazed at Elodie with the gormless expression of a drunken teenager and said, 'Aren't you considerate? Of course, you must sit here. Enjoy yourselves!'

The eye-dagger wielders tutted and whispered about how outrageous it was that those in the lower priced rows could just walk in with such effrontery, but their targets did not hear because the band started playing Maureen's theme song as she walked on stage to a standing ovation. She placed a hand over her heart, bowed in gratitude and, when everyone sat down, started singing.

After the first number, Maureen asked what she should perform next. The din as the crowd shouted out the titles of her countless hits would have lifted the roof off the Hollywood Bowl if it had one, but all went silent with the first notes of 'Hitching a Ride on the Love Train': the composition that had earnt her the Oscar for Best Song.

After she finished and was chatting with the audience, she started teasing punters in the boxes immediately in front of the stage, saying, 'These folks won't have a clue what I'm talking about because they're here on a freebie, and probably don't know my music.' Maureen looked down at them where some were squirming, then her face lit up. 'Well, what a wonderful surprise, my friend the esteemed Doctor Elodie l'Archambeau from France is here.'

Elodie blew her a kiss as Maureen said, 'Honey, come backstage after the show and we'll go for a drink.'

Cordelia could not resist turning round to the tutty people in the row behind and smiling at them. They looked equal amounts of crestfallen and deeply envious.

'How do you know Maureen?' Cordelia said as they waited for her after the concert.

'I curated the shoes at her Musicals Museum in Las Vegas. She has a vast collection of extraordinary costumes and memorabilia worn in musical films and theatre.'

'And whose shoes did you woman-handle?' Cordelia asked eagerly.

'Dozens, including Elvis, Ginger Rogers, and, most exceptional, the black leather and suede stilettos worn by Marilyn Monroe in the "Running Wild" scene from *Some Like It Hot.*'

'Want. Badly. Just think what I'd discover if I psy-commed them.'

'We'll make it happen! Imagine if you came out of the trance and were able to play the ukulele like Marilyn did. We could form a duo. I play the piano accordion. It will only be a matter of time before we have a recording contract for our niche performing style.'

+++++++

Maureen settled back in the red leather booth of the Catalina Grill, an old-school Hollywood bar and restaurant, the type of place where osso bucco and creamed spinach were washed down with the finest Martinis in town, and cheersed Elodie and Cordelia.

'Honey, tell me more about your Shoeseum. It sounds like nothing I've heard of before.'

The mistress of House of Tanner needed no encouragement to speak about her beloved shoe collection and the unique interpretation format she had conceived. Maureen was fascinated.

'You must come and see it when you're next in London. I have shoes that belonged to Lorenzo De Santis,' Cordelia said.

'I knew him. We worked together on *Ring Them Bells* and had a short-lived romance. One of those film-set love affairs that does not survive post-production. We'd play Scrabble in his trailer. What a cheat he was. He once tried to persuade me that "zyyonku" was a real word because he had a Z and two Ys in his tiles. Said it was a Zambian antelope and intersected the k in the paltry "oak" I had laid down. I realised he was trying to juke me but let him have it otherwise he would have sulked. I still have good memories despite him being high maintenance.

'And yes, I would love to see Shoeseum. I'm planning a farewell tour and London would be the first overseas city we play. You must come to my museum in Vegas. The collection is something else especially the magical flying shoes worn by Derry Daffodil when she tap danced with Bertie Tidewell over the arc of a rainbow in *Cruising Through the Heavens*.'

'That was the first film musical I ever saw! My guardian Celestine took me and my brother Rex to see it when we were nine. We begged her to send us for tap dancing lessons and kept them up for years. Even now, we can still shuffle off to Buffalo. Do you have any exhibits from *The Sound of Music*? It's one of my favourite films.'

'Yes, I do. Several. My highlight is the violet crêpe de chine puff sleeved shirt-waister dress worn by the Baroness in the scene where she reluctantly plays ball with the children. I also have the wimple that Mother Superior wore when she says to Maria, "What is it you can't face?", which always make me chuckle if you listen with a certain type of ear.'

Cordelia woke up most days loving her existence, but just at that very moment, her cup of love runneth over to be drinking cocktails opposite one of popular music's legends and sitting next to her fabulous new friend. She never took for granted that she had triumphed in the lottery of life with her upbringing by Celestine, sparkling career and, more than anything, being twin to Rex which was the greatest jackpot anybody could win.

How mundane it would be if I was married to an Orpheus type, mother to a herd of delinquent brats, and never had the urge to go-go dance in a cage. And if that was me, what would Rex have been? A statistician in the planning department of a local council in the Home Counties. He would wear slacks and be founder of the sudoku society that met in the disused canteen of the Town Hall, she thought.

Cordelia was jolted her out of the nightmare of what might have been when a fan approached the table and asked Maureen for her autograph.

'Sure, honey, and you should ask my friends for theirs. I'm just a singer, these two are world class authorities on shoes.'

The fan looked nonplussed and reluctantly stuck a scrap of paper in front of them.

'You're a leftie,' Cordelia said as Elodie signed her name. 'So am I. Rex is too. We have a very exclusive club, called the Left Leaning Society. It's just me and Rex. Do you want to join? We play a game where we draw or write something with our right hand and the other must guess what it is. Naïve art has nothing on our creations.'

'I will not rest until I am a member. How do I make that happen?'

Cordelia placed a notebook and pencil in front of her. 'Time to audition.'

Elodie shakily made some marks on the paper. It was a bulbous shape with a long narrow pointed something or other.

'Elephant head and trunk or perhaps a narwhal?' Cordelia questioned, turning the page upside down and peering at an angle through her eyelashes.

'Close. It's one of Marilyn's stilettos at Maureen's museum.'

'Welcome to the Left Leaning Society, comrade. You're so bad with your right hand, you're good!'

'You two are cute,' Maureen said. 'How long have you known each other?'

'About thirty-six hours,' Cordelia answered.

'In this life,' Elodie chipped in.

'Fast friendship, can't beat it. When are you off back to Europe?'

'Tomorrow afternoon.'

'Then 1 a.m. is a good time to say night night. Cordelia, I can't wait for you to come and see the Musicals Museum. And Elodie, I'll be so pleased to welcome you back. Anytime. Call me.' Then as she stood up to leave, other diners started applauding and the three of them walked out of the restaurant to loud cheers.

++++++++

'*Bonjour et bienvenue* Cordelia. I am Colette, the captain, and this is Boniface. He is in charge of the cabin and will look after you very well. *Bonjour* Elodie, I hope your time in Los Angeles was memorable.'

Well, he certainly puts the dolly into trolley, Cordelia thought smiling at the pretty flight attendant who looked so neat in his uniform.

'*Bonjour* Colette. *Bonjour* Boniface,' Elodie said, kissing each one in turn. 'We went to the desert, sang country and western songs in a saloon and the next day found a big golden nugget.' Then, turning as another young man approached from behind, said, 'Ah, Cédric there you are, *bonjour*. Cordelia, this is Cédric my personal assistant. He and Boniface were married before we left France and spent their honeymoon driving up the Pacific Coast Highway to San Francisco.'

'*Bonjour* Elodie. *Bonjour* Cordelia. We stayed a night at the Madonna Inn. It was mad! We wanted the suite called Bridal Falls, but it was booked so we chose Caveman instead. The room was lined with rocks and the shower was a waterfall. Boniface was enamoured and now I am convinced I married Fred Flintstone.'

Boniface grinned and said, 'Yabba dabba doo.'

'I'll pilot us the first few hours and Colette will fly the remainder then I will come for drinks and dinner with you. And I have a plan for our entertainment afterwards so don't go anywhere,' Elodie said to Cordelia.

'Perfect. I have some work to do. Our trip to the desert has given me ideas for footwear. I need to make notes and do some drawing.'

Quinn's boots had made her want to do something bold with beasts for Footloose and after much sketching, she put down her pad content with what she had achieved.

Elodie walked into the cabin and sat down opposite her. 'I think we need a drink now, don't we? Champagne?'

Boniface poured two glasses.

'You can leave the bottle, thank you. *Santé*! May I look at your illustrations please?' she said to Cordelia who passed her sketchpad. 'Ooh, boots. What are they made from?'

'The drawings are mood boards to give me inspiration. They will never be manufactured because the skins come from endangered species which I would never condone using,' she replied avoiding Elodie's gaze, and thought, *Here I go, being evasive about Footloose. Is it dishonest to obfuscate?*

'How clever you are. If you ever do make them from sustainable animals, I'll order a pair in every colour. Are you hungry? If so, we can eat dinner. Let's go into the dining room.'

Boniface had set the table with white linen, and gold rimmed navy blue porcelain plates designed for the plane. Cordelia sat down.

'Tagliatelle with truffle butter — divine.'

'It's the most popular dish at West Hollywood's Araminta trattoria. So simple and so delicious. Cédric arranged a takeaway to be delivered to the plane earlier.'

Pudding was sfogliatelle followed by coffee. When the table was cleared, Elodie said, 'I would normally suggest a digestif, but we need to wake up for our next activity so how about more Champagne?'

'Oh, must I? Yes, I must. Fill her up, Boniface!'

'Close your eyes. I have a surprise for you.' Elodie led her into a room at the rear of the plane. 'Now you can open them. This is Elodelia's nightclub in the sky!' she said as 'Devil in the Rhythm' played over the sound system. 'I had a dancefloor installed which can be covered if I need this area for work. Cédric helped to design the laser lighting system to encourage a dream-like state.'

'When I am World President-for-Life, I will decree that mirror balls are mandatory in every room, and that dancing is prescribed by doctors. It makes me so happy,' Cordelia shouted above the pulsing one hundred and twenty beats per minute tune.

After two hours of non-stop dancing, their euphoria was supersonic.

'Greatest night ever,' Cordelia panted, taking a break and gulping down water.

'We have three hours before we land. Do you want to rest?'

'Yes, best to leave wanting more. I'm too psyched to sleep, but I'd like to lie down.'

Boniface brought them fleecy cotton pyjamas, heavy duty earplugs, eyeshades, and a blend of geranium and ylang-ylang essential oils to douse on the pillow for relaxation.

'You have the master bedroom. It has a bathroom with everything you need so you can have a shower before breakfast. Sleep tight,' Elodie said, closing the door.

Cordelia was unable to reach the land of nod but she dozed along its ramparts for a while which was enough until she got out of bed for her ablutions.

Elodie was already up and drinking coffee at the dining table. '*Bonjour ma belle.* Caffeine?'

'Tea please,' Cordelia replied.

Boniface brought a china teapot and cup. It was not just any tea, this was first flush loose leaf from Paris' impeccable Mariage Frères.

'Would you like to eat something, Cordelia?' he asked handing her a plate of warm croissants.

'They are from my local boulangerie and were frozen for the plane so I'm afraid they are not freshly baked this morning. But they are freshly defrosted and warmed in the galley oven,' Elodie said apologetically.

'I would enjoy them even if they were stale. I'm so loved up with everything about this jet.'

'This is the first of many journeys together so I hope you will always feel that way.'

They sat quietly finishing breakfast and then Colette announced over the address system, '*Bonjour* Elodie and Cordelia. We have forty minutes before we land, please get ready to take your seats.'

Cordelia strapped herself in and stared out of the window but it was overcast in the Paris region so there was little to see as the plane came down at Le Bourget Airport.

'Wonderful, thank you. Everything was superb,' she said effusively to Colette, Boniface and Cédric, shaking their hands before disembarking and saying to Elodie, 'Now I'm spoilt forever and not even first class will suffice.'

'I'm so grateful to have this luxury. I do fly commercial too, but the size of their dancefloors always disappoints me. Now, do you want to go into the city in a taxi or on Nike? Depending on traffic it could be forty-five minutes, maybe less if I can weave between vehicles. Our luggage will follow by car.'

'Who would choose a car when they could be sitting pillion with a woman who defies the laws of physics and is the motorbike driving equivalent of capillary action?' Cordelia replied.

+++++

Elodie lived in the 9th arrondissement, a few minutes' walk from le Palais Garnier. When Cordelia discovered that, she responded ecstatically. 'It's my absolute favourite building in Paris. The foyer! The staircase! The more-is-more and then add some more-ity of it! But I'm in love with your apartment too. Streamline Moderne, so chic.'

The lunch menu, specifically requested by Cordelia, was omelette aux fines herbes and a bottle of Sancerre, then crème brûlée matched with Sauternes for dessert.

'Did you know you can no longer get an omelette in a Paris restaurant? I try each time I'm in the city. I think it's something to do with them only having pasteurised liquid egg in the kitchen in case of salmonella,' she said.

'Then you must always come here in future when you need one. My chef Véronique makes them taste extra special with butter from cows grazed on wildflowers that grow only on her parents' alpine farm in the Auvergne. Now, if you are ready, do you want to look at my shoe collection? I'm nervous. What if you are not impressed?' Elodie said with a slight frown of worry.

She need not have been. Cordelia was stunned at the size and range. It included Indian paduka wedding shoes with toe-knobs formed of ornamental silver, and medieval poulaines with ultra-long points that extended ten centimetres from the toe.

'Catholic priests called them Satan's Claws because they prevented the wearer from kneeling and praying. Men who wore them were accused of sexual deviancy because the long points were considered to be phallic,' Elodie expounded.

The footwear was displayed on glass shelves in her laboratory where they had been X-rayed, carbon-dated and examined under a microscope. This was Elodie in professional rather than playful mode. Both suited her.

'Unbelievable!' Cordelia said. 'Do you want me to psy-comm a pair and tell you the story of the owner? I have time before I leave for London.'

Elodie chose simple flat black leather ankle boots tied with a crude lace at the midfoot. They had belonged to Piero Cellini, an apprentice in Leonardo da Vinci's studio in Florence.

As Cordelia held them, she pictured a young man with long dark hair dressed in a green velvet gown, sitting side on to the painter: a heavily bearded man of around fifty. He was standing by a canvas with brush in hand looking intently at Piero. 'Try that smile again,' he instructed. 'But make it imperceptible.'

'You'll never believe this,' Cordelia said incredulously, exiting her meditation. 'Mona Lisa is a portrait of your shoe boy! Lisa Gherardini did none of the sittings because they were the only times she could see her childhood friend Bartolomea. After Lisa married, her husband forbade them from ever meeting. She arranged with da Vinci for her cousin Piero to take her place.

'They had a family resemblance but not enough of one as it turned out because when the painting was completed, it didn't look like Lisa. That's the reason it was never delivered to Francesco del Giocondo even though he had commissioned it. I've heard the theory that the painting is a self-portrait of Leonardo so the hypothesis that it's not of who it's meant to be is already out there, but now I know the real story.'

Elodie looked stunned. 'You learnt all that through the boot and nobody else knows this? Do we have time to visit the Louvre and say hello to Piero? Should we ask him if he wants this fact to be a secret or can we reveal the news?'

'Unfortunately, there are limitations to my psy-comm skills and although I can see and hear the characters, they don't know I'm there. There's no scientific basis to my ability so I only mention it to the open-minded. I've tried before to enlighten non-believers about it being a form of extra-sensory perception but they thought I was talking rubbish. It's so tempting to announce this news but if folk knew how I'd discovered it, they would think I'm barking.'

'What are you barking at?' asked Elodie, not understanding the idiom.

'Barking mad. English slang to describe someone insane. It may be related to brain damaged rabid dogs that act crazy.'

'Well, I believe you,' Elodie said sincerely. 'I trusted you from the moment we met because I'm convinced we were connected in a previous life. Our friendship was immediate. Having the same birthday might mean we were twins!'

'I would love it if that was the case. It would explain why I had such a strong sense that we already knew each other. I hope that in all my past and future incarnations I have been and will be a twin. But if we really want to make our heads spin with possibilities, what if we were not twins, and were not acquainted at all, but instead are reincarnated as each other? Don't forget the scar in our left eyebrows. Of course, we'll never know unless my psychomatricks abilities have a past-life clause that I am yet to discover.'

'What a thought. Although if I had a choice, it would be that we were sisters rather than each other. Unless we *were* sisters but I was you, and you were me.' She paused, then said, 'Now my brain is barking at the effort of trying to work out that concept.'

'We need Rex to apply his analytical brain and do a Venn diagram or a flow-chart. He says maths is the answer to everything. Of course, he forgot that Champagne is actually the answer to everything. Anyway, back to Piero, at least *we* know the truth and are so excited with the knowledge. And you have so many incredible shoes and a cellar full of delicious Sauternes so I'll be back to discover what other surprising stories your collection is harbouring.'

Elodie nodded keenly. 'I can't wait to learn more about my shoes. What a spectacular talent you have but now you must leave and I am *désolée*. Are you sure you don't want me to fly you to London?'

Cordelia assured her host that Eurostar was swifter door to door and having seen Elodie's inspiring collection, she needed some time with a sketchpad.

'Miss you already, please come to HoT soon,' she said, blowing a kiss as the taxi pulled away, a cowbike boot shaped hole in her soul.

+++++

'Rexicles, I'm back and need a sausage sandwich. Have you had breakfast yet?' Cordelia asked him on the phone the morning after returning from Paris.

'If you are suggesting one of Antonio's bangers then I am obliged to eat a sequel to the breakfast I had earlier. See you in the caff,' he replied.

Cordelia was pleased there was room on her preferred table by the Art Deco wooden panelling in the corner of the café so she sat down and chatted with the man sitting opposite. She discovered that he made a living as a water diviner.

'Do you want to see my pendulum?' he asked, pulling out the tool he used to determine the presence of underground water. As a practitioner of a speciality most people did not believe was real, Cordelia had empathy and was fascinated.

'What happens when you sense water?'

'The pendulum swings and the muscles in my hand twitch,' he replied. 'In London, there are so many underground streams and rivers that I rarely do it here, otherwise I'd be in a constant spasm!'

Cordelia wanted to know more so she could try it herself but Rex had arrived.

'Did you bring anything back from LA?' he asked eagerly, kissing her and sitting down.

'Not Bette's shoes, darn it, they were taken out of the auction. But I met my new bestie, Elodie. You'll adore her. Everyone does.'

'You know I don't follow the herd, so I shall studiously decide not to adore her.'

'Good luck with that. Totally irresistible and unaware of the effect she has. She's all heart. Calls me Coeurdelia.'

'What do you call her? You're usually good on nicknames.' Rex was not bad himself, having for years referred to his sister as Drug Delia, or D'Rug for short.

'She-She. Because she's ultra-chic, and because "El" sounds like the

French-English translation of she.' Cordelia blushed. 'Trying to describe the reason for a nickname is sometimes a bit embarrassing, isn't it?'

'I think it's cute. Sounds like the name a Chinese heiress would give to her lapdog.'

'Thank you for that, Tyranno. I shall ignore it. Anyway, remember how when I first met Oscar I was dazzled because whoever he's with feels as if they are the only person who matters. I thought I'd never know anyone more enchanting than him. Well, Elodie has his sweet nature, and charm to the power of ten recurring. And she has a shoe collection that makes me drool.'

'Tell me more, but I'm determined not to succumb.'

'Wait until you hear about her connection to your favourite Champagne house.'

'Oh, now I'm interested.'

Rex was enthralled to learn that Elodie was descended from Apolline Bonheur who, in the nineteenth century, had established Champagne as the ultimate high-status libation. She had built on Barbe-Nicole Ponsardin Clicquot's innovation of what came to be known as the *méthode champenoise* where the wine undergoes a secondary fermentation in the bottle with the addition of sugar and yeast. Bottles are stored at a slight angle on racks with the neck pointing towards the ground. Slightly rotating the bottles regularly over months coaxes the sediment into the neck for removal before the bottle is sealed with a cork and muselet.

Apolline was a pioneer by deciding to focus on ultra-dry sparkling wines in order to appeal to the English market instead of the sweeter versions that were widely popular in France. Her biggest coup was when Britain's King George IV proclaimed he would never drink anything other than Bonheur brut. From then on, every royal family in Europe, all their courtiers, and any social climber took his lead.

As a widow, Apolline was permitted to own a business, control her own finances and move freely in society in a way that would have been impossible as a married or unmarried woman. Her husband's death was a most positive occurrence, and she was able to rescue some of the fortune she brought into the marriage which he had largely squandered by gambling and amorous activities he pursued outside the marital home. This prompted her decision to establish a trust, funded by company profits, and bequeath it to the female line of her descendants as long as they chose a career that was beneficial to society.

Which is why Elodie l'Archambeau was a doctor twice-over. Her first doctorate came from medical school which eventually led to her profession as a surgeon specialising in reconstructive surgery. She volunteered every three months with Rebâtir, the humanitarian charity she had established, that worked in more than a dozen countries to rebuild the bodies of civilians maimed by explosives in current and former war-torn regions. Hence owning the largest private jet on the market, with enough cabin space to carry medics and equipment, and if necessary, room to evacuate patients from hot zones on a plane with the call sign F-DOAM which stood for France-Doctor on a Mission.

She had already proved herself as a philanthropist, so the PhD and her research into shoes did not breach the conditions of Apolline's bequest. Elodie met all the criteria to receive the Bonheur bounty and as the only girl child born into the family for decades, it was considerable indeed. She never forgot that her riches had not been earnt and felt a moral obligation to use a significant proportion for the benefit of humanity, supporting numerous charities and, over the years, funding the annual training and living expenses of hundreds of medical students from developing countries.

'Maybe my resolve is fracturing. I can't resist kindness. And I hope she travels with crates of her Champagne so she's not at the mercy of... I can barely bring myself to utter the word... Prosecco,' Rex said with a shudder.

'She most certainly does and also carries two glasses in a vintage binoculars case. Plus, she takes her piano accordion to accompany the disco tunes she sings in karaoke lounges.'

'Okay, that's it. When can I meet her?'

'Next month. She's coming to visit Shoeseum.'

'I'll have a new suit made.'

'See, you're wavering and you only do that when you've got your sexy on.'

Rex sighed. 'If only my sole concern was to impress a beautiful French doctor with my sartorial scrumptiousness, but those with a cause are becoming more voluble. A teenage influencer with millions of followers posted a video of themselves in a Free Your Feet T-shirt and threw beanbags to knock over shoes balanced on a shelf into a dust bin.

'The comments underneath were scathing about the buyers of real shoes, describing shoe designers, producers and retailers as a cartel of cruelty. I don't want to be a drama queen... well, not in this exact moment, but I suspect the first shot in a revolution has been fired and we supplied the bullet.'

'I tried to forget that twit Nigelchizadek when I was away but I'm worried that his Free Your Feet slogan is so similar to our Free Range Feet. If the two are conflated then Footloose's brand reputation will be damaged by being connected with something we have no control over. I just want loveliness not aggravation. That's why I became a designer and not a debt collector. We need a diversion from all this disapproval. I'll go and see Lancelot. What will you do?'

'Well, to paraphrase Dame Shirley Bassey: "numbers are forever and are all I need to please, stimulate and tease me." I shall play Pi-ainting By Numbers and lose myself in maths.'

Like many mathematicians, Rex found numbers captivating and was so devoted to formulae that he had designed a painting-by-numbers game using pi to the twentieth decimal place. There were several versions, based on fractals found in nature — repetitive geometric patterns like the ones in ferns, romanesco and the cross section of a nautilus mollusc with its multiple chambers. His choice of jewel-coloured hues assigned to the numbers and letters caused much argument in grapheme colour synaesthesia forums with participants disagreeing and claiming that four could not possibly be emerald, and that surely it was commonly accepted that F was black and not sapphire.

But although Lancelot and Archimedes temporarily distracted Cordelia and Rex from The Predicament as they called the issues caused by Footloose, cats were already out of bags, genies out of bottles and discord was increasing.

Chapter Five

As a slogan, 'Free Your Feet' was an astounding success and made many people think about feet in shoes being comparable to battery hens in cages. A coalition of individuals who cared about sustainability and avoided buying 'stuff' because of its environmental impact, plus keyboard warriors, and band-wagon jumpers formed the Foot Freedom Liberation Front. Activists adopted the Bath benders' technique of gathering outside shoe shops, accusing the staff of being worse than peddlers of foie gras, and acting menacingly to prevent customers entering.

Front members took jobs in shoe factories and, in a coordinated move, worked slowly enough to interrupt production schedules; disrupted the supply chain when their moles in logistics companies sent deliveries to the wrong address, usually a vacant building; and they hacked into online shoe retailers so the Foot Freedom logo and skull and crossbones pictogram that warns of acute toxicity hazard popped up on screen. Anyone wearing real shoes became a target and some militants threw red paint on the pavement in front of them. It turned out to be water based and was cleaned up by the perpetrators so they could make their point but not be charged with criminal damage.

Melchizadek saw what was happening globally, claimed intellectual property rights and anointed himself as the public face of the international movement. It was useful for believers to have a figurehead to rally round, and for the media to have a representative of the crusade to communicate with. To many people, he was an authentic warrior for change and his humble and honest circumstances appealed to the like-minded around the world. He gloried in the attention and the public stage it presented to disseminate his dogma and he hired a manager to monetise his new fame with official merchandise bearing his rising sun motif quickly hitting the shops. 'Don't Treat Your Feet Like Meat' was trademarked, and a renowned pop artist commissioned to draw the veal calf in a box for use on branded placards in order to deliver the message more effectively.

He appointed an agent to secure media opportunities, the first being a syndicated radio show where every pronouncement he made sounded as though it was written in capital letters, 'MY PEOPLE WILL NEVER BREAK THE LAW BUT THEY WILL BREAK YOUR DESIRE TO BUY SHOES', and clumsy attempts at being profound, 'IT'S NOT THE SIZE OF THE WAVE THAT COUNTS'.

Melchizadek had a sizeable number of listeners but many of them thought he was a joke. They tuned in for entertainment and scorned him, but he had enough true believers to make a difference. Yes, he was a self-aggrandizing buffoon but his words had consequences and the intimidating tactics practised by supporters of the ideology were having an effect. Real shoe advocates became scared to wear them in public after news reports of celebrities attending shows at New York's Fashion Week being verbally abused for their devotion to high heels.

House of Tanner's production team devoured Melchizadek's proclamations. They impersonated his declamatory speaking style, and made up gobbledegook such as that tiptoeing should be mandatory to prevent heavy footfall throwing Earth off its axis. Then one day, Cordelia overheard them discussing the announcement he had made about being in business with Footloose to license virtual Jesus sandals bearing his logo. She dashed into Rex's office and closed the door.

'Mel-End is claiming to be collaborating with Footloose. I don't want that wassock anywhere near us. Jill Mitchell better tell him to walk on toot sweet.'

Rex pointed to the business page of the newspaper on his desk.

'There's another complication,' he said.

'Oh no, what?' Cordelia asked, nervous at the serious tone of his voice.

'Vietnam's largest shoe manufacturer has gone out of business citing the actions of Foot Freedom Liberation Front as the cause. Shoes are not selling in shops so there are stockpiles in warehouses. No point making even more if there is no demand. The factory was a major employer. If Footloose is associated in anyway with that fool, it will be terrible PR.'

'In that case, Jill will have to make an announcement refuting his statement.'

The next day, a press release from Jill Mitchell was sent out in which she insisted she had never heard of Mr Melchizadek and the Foot Freedom Liberation Front, that there was no commercial relationship between them and would be none in the future. A cease-and-desist letter was sent to him but even so, the following week he claimed again on his radio show to have a partnership with Footloose and encouraged his followers to download and use the app. Was he chancing it believing that, with his sway over so many people, Jill would relent and enter a business alliance, or was he just a pudden-head? Probably both.

'Melking it for all it's worth,' said Cordelia with venom.

'He's a menace. How can we stop him?'

'Let's take Blanche for a walk and open our synapses.'

As they strolled, they discussed ways to silence him. Hit man was number one. Revealing him to be a hypocrite was second.

'Under the face-fuzz, I bet a privately educated poor little rich boy resides,' Rex said.

'I have it! If I can get hold of one of his scabby sandals, I'll give him a psy-comm investigation.'

'Doesn't Ed, the son of Oscar's cousin, work as an intern at the station where Mel-End records his show? Did I imagine it, or does Ed have the awful task of massaging his nasty feet beforehand? I bet he could be persuaded to "lose" one of the sandals.'

'I know what we can do. It's "Take Your Dog to Work Day" on Thursday. That's when he broadcasts his stupid show. Ed can borrow Blanche who will quietly pick up a sandal and chew it so its unwearable. I'll still be able to read from it though.'

And so it was that Cordelia discovered Melchizadek was a fraud from a super-rich family. His given name was Hugo Spencer-Lottway and he had been educated at a leading single sex boarding school where he was unpopular for being annoying and attention-seeking, telling tales and acting puerile but never in an amusing manner. The teaching staff despised him, more so after he said to the newly qualified maths tutor, 'My monthly allowance is larger than your salary.'

'Everybody's allowance is larger than my salary,' she had answered, 'I'm a teacher.'

His hatred of footwear began when he was punished for a misdemeanour by having to unthread and then rethread the laces of every pupil's muddy rugby boots. As an adult, he recognised that the only individuals who would listen to him were impressionable and easy-to-manipulate innocents — hence appointing himself as chief of the Bath bender brigade. And while his clan members were shivering through damp winters and surviving on fresh air and cabbage soup, he was comfy in his Royal Crescent townhouse eating fast food and living on his trust fund.

'Top sleuthing, sistina. We have enough to muzzle the false prophet,' Rex declared dramatically. 'I shall get to work with the dark art of reputation destruction.'

'Don't you ever worry about having all that power?' Cordelia asked him.

'Hmm, let me think for a nano-second. No. But I promise only ever to use my supreme authority for unmasking phoneys,' he replied.

'Think of what Celestine would say if she clocked that you could fiddle with other's lives in this way.'

'She'd look at me with a raised eyebrow and say "precious jewel, behave yourself".'

+++++

A statement from Jill Mitchell was released denying the spurious claims from Melchizadek, and soon, Rex-generated memes were circulating with images of him bearing an extra-long Pinocchio nose, fingers crossed behind his back, and cartoons of his pants on fire. Rumours spread that he was from a well-to-do family made wealthy through an asset-stripping hedge fund where employees of the companies it bought at knock-down prices were treated as dispensable casualties; that his claim to be an activist living his best socialist eco-life was pretence; and the whole Free Your Feet campaign was a ruse to exploit believers, build a personality cult and add to his already considerable fortune. It was all true.

Social media was brutal in its response and the hashtag 'WreckDek' trended repeatedly. Disgruntled listeners flooded the stations that broadcast his show with emails demanding he be taken off air, sales of his branded merchandise plummeted, and some people who had bought it, posted videos of themselves using the clothing to wash the floor or line the cat litter tray.

The Bath benders were filmed in tears sending plaintive messages begging him to confirm the reports were untrue but he failed to respond to any of the accusations. News camera crews gathered outside his house and waited to doorstep him but they were wasting their time because he had already decamped to Tenerife to live as a surf bum. A journalist on holiday spotted him at a beach and reported that Spencer-Lottway's fatuous statement, 'It's not the size of the wave that counts', was true when it came to his talent at surfing because he was unable to manage his board even if the wave was a mere dribble.

To the great relief of Cordelia and Rex, nothing was ever heard from Melchizadek again. He had scuttled off into oblivion and Footloose was no longer at risk by association with an imposter.

+++++

With the unmasking of Melchizadek, direct action by the Foot Freedom Liberation Front eventually slowed but it was too late, the harm inflicted on the shoe industry was profound and it had happened shockingly quickly. Millions of people had stopped purchasing footwear and although Cordelia and Rex were loath to admit it, the popularity of Footloose triggered a chain of unintended consequences.

Not only had the decline in sales forced bankruptcies on shoe producers and retailers with the blow that had on livelihoods, but related businesses, such as shoe repairers and the makers of laces, inner soles and corn plasters, were also affected. Shining footwear was a thing of the past so shoe polish became a memory of the days of leather and instead was sold as a plug-in retro fragrance for the home; shoeboxes were transformed into high-value collectors' items at auction; and sweaty socks, traded the way used knickers are to men with that tendency, were a lucrative niche with enterprising sellers rubbing Stinking Bishop on them to fake the cheesy aroma. Consumer behaviour worldwide changed entirely and it was Cordelia and Rex who had inadvertently provoked it.

'This was not supposed to happen. I just wanted to create something gorgeous for me and the other freaky footers to wear, not destroy an entire industry. Now I understand why we need Jill Mitchell. What if we had been blamed for this disaster? It's bad enough knowing we made it happen without the thought of someone vengefully smearing brown shoe cream on the front door handle if they knew it was us,' Cordelia said mournfully.

'I know,' replied Rex. 'What's happening is absolutely horrendous. I'm not sleeping well, and I don't suit eye-bags.'

'Is there anything we can do, apart from hypnotising the entire world population into spending big on shoes again?' She cared deeply about the economic injury Footloose had inflicted to all connected with the making and selling of shoes. Not even House of Tanner, the leading purveyor of luxury shoes, was immune to the collapse of the industry and so the production team was having an unplanned holiday.

'I do have a suggestion but you won't like it.'

'Don't tell me. I have to bathe in cold baked beans as punishment,' she said, shuddering at the thought.

'Worse. You're going to publicly support Pauline Westwich and her Best Foot Forward campaign.'

'No, no, and thrice no,' she said insistently. 'I can't be associated with that hate-spewing woman.'

'I know, she's vile but we need her influence.'

Which is how Cordelia found herself inviting the leader of Moral Universe to tea at Café Majestic. As usual, she looked splendid that day in a red and black dress with a skirt that flared out with ruffles and more ruffles to the ankle, hair scraped off her face, and a fresh gardenia pinned above the left ear. All heads apart from Pauline Westwich's turned when she entered the room. They always did. Cordelia had no trouble identifying her guest. Mousey hair in a shortish non-descript style, taupe acrylic reversible cardigan which was taupe on the inside too, cream slacks, and fawn slingbacks. *Multiple pairs or did she go back to the cemetery and retrieve the missing one?* Cordelia wondered, trying not to picture her nocturnal activities.

'How do you do, Ms Westwich?' Cordelia said, holding out her hand.

She jumped as the woman loudly snapped, 'It's Mrs.'

Cordelia sat down, arranging her skirt so it was not a trip hazard and looked attentively at Pauline who said, 'I don't approve of such opulence,' disparagingly eyeing the gilded and mirrored *Belle Époque* salon.

A waiter came to take their order.

'What can I get you, Mrs Westwich?' Cordelia said.

'Tap water is adequate,' Pauline answered.

'Ice and a slice of lime?' the waiter enquired.

'Just water,' she replied curtly.

Adequate? Adequate? Cordelia repeated in her head, *What does that even mean?* Then smiling at the waiter, she said, 'I'll have smoked salmon sandwiches, lemon and pistachio cannoli, a pot of Rose Pouchong tea, and a glass of the English fizz please.'

She was obliged to spend a disagreeable hour courting this intensely unpleasant individual because of Best Foot Forward, a loose coalition of interested parties concerned with shoes whether that was designing, making, wearing, mending, selling, shopping for or fetishising. It had started as a grass roots resistance movement against the Foot Freedom Liberation Front. Pauline Westwich, the founder, was able to persuade her hinterland of hundreds of thousands of devoted admirers who longed for the world then, not the world now, to promote its aims of bringing back real footwear.

At first, they participated in simple marches up and down high streets dressed in their Sunday finery and said (being far too polite to shout), 'Shoes are nice. Please wear them,' and, 'We won't eschew the shoe,' which sounded to passers-by like multiple sneezes. It was obvious by the lack of decibels and snappy slogans they had never protest marched before but with practice they became more effective with their messaging and the stroppier, 'We refuse to lose shoes,' could be heard, but only just, echoing down the road.

Pauline encouraged them to ramp it up with counter demonstrations outside shoe shops where they created human corridors for staff and shoppers to walk through, safe from the Footwits as the Foot Freedom Liberation Front was nicknamed by its adversaries. Just as at a military wedding where the married couple processes underneath an arch of ceremonial swords, members of the Best Foot Forward taskforce did something similar but instead of rapiers, they held up shoes. The world had never seen so many slip-ons in one place since Val Doonican headlined at the London Palladium.

Support took many guises. In its early days, the residents of the English town of Shoeburyness had no idea why the municipal sign was repeatedly stolen but were thrilled that increased tourism added considerably to the local economy. When they discovered that shoes had become a thing, canny owners of events spaces began to market them for footwear conventions, and townsfolk were shocked when police officers came across groups of attendees huddled in bus shelters sniffing shoe polish. It soon became so commonplace that pensioners were nervous of catching the bus for fear of falling over if they accidentally breathed in the fumes.

Heritage groups were formed to preserve the skills of cordwaining and cobbling, and the two Members of Parliament for Northampton jointly tabled an Early Day Motion to recognise the area's centuries-old reputation as one of the world's great centres of footwear production.

Chicago had a chapter that met in a strip club where scantily clad dancers in stilettoes tottered around the stage and, in exchange for a generous tip, would permit customers to caress the heels, maintaining the no body-touching rule.

In Italy, there was an active faction of men who wanted the law changed to force women to wear heels because they found them sexy. Some females joined in by lobbying Italian lawmakers, saying, 'Heels make us look feminine and feel subservient. Men like that,' causing feminists to roll their eyes and utter expletives.

Fetish clubs reported increased attendances and all attention was on the punters shod in thigh high spike heeled boots. In a Buenos Aires nightclub, the waitresses were issued with mink-lined mules to wear as part of their uniform.

During Paris Fashion Week, the most popular show was a fringe event, nothing to do with frocks, but all to do with footwear. Supermodels strutted down the catwalk in lofty platforms competing in the Sashay Stroll and giving it plenty of attitude.

An enterprising shoe propagandist made a deal with a retailer of children's princess outfits to include a note in the packaging to remind the child that Cinderella would not have attracted Prince Charming if the glass slipper had been digital.

At Sydney Mardi Gras, the centrepiece of the parade was a giant rainbow coloured wedge sandal on wheels, a banner printed with, 'Always Put Your Best Foot Forward'. It was unconnected to the campaign but claimed by them in any case.

Cordelia listened to Pauline's report on the multifarious activities then took a sip of tea and said, 'This cause is obviously something you care about, Mrs Westwich.'

'I care about all my causes but this one is personal. My grandfather was in the grommet eyelets trade and sold them to shoe manufacturers. If he'd been alive now, he would have gone out of business because of the callous actions of the Foot Freedom Liberation Front and that appalling Footloose nonsense.'

Cordelia bristled at the insult to her superlative concept and tried not to glare at Pauline then said, 'I'd like to help Best Foot Forward in any way I can.'

'And what do you think that might be?' Westwich said brusquely. 'Your sort of business is hardly standard fayre. My followers are genuine traditional hard-working folk, not like the precious lot who wear what you sell, lolling around all day reading glossy magazines.'

Vicious, but don't take the bait, and besides, HoT clients are too busy running the world's leading companies and global organisations to read magazines, Cordelia thought, then replied, 'I have a high media profile and can pull in some favours to help with publicity.'

'You're not the only one who can do that. Richard Nailer is in charge of public outreach, and he understands folk of our ilk,' Westwich said dismissively.

Who's Richard Nailer? Cordelia thought, trying hard to keep from cowfing, the trick of audibly saying 'cow' but disguising it with a cough. *And to think that Blanche had her soft mouth round one of those horrible canvas monstrosities. I need to leave this person's company, she's unbearable.*

Cordelia asked the waiter for the bill, paid it, and said, 'Mrs Westwich, it sounds as if you have everything you need. Even so, I'll do what I can to support the aims of the campaign. Good afternoon to you,' then stood up smiling from the teeth outwards and elegantly walked out of the room waving to a couple of acquaintances who were taking tea.

++++++++

'Pauline Westwich is the most objectionable piece-of-work I have come across. No manners, no humour, no appeal. She doesn't want our help so that was a waste of time,' Cordelia said as she walked into Rex's office and flopped on the sofa.

'I'm sorry, was it awful? Give me the gruesomes.'

'She has a gripe against HoT and didn't care for me at all. How can that be? Who doesn't like *moi*?'

Rex thought for a while. 'Michael Norrington didn't. Remember when his face accidentally connected with your elbow as you were demonstrating kangaroo boxing techniques in the school playground?'

'Yes, but he got five pound from the tooth fairy when most children at the time received fifty pence and he spent it all on sweets so I don't know why he was so upset. Anyway, WestBitch. Three words. Wears elasticated waistbands. Never owned a natural fibre in her life. I went to shake her hand and was zapped with static electricity. When I offered to fund Best

Foot Forward and score some publicity, she made it apparent I was not needed. Said that Richard Nailer was already helping. I pretended to know who he is. Have you heard of him?'

'Let's have a look,' Rex replied, checking online, and reading a business page. 'Yes, here he is. Nicknamed "Discount Shoe Supremo". Loaded. Owns factories in South-East Asia mass producing cheap footwear for bargain shops across the globe. Seems they are all moth-balled because of you know what. Urgh, when he introduces himself, he says, "Richard Nailer's the name, but you can call me Rich because I am".'

Cordelia shook her head and sighed, 'Not another nitwit. That's two who have entered my awareness since we launched Footloose. I didn't invite them in and I want them out of it. I long for my stress-free life back again.'

Rex glanced through more web results. 'Cheeky git! You don't want to see what he's been saying about Footloose. Brutal.'

'No, don't tell me,' she pleaded. 'I know we're protected in our HoT bubble and I may sound completely naïve, but is that what the real world is like — full of nastiness? How depressing. I must recover from WestBitch's malevolence with some radiance. I'll take Blanche for a walk. She's the antidote to all that is ugly and mean.'

But not even Blanche therapy was powerful enough to protect Cordelia against the furies unleashed by Footloose, with the most furious of them being Richard Nailer. He did not just have a bee in his bonnet, he had the entire hive in his hairdo because Nailer was every buccaneering businessman, win-at-all-costs, exploitational narcissist rolled into one. His business mantra was 'Expansion, Profit, Repeat', so when shoe sales collapsed, his entire business model was rent asunder. He blamed Footloose and his response was to condemn it through social media, his preferred weapon.

'Does he even know what lowercase means?' Rex said reading out loud @ShoeSupremo's latest tirade. 'FOOT LOSER! FOOT USELESS!

SHUT-LOOSE!'

'Dreadful shouty man,' replied Cordelia. 'I bet that's how he speaks, as though everything is blasted through a megaphone.'

Richard Nailer was the type of bombastic balloon who pontificated but never engaged and that applied to his social media technique too. If he had bothered to respond to the thousands of messages posted in response to his, it would have been an interesting conversation because his bellicose attitude towards Footloose had made the general public think about the wider ramifications of not buying real shoes, and how that impacted on those who depended on the footwear industry for employment.

Cordelia had made the decision to mute him preferring beauty and positivity in her life of which he was neither. Nevertheless, she was rather gripped by what he would say or do next and she asked Rex to filter the nastiest comments and just give her general updates. He decided not to tell her that Nailer referred to Jill Mitchell as 'Slutloose' and had claimed her money was inherited from Daddy. 'Behind every wealthy woman is a wealthy man who gave her the dosh,' which would hardly make it into the Oxford Dictionary of Quotations but said much about his attitude towards successful women.

'Should Jill respond to any of his provocations?' Cordelia asked Rex one day after more tirades from Nailer. 'If she doesn't then she'll either be perceived as a wimp who accepts the bullying, or that she has dignity and refuses to paddle in the gutter where he resides.'

'It's tempting but tricky. The media loves a spat and if we draw attention to Jill, they might start delving into her background. Annoying as it is, we must ignore everything.'

'I daydream about meeting him, pretending to be Jill and asking what his mum thinks about all the abuse he spews. Bet he'd crumple when challenged, bullies usually do. But as I can't, I'm compiling the A-Z of adjectives to describe him instead. Very satisfying. It starts with

Argumentative, Belligerent, Crude, Despicable.'

'Or you could have Disgusting,' Rex interjected quickly, 'Apparently he picks his nose in public.'

Cordelia shuddered. 'N for Nauseating then.'

If Nailer's social media campaign had been insulting but childish, what he did next was acutely destructive. A denial-of-service incident resulted in Footloose being off-line for two hours until the cyber security team in India restored normal operations. After the attack, he gloated that an enemy of Footloose had succeeded in interrupting normal business.

'No doubt it was a supporter of real shoes and real jobs,' he claimed. 'Someone impervious to the joke that is virtual shoes. Footloose is like the Empress' New Outfit.' The latter comment would have had more effect had Nailer checked the accuracy of his metaphor.

'Call Me Rich must have been the culprit because the cause of the outage was not public knowledge. How would he know unless he had ordered it?' Rex said with frustration.

'He certainly takes the O out of discount. Will it have a lasting effect on the business?'

'No, but now we know he's done it once, he might be tempted again, so our security team will be the cyber equivalent of hungry bull mastiffs in a bad mood.'

'Reassuring,' said Cordelia. 'Anyway, I'm off Top-Decking. Want to come?'

Top-Decking was one of her pastimes when she needed to think. It entailed sitting on the front seat of the top deck of a bus and looking at the urban landscape, notepad and pencil to hand, as it trundled along its route. She always saw something that spurred her creativity. Her favourite route was the number 139 because it went along Oxford Street towards Marble Arch where the Art Deco Queen of Time statue above the main entrance to Selfridge's department store hailed shoppers. It had not only inspired a House of Tanner design but was the model for her greatest fancy dress triumph when The Weasel Pleasure Gardens hosted a costume party with the theme of 'queen'.

The bash had a plethora of Elizabeth Is, Titanias, and chess pieces, but nothing as glorious as Cordelia. She did not make an entrance, instead appearing when a curtain was drawn back to reveal a *tableau vivant* with her standing on the prow of the Ship of Commerce on the Sea of Eternity. Her skin was sprayed gold, she wore an ultramarine gown decorated with gold inlay and blue faience tiles, and on her back were metallic wings. In one hand, she held a golden globe and in the other, a sprig of leaves. Nymphs and bare-chested male attendants crouched at her feet, holding models of crescent moons. Cue whoops and wolf whistles from the other guests.

'I'd love to but I need to stay and check whether Call Me Rich's little trick has affected the numbers,' Rex said.

Cordelia's eyes glazed over. Not for the first time was she thankful that she and Rex were sense and sensibility: she, all right brained, and her little brother by ten minutes having a well-developed logic and systematic muscle in his left brain. She could never do what he excelled at, nor did she want to, likewise him with her. But together they were the full banquet where the multiple courses were perfectly attuned.

Chapter Six

Thursday was Elodie's first visit to House of Tanner and Cordelia was excited and a little apprehensive. What if Rex was not impressed? She re-touched her lipstick in the mirror and nodded in approval at the screen goddess who looked back at her. 'I should be Paulette Goddard more often.'

That day she wore her own hair down, and a lavender tea dress with nipped in waist and floaty skirt below the knee. On her feet were rose-pink loafers — real shoes rather than a Footloose fancy which might invite discussion and the risk of giving anything away about its real ownership.

She was only waiting a few seconds on the street before Elodie pulled up and dismounted Nike, removing the crash helmet and shaking loose her hair making it swish from side to side like a shampoo commercial. She was clad in maroon coloured leathers with signature matching cowbike boots and looked impossibly glamorous.

'*Ma chérie,* how I missed you,' she said, warmly hugging Cordelia.

'I'm soooo happy you're here. Welcome to House of Tanner. I can't wait to show you the empire,' Cordelia replied hugging her back. 'Oh, you smell just like you. What perfume do you wear?'

'It's made from Bonheur. I designed it just for myself. Champagne aromas are lost during distillation so botanicals to replicate the tasting notes are added, plus rose for the bushes that traditionally grow in vineyards.'

'I've always wondered why roses are present in every winery I've been to. They look beautiful but is there another reason?'

'Yes, aphids and fungal diseases land on them before they do on the vines, so roses act as an early warning system.'

'How clever. They are floral guard dogs. Now, are you ready for the tour? So much to see. And I'm saving the best for last: Rex. We'll have dinner together at The Weasel.'

Elodie was captivated by House of Tanner — the grand lobby and staircase, the design studio, the workshop and, most of all, the showroom, known as Boudoir of Pulchritude, a luxurious chamber lined with midnight blue velvet printed with images of purple belladonna flowers for their association with bewitchment. Each new season's shoe was presented on the head of a caryatid which was modelled on marble female figures that supported the architrave of a temple in the Acropolis. A curule seat, its curved U-shaped legs painted in old gold, topped with Tyrian purple upholstery was positioned in the middle of an archway decorated with fresh flowers.

'Clients sit on the seat and place their feet on a damask cushion for us to measure because the shoes are handmade for a total fit. They choose which shade of cushion and that says a lot about their current mood or personality. Red, the colour of passion, is linked to sexuality, pink is about romance and joy, and turquoise is calming and enhances empathy and compassion. Most choose the red cushion which suggests to me that HoT customers don't just think about their feet!'

Elodie sat down. 'I once met an Iranian stonemason who told me to stand or sit in the middle of an arch because that is where the energy concentrates. I can feel it in yours even though flowers do not create the pressure that stone does. And I like this idea of colour symbolism. What does the orange cushion reveal about me?'

'It describes you so accurately. Warmth, spontaneity and optimism. Now, if you pass me your feet, I'll show you what we do.'

Cordelia made a note of all the dimensions because she was designing a pair of cavalry boots as a surprise gift for Elodie to wear during her work with Rebâtir. She had never created footwear more apposite because they were to be made in indigo leather as a nod to the colour of Pinot Meunier, one of the three permitted grape varietals in the Bonheur blend, and decorated with hand-tooled images of the caduceus, the emblem of doctors where serpents coil around a staff topped with wings. Ancient Greeks considered snakes to be sacred and they were often used in healing rituals. The wings represented Hermes, messenger between the gods and humans, and patron of travellers.

Elodie was already awestruck with House of Tanner but when they entered Shoeseum and she saw the extent of the shoe collection and what Celestine had created from Cordelia's imagination, she was flabbergasted.

'You actually have a pair of Pulcinelli's boots?' she said in disbelief pointing to red cloth flat-soled boots to mid-calf with red satin ribbons for wrapping around the legs. 'I'm obsessed with knowing what his voice would have sounded like.'

Pulcinelli was the icon of an exclusive musical clique known as *castrati*, possessors of transcendental singing voices, a bequest of having been castrated as children to retain the purity of their voice beyond adolescence when it would normally break. They were believed to be free from original sin which made them angels on Earth. Lacking the testosterone levels of other males meant a castrato's bones did not fully harden and grew longer than average. They were typically tall with large rib cages and it was the latter that as adults increased their breath capacity and gave them the capability to hold notes beyond what was thought humanly possible. But it was the pitch of the voice that was so extraordinary, similar to a soprano but with a richer sound, and a wider octave range including reaching a high C without straining their vocal cords. No one alive in the twenty-first century had heard a castrato sing in person. A 1904 recording of Alessandro Moreschi, the last castrato, existed, but by then his voice was no longer in its prime.

'We hired a countertenor to play Pulcinelli for his If the Shoe Fits episode because that is the nearest register to a castrato but a modern-day singer could never communicate how ethereal he would have sounded so we have to imagine it. At least I know something of his personality because when I psy-commed his shoes, I discovered how completely delightful he was. I think you'll agree when you've had his virtual reality experience.'

Afterwards, Elodie emerged from the pod, eyes wide, and fanning her face. 'Is it hot in here? I need to sit down in a bath of ice. I'm infatuated with him.'

She had learnt that, despite everyone in high society knowing Pulcinelli was mutilated, the jealousy he aroused in straight men was remarkable. Why would the absence of testicles elicit such resentment? Because so many women fancied him. What Pulcinelli offered was all the bliss and none of the risk. On a scale of one to ten, his swoon-inducing ability was a perfect score.

As a child, he had been discovered by fishermen in a coracle washed up on an Italian Adriatic beach. They took him to a nearby monastery where the monks gave him work as a kitchen hand. Traumatised, he did not speak for several years and no one knew his name or where he came from. The brothers called him Francesco after the basilica of Ravenna, and Il Mistero because his origin was a mystery. He was encouraged to sing at mass and that liberated him; he found his voice and was then able to speak. His monasterial family loved Francesco the boy but they loved his singing more and even though the operation was never legal, he was secretly castrated to retain his God-given celestial tones.

As Francesco aged into a young man, appreciation of his immaculate singing and beautiful face was spreading. Handel was the first composer to hire him as a professional, casting him as the titular role in *Giulio Cesare* for its London premiere. His performance was described as, 'Masterly, with unrivalled elocution. The voice is rich, full, and penetrating, and he sings with great fire'. That was enough to turn him into the most adulated performer of the eighteenth century with patrons vying for his attention.

He could name his price for private performances and as only the wealthiest could afford him, he was familiar with the palaces and great houses of Europe. And, as Cordelia discovered, he was especially familiar with the bedrooms. But Pulcinelli was no rogue. He fell for every woman he was intimate with and they with him, being the most considerate lover. Incredibly, despite so many prominent married men being cuckolded, he was never challenged to a duel. To do so would have risked extinguishing the voice of the century.

'You are a genius. I have never been as impressed. My shoe collection is nothing unless it is united with yours. It needs the Coeurdelia treatment, and to be seen and appreciated in Shoeseum. Would you accept it on permanent loan?'

Cordelia felt breathless with excitement and a choral blast of the line, 'And all the people rejoiced' from 'Zadok the Priest' played in her head as she relished the idea of being able to admire Elodie's collection whenever the urge took hold.

'It's the greatest suggestion anyone has ever made. Life could not be any more fabulous than it is right at this minute,' Cordelia said euphorically.

'Wait until your mirthday tomorrow, it might get even better. I have a plan.'

Mirthday was the word coined by Cordelia and Rex to describe the once-a-year special day they reserved to celebrate their birthday as individuals rather than sharing it as twins. Cordelia had picked the date of the platform shoe being re-introduced by Salvatore Ferragamo, the exceptional Italian shoe designer, who had been much in demand with Hollywood stars, including Carmen Miranda and Marlene Dietrich.

'What a treat,' she said in response to Elodie just as her phone rang. It was Rex calling from The Weasel's private dining salon.

'Me and Blanche are sitting in the Majolica Room and awaiting the two of you.'

'Coming, babe. Three minutes,' she replied.

Rex was always fastidious about his wardrobe but had planned his outfit with even more deliberation for his first meeting with Elodie. His new suit, single breasted windowpane check, woven in the colours of the company logo, was worn with a dusty pink shirt, cufflinks embedded with Blue John, and a purple spotted tie. He was nervous but shouldn't have been.

Elodie took his hands, kissed each cheek, and said, 'Rex, please tell me that you win every best dressed man award there is. You are therapy for the eyes. And with such a superb intellect, you are the epitome of beauty and brains. Coeurdelia said House of Tanner would not exist without you.'

His heart fluttered and he heard the sweeping strings of a full orchestra playing the crescendo of the adagio in Khachaturian's *Spartacus*, one of the most tender pieces of music ever composed. *Now I understand*, he thought, feeling as if the sun was shining just for him. It was a *coup de foudre* and his glacial resolve to be unmoved melted in an instant.

'Who is this gorgeous creature?' Elodie asked, sitting down and stroking Blanche who immediately jumped onto her lap.

'She only ever does that to family,' Cordelia said in surprise.

'Then I must be family.' Blanche agreed and snuggled in even closer. 'And your handsome Oscar, will I meet him?'

'I did think about it but couldn't chance the destruction of creation if you two met and multiplied each other's galactic-level charm, triggering the second Big Bang. That or one of you would cancel the other out and I need you both in my life with your superpowers undiminished.'

Elodie giggled. 'But the Big Bang might create a new planet for us to live on where everything is full of joy so it's worth the risk.'

Dinner was very jolly, made more so by the Jeroboam of Bonheur Elodie had brought as a gift for Rex knowing it was his favourite

Champagne. He told her all about his orchestra conducting lessons, that the date of his mirthday was chosen to coincide with Dolly Parton's birthday, and details of the monthly card club he hosted at home in Spitalfields.

'I often play cards with friends and I've always wanted to learn canasta,' she said.

'Then I shall teach you now. I normally play with four but we can do it with two,' Rex offered, pulling out a deck of cards from his bag and dealing them.

'Oh, you're a natural. How long have you been a card player?' he said a while later with a little 'huh' in his voice after she won yet another game. He wasn't used to losing.

'I love to learn and you are an excellent teacher. My English nanny Felicity taught me how to play *chemin de fer* and other games when I was eleven. I set up a secret card academy at my strict boarding school and instead of us focusing on Latin revision in the evenings, we were gambling our weekly allowance on the ace of diamonds.

'My friends were envious of me having Felicity because she was young and, under her professional exterior, was great fun and very naughty. I have her to thank for speaking fluent English. She even taught me some regional terms and accents.'

'Go on, say some and we'll try and guess where,' Rex begged.

'Hmm, let me think. What's this: "ey up, babby duck",' she said to clueless expressions from the other two. 'Lincolnshire yeller belly, can't you tell? How about this one: "dinna droon the miller". Again, blank looks. 'Don't drown the miller, as in don't dilute the whisky. Okay, last one: "Meet me at booss shell-aah". Nothing. 'That was my finest Geordie accent asking you to meet me in the bus shelter. Are you sure you two are British?'

'We're Londoners, She-She. Centre of our own universe and unaware of anything that happens beyond the final stations on the underground network,' Cordelia said in their defence.

'I'm going to call Felicity and ask her to come and give you lessons in lingo so you're no longer twa bubbles aff the centre, lassie,' she laughed.

'I'll see your Scottish dialect and raise you Esperanto: *vi rava Franca virino*,' Rex said flirtily.

'Ooh, Rex, I don't know what you said, but I like the tone of voice you said it in.'

'*Ankaŭ mi*! I try my utmost to sass up the least sexy language on Earth. I took evening classes for a while and naturally assumed that all the other learners would be like me and prioritise learning swear words and how to order a glass of beer. Wrong. One of them wanted to know how to say, "When is the next train to Pullton?" A town that should be renamed Dullton because its only claim to fame is being the birthplace of the man who devised the nation's most boring sandwich filling — bread sauce.'

'I'm so impressed with your linguistic prowess. Can you translate this: what is the best Champagne?'

'Darling, I can answer that in one word: Bonheur. But I can show off if you want. Your question is *kio estas la plej bona ĉampano?*'

Elodie beamed at him, mouthed, 'You're so clever,' then sighed, 'I wish this evening would never end but I must go.'

'So soon? Please say no,' Rex cried.

'You can't leave because you are the prisoner of London's most adoring dog,' Cordelia said, smiling at Blanche who was asleep with her head on Elodie's feet.

'She's so beautiful. I don't want to wake her, but I have something to arrange for your mirthday. Corsets and ballgowns are not necessary. Apart from that, everything else is a surprise.'

++++++

Wish I had more not-knowing-ness in my life, Cordelia thought as she waited outside House of Tanner the following day. Sebastian managed her diary so efficiently that her schedule was fixed from hour-to-hour so having no clue of what she was doing that day was liberating. *I need more of the adventures I had before my self-inflicted work tyranny stole all my time.*

A cab drew up and she noticed queasily that it was covered with Footloose advertising. *What if She-She mentions it and I have to comment and act as though I have no connection? I'll blush and as a poker player, she'll notice my tell.*

'Blanche wanted to say good morning before we leave,' Cordelia said as Elodie stepped out of the taxi.

'*Bonjour* beautiful,' she said tickling Blanche under her chin. 'And *bonjour* beautiful,' she added, tickling Cordelia under her chin too. Elodie seemed not to have noticed the Footloose branding that had turned it from a black into a multi-coloured cab.

'I'm so excited about my plan. It was such fun to plot. This is Serena and she'll drive us today.'

First stop was Millfield Lane. Cordelia wondered if they might be going to the Triangle Pond on Hampstead Heath, one of several natural open air bathing pools originally excavated in the seventeenth century as reservoirs for London's growing population. She was right.

They walked up the wooded pathway where green and yellow dappled light peeked between the trees, through the gate in the metal fencing and down an incline to an expansive stretch of water surrounded by mature woodland. It was completely enclosed and protected from Peeping Toms. Unusually the place was deserted.

'Where is everyone? I've never seen it empty before,' Cordelia asked.

'I rented it exclusively.'

'I didn't think that was possible.'

'It's not normally, but they said yes when I enquired. And no need for a swimsuit because the rules don't apply.'

They went into the changing room and disrobed then slipped into the water with a shock at its cool temperature, adrenaline powering them as they set off towards the centre.

'Is it too deep to stand up?' asked Elodie.

'Yes, and we have to keep swimming to escape lamprey that lay in wait to ambush us if we stop and tread water,' Cordelia blurted out with a note of hysteria.

'What is lamprey?'

Cordelia was paranoid about the primitive parasitic creature with a toothed sucker mouth that attaches itself to a host and feeds off its bodily fluids. Her logical mind confirmed there were no lamprey in the pond, but her illogical mind insisted otherwise. *Why did I mention lamprey? Nobody needs that vicious brute in their nightmares,* she thought, and then said, 'Lamprey are like eels, *l'anguille,* and it makes me shiver to think they might brush past my legs.'

Elodie yelped, 'Urgh,' and increased her pace momentarily until slowing for Cordelia to catch up. They swam the perimeter of the pond in tranquillity, past the heron wading in the shallows, and the fox snoozing in the sun where the meadow met the woodland, and they spotted the iridescent blue flash of a kingfisher as it dived under the surface for a snack. When they got out, skin tingling and enlivened, Cordelia discovered that Elodie had arranged aromatherapy toiletries in the shower and white towelling robes for drying off.

'Are you hungry? I am,' Elodie asked after they had dressed.

'A little nibble would be just the thing.'

'Good, here is Véronique.'

It was indeed Elodie's chef who led them to a table with two chairs set up on the grass, linen tablecloth, silver cutlery, two glasses, and a bottle of Bonheur. Elodie expertly opened it — the carbon dioxide escaping like a whisper — poured the Champagne, and passed a glass to Cordelia.

'*Santé*! I asked Véronique to make you a special omelette and she foraged for mushrooms earlier this morning. And for our *mise en scène*, I thought of recreating the setting of Manet's *Le Déjeuner sur l'herbe*, but I don't like that one woman is naked, the other is semi-clothed and the two men are fully clad. I'm all for equality. Either the men are also *déshabillés*, or the women are clothed.'

'I'm with you. It's just an excuse to see boobage,' said Cordelia who was able to multi-task by eating enthusiastically whilst critiquing art. 'Véronique, you deserve the *Legion d'Honneur* for your knack with eggs! But how did you cook such flawless omelettes out here? '

'*Merci beaucoup*,' Véronique said looking pleased. 'I practise a lot on a field kitchen because I travel with Elodie for her medical work.'

After lunch, Cordelia said, 'I'm not hijacking your marvellous plans for today… well, actually I am, but as we are so near to one of my top museums, do we have time to pop in? There's something I want to show you and once you have seen it, you will never unsee it.'

'Of course. And now I'm intrigued.'

They walked up through the Heath past a tree with a hollow trunk, climbed into it and sat for a while as Cordelia explained it had once been used temporarily to imprison Ned Shepton the notorious cutpurse who prowled the area in the 1760s. She described how the Heath was a danger zone for coach travellers because, apart from the years when Fletcher and the Arrows saved the day, rampant highwaymen made traversing it a terrifying prospect.

'Who was Fletcher? Was he famous?'

'He was a she although only I know that. I have a pair of her boots and I psy-commed them. She's magnificent and warrants her own superhero film franchise,' Cordelia said revealing more of Charlie Bennington's story.

'I adore her.'

'Oh, I wish you could psy-comm too. It's like having access to a vast library packed with the most extraordinary yarns. If only I was able to bring all these incredible tales to the big screen. I've done it in a limited way at Shoeseum, but there is so much more that could be achieved. And House of Tanner would design the shoes!'

Cordelia was taking Elodie to Bellford House, a late eighteenth century cream stucco mansion designed by John Nash using his signature symmetrical neo-classical style. Now it was a museum full of art treasures including paintings by a rollcall of superstars: Rembrandt, Vermeer and Gainsborough. She asked Elodie to close her eyes and led her along the pergola, trailing with fragrant plants, to the grand entrance.

'What can you smell?'

'Jasmine, honeysuckle, art.'

'Is correct. *Très* good *nez*!'

The house had been on Cordelia's list of fascinations ever since she and Rex first visited as children with Celestine. Rex had stood for ages by the painting of a galleon and sniggered when he noticed how many penis-shaped images it contained. Celestine laughed when he pointed them out and said the painting thereafter would be known as the Membership.

Cordelia beckoned Elodie over to look. 'Spot the *zizi*.'

Elodie scrutinised it for a few minutes then started giggling so hard her legs gave way and she slumped to the floor, holding her stomach.

'Do I need to call the first aider?' the docent asked sarcastically, looking annoyed that they were being frivolous rather than earnest and reverential about the exhibits.

'She always has this response to art. I usually bring smelling salts,' Cordelia replied pulling Elodie upright.

'Did my mascara run?'

'No, still intact. Top quality to be Membership-proof. Now, one more glory to show you and then I'm back to my state of bliss where I know nothing of what will happen next.'

They entered a room where dozens of eighteenth century shoe

buckles were displayed and Cordelia pointed to a pair encrusted with Burmese rubies.

'These belonged to Joséphine, Duchess de Roches-Villeroy, a fascinating creature who I can never get enough of,' she said, sighing at the collection.

Elodie looked at her in disbelief. 'But she's one of my heroines too. We studied her in history at school. The French are proud of her influence on European fashion. Apolline owned her portrait, which I inherited, and I also have a pair of her shoes. Not only that, but our next stop may or may not have a connection with Joséphine. That's all I shall say because this day is all about surprises.'

'You have her shoes? May I psy-comm them? From what I've read, she had a mischievous attitude to life. Just the type of person I like.'

Joséphine, Duchess de Roches-Villeroy, had fled revolutionary France for England in 1793 after her husband Hercule was executed during the Reign of Terror. She arrived in London with just her maid, two footmen, a chest of jewellery and gold coins, a trunk of wigs, clothes and shoes, and her reputation as one of the great party hosts. Fortunately, she was already acquainted with the highest in society who helped her to settle in, although some may have regretted that each time she cleaned up at the high-stakes card games she hosted at Tellering Hall, her Palladian villa in Chiswick.

Cordelia and Elodie were heading there to climb a tree and take afternoon tea. It being Elodie, she had called the heritage organisation that owned Tellering Hall and asked to install a temporary tree house. The manager she spoke to said that normally it would be a definite no but he could make an exception for her because she was polite and he liked the sound of her voice. Then he asked what cake she was serving.

'Victoria sponge with fresh cream and gooseberry jam, sprinkled with edible flower petals. It's a favourite of my friend Cordelia Tanner. I shall send you a whole cake for yourself as a thank you for being so kind.'

'How lovely. And Cordelia, we know her well from when she worked with us to recreate historic footwear for an exhibition at one of our other properties. She might be interested to know that we have just restored the duchess' famous carriage. And it's having a test drive soon, pulled by four horses descended from the ones she kept.'

Elodie was thrilled to hear the news. The carriage in question was a landau that looked like no other. Joséphine had designed it in the shape of a Pompadour shoe impractically covered in baby blue silk brocade and with matching upholstery. Whenever she was driven through the streets, the public waved and shouted felicitations, and little boys chased alongside hoping to catch one of the bon-bons she always handed out.

'*Incroyable!* Would you like me to test-drive it with Cordelia on the day we visit the tree house? How prestigious for such a respected shoe designer to be the first passenger in the refurbished carriage.'

He could certainly appreciate the prestige factor and thought it would be good for publicity, however, the reality was that the carriage was too precious to be handled by a non-professional. But when Elodie told him she owned horses and had once represented France in the World Equestrian Games in the carriage driving category, he relented and said yes. What she failed to mention was that, as a teenager, she had also been a jump racing jockey and winner of several races.

'This is one of the most glorious days of my life. How did you wangle us a ride?' Cordelia said when she climbed into the carriage with Elodie at the reins.

'I mentioned your name and that opened the stable door,' she replied. 'Ready? Hold onto your hair!'

What Elodie meant by 'drive' was not the stately procession the house manager might have expected and she quickly coaxed the horses into a swift canter that Joséphine no doubt would have whooped at as Cordelia did.

++++++

'It's extraordinary because anyone else would get an emphatic "sling your hook" but she's a yes whisperer,' Cordelia said to Rex the day after, telling him about the excursion. 'Nobody ever says no to her, not even jobsworths who normally take satisfaction in being intransigent. She could so easily be a spoiled madam with a sense of entitlement but she's guileless.'

'And what about the treehouse?'

'Very simple. Planks with scatter cushions for a nap after egg and watercress sandwiches, a pot of Darjeeling, and Victoria sponge.'

'Was it delishment?'

'It was so light that were it not for the liberal wedge of jam and cream, it would have floated into the air.'

'Where did you go after snoozles?'

'You know how much I love the architecture in Fleet Street and we were driving east on Embankment so we did a detour.'

Cordelia had introduced Elodie to the spire of St. Bride's Church, the original model for tiered wedding cakes, and pointed out the former newspaper headquarters fashioned in an Egyptomania meets Art-Deco-in-a-classical-Greek mash-up style inspired by the discovery of Tutankhamen's tomb in 1922. Then the *pièce de résistance*, a black glass and chrome Streamline Moderne edifice next door with its sensuous curves resembling a cruise-liner that had moored in a street of stone buildings.

'I'm speechless and want to be hypnotised to forget so I can see it for the first time. Could we walk away then turn round and I can look at it all again. It makes my eyes very happy,' Elodie had said.

Cordelia continued regaling Rex with details of the activities. 'She's so full of enthusiasm about everything that it felt like a constant reward. Seeing as we were close to St. Paul's, I thought I'd take her to the Whispering Gallery to hear how she'd perform at the swear wall,' she said, referring to a game she and Rex had started as teenagers after their first ascent of the two hundred and fifty-seven steps up to the cathedral dome. They had stood each side of the circular space and took turns to whisper rude words at the wall. Sonic waves crept along its curvilinear surface until thirty-three metres away the other one heard the sound and had to guess what was being said. Cue much giggling.

'And how did Elodelicious score on the Profanity Scale?' Rex asked.

'Prodigious. I gave her extra points for her French phrases. Then she asked if I was in the mood for dancing and, of course, I always am, even more so when I have the right number of sparkles on my *schmutter*. She-She thinks of everything, and we went via a hotel room to get changed into gear worthy of the dancefloor. Serena dropped us off in Limehouse by a crumbling old theatre straight out of a penny dreadful novel where the ventriloquist doll in the props basket comes to life with evil intent.'

Cordelia revelled in uncovering secret corners of London in a hobby she called hiddenism but she had not before come across the dilapidated former music hall down an alleyway near the Thames. There was still an air of menace about the area from its days as a playground for roistering sailors who kept the pubs and brothels busy. It was easy to picture Charles Dickens quietly observing drunken fights, criminality, and the adventure tourists from the West End who went there to slum it and to use the opium dens in the narrow, foggy streets of nineteenth century London's original Chinatown.

'"View From Groove Mountain" was playing as we walked in so I sprinted to the dancefloor where the stalls' seats used to be. Lost in music as the song goes. Elodie even hired professional dancers to ensure the standards were high. The playlist was an all-time best. Top tunes, and the lighting system made me hallucinate.

'At one point, I thought I saw Lancelot. It was brilliant. Me and She-She were dancing for hours. Then when my appetite was calling loudly, it was time for a fry-up at an all-night caff after which we drove to Greenwich and arrived at the observatory at sunrise. As dawn broke, we jumped from one side of the prime meridian to the other.

'When I returned home, the HoT lobby was full of tuberoses and smelt gorgeous. Elodie had arranged it knowing how mad I am about them. She has an incredible memory because I mentioned a while ago how Harriet doesn't supply them to her clients because their fragrance gives her terrible flashbacks.' Cordelia had mentioned how tuberoses reminded their florist of a nightmare hangover involving tequila slammers and Lego.

'Poor lass can't go anywhere near a toy shop without feeling nauseous. Such a shame for her, and for us. They are perfect for HoT, being the Victorian symbol for voluptuousness,' she had said.

Cordelia carried on describing the day to Rex and said finally, 'Anyway, it was a blockbuster mirthday and yours is coming soon so prepare to be astonished. I don't know what she's planning but it'll be on a grand scale because that's what she does.'

Rex sighed and a dreamy expression crossed his face. 'I know I've only met her once but we were immediate friends and I can't imagine life without her. Ours was never dull before, but it's as though she has transformed the world from sepia into technicolour and I love it.'

Chapter Seven

'Dearest Cordelia,' Violetta trilled musically as she greeted her guest. 'And where is our darling?'

Blanche dashed towards her, tail in a circular motion like a helicopter blade, to be rewarded with vigorous stroking and baby talk.

Violetta was the owner, with her partner Dorothy, of Heartwood, the only extant work of arts and crafts architect, Edith Brookhampton. The exterior was a combination of half-timbering and green, purple and white glazed brick to represent the colours of the Suffragist movement. It had mullioned windows, an asymmetric gabled roofline and decorative Elizabethan chimneys.

Inside, each room was panelled with wood sourced from windfall trees; the parquet floor tiles were laid out in sunburst patterns. The ornate oak staircase that dominated the hallway had been carved by craftsmen who worked on the interior decoration of the Olympiana ocean liner.

Cordelia had chanced upon Heartwood on a morning walk when Blanche trotted through a wrought iron arched gateway. Her calls were ignored so she followed the dog into an enormous private garden. Sculptures, both modern and classical, some on plinths in the grass, others set on alcoves in the perimeter wall, drew the eye. At the bottom of the garden was an unexpected sight — a structure that resembled the ruins of an Egyptian temple with a line of soaring sandstone columns forming the walls of the rectangular hall. It was dominated by the statue of a human female with sculpted stone foliage instead of a head.

She stared for some time, wondering what its significance was then turned round as she heard a bark. Blanche was sitting by a table under a tree where an elderly couple was exuberantly talking to her. The taller of the two noticed Cordelia and greeted her. 'Good morning! Do come and introduce this delicious creature to us.'

'Meet Blanche, without doubt the most beautiful dog at this table. And I am Cordelia, her devoted guardian. How do you do?'

'How do you do? I'm Dorothy, and this is Violetta. Would you like to join us for coffee, my dear?' she said and rang a school bell hanging from a post behind her.

Soon after, a young woman in a formal black suit approached the table.

'This is Hope, our butler,' Dorothy said.

Hope nodded politely to Cordelia who wondered if that was her first or last name. As it turned out, it was both.

'Hope is a trained barista too so whatever you're in the mood for, she can make it,' Dorothy said. 'And we have freshly baked viennoiserie. Can we persuade you?'

'I have entered the Garden of Temptation and I willingly submit.'

This was the start of a warm friendship with Doroletta, as Cordelia nicknamed her hosts. Dorothy McInnes, emeritus professor of archaeology, and Dame Violetta Veronese, eminent concert pianist, and noted interpreter of the works of composer Cynthia Fender. Violetta had never retired, just ceased touring, and was so popular she always sold out her lunchtime recitals at the Wigmore Hall which was an easy ride down the hill from Highgate and back again in time for afternoon tea.

The garden temple was a replica of the one Dorothy had uncovered in Egypt several decades previously that honoured a hitherto unknown deity called Haljesta who, as Dorothy's research revealed, was the goddess of revels, conviviality and tolerance. This was a remarkable find for someone at the start of their career and she became an inspiration, principally with girls and young women the world over; many of whom went on to study archaeology.

'We throw an annual shindig called Jubilation on Midsummer's Day, the anniversary of the discovery. It's quite the scene. The flock of Monkey Business Ministries comes and glorifies our goddess with zeal. Are you familiar with them?' Dorothy asked Cordelia who shook her head.

'Monkey Business Ministries is for those people who worship a party and want to be part of a congregation but have no religious tendencies,' she continued. 'They meet at a deconsecrated Anglican church. The MC is called Drag King Wenceslas. She's marvellous and produces Jubilation for us.

'The neighbours always complain about the noise even though the festivities end by sundown. We'd invite them too if they weren't such a dreary bunch, so each year we warn the local police station to expect some angry calls, and without fail they act as predicted. You must come to our next do.'

'Thank you. I'd love to,' Cordelia replied eagerly. 'And I'll be at the Monkey Business service this Sunday. Do I need to take anything with me?'

'Just an open mind.'

'It's never been closed.'

They chatted animatedly for another hour, and Cordelia enthusiastically accepted Violetta's offer of piano lessons, and Dorothy's suggestion of exploring artefacts of the British Museum's archaeology collection that were not currently exhibited.

In return, Cordelia, who had almost wept when her hosts mentioned they were still grieving the death of Xerxes their treasured Staffordshire bull terrier, said, 'How about Blanche coming here for a visit without me sometime? I know she cannot replace Xerxes but she's very good company.'

So, twice a week, Dorothy and Violetta sent their driver Frankie to House of Tanner to collect London's most loveable dog and Cordelia tucked her up on the back seat of the Daimler and waved her off.

'You are so lucky going to Heartwood. Doroletta are two of my absolute favourites.' She said that about every captivating person she met but always meant it.

If Blanche could have replied, she would have said they talked endlessly about her and were particularly intrigued by psychomatricks.

'Does it have to be shoes for you to do a reading or will other belongings work?' Violetta had asked over lunch one day, and when Cordelia said it could be any personal object, she left the room and returned with a burgundy leather briefcase. 'This contained my music scores when I was on tour.'

Cordelia took it and said, 'Let's see what it reveals,' then started to meditate.

Dorothy nudged Violetta and whispered, 'Will I be shocked?'

'I do hope so, dear!'

Cordelia opened her eyes, chuckling. 'First violinist *and* bassoon player in the Berlin Philharmonic?'

Violetta tittered. 'People talk of a rock and roll lifestyle. Well, in classical music, we describe it as *allegro con brio*.'

'Tell us more,' Dorothy implored, 'I've never seen Violetta blush like this. I thought I knew about all her skeletons.'

They were most impressed at Cordelia's talent, especially Violetta who had forgotten many of the escapades she'd been involved in during her years on the road.

'Gosh, did I really get up to that?' she had said when Cordelia reminded her of streaking through the corridors of Copenhagen's Amalienborg Palace for a dare after she'd appeared in a concert there. And most subversive, smuggling Marmite in her hand luggage through customs into the USA.

'I wish you could do it on one of my trowels, because some of us old stone wranglers lived a rock and rock lifestyle! But all my field tools are currently in an exhibition at the Smithsonian Museum of Natural History so I have nothing to show you apart from this tattoo,' Dorothy said, pulling back an ear lobe and revealing a small feather acquired in Papua New Guinea at an initiation ceremony with the Tanufian tribe in which adolescent girls were marked with facial tattoos for beautification. 'I still remember how dashed painful it was. The tattooist tapped a pattern by pricking my skin with a thorn into which squid ink was soaked.'

When she said it was based on a bird of paradise, Cordelia exclaimed, 'So is the logo on my shoe business.'

That was not the only factor they had in common, for Doroletta had met at Libertas when they individually took solo holidays to recuperate from months of non-stop work.

'We hadn't yet met and one night both of us decided to go for a midnight swim in the outdoor pool. It was the full moon on Midsummer's night. The scent of jasmine was intoxicating. That's why it grows here in the garden, to remind us of our perfect first meeting,' Violetta said wistfully.

'As we gazed at the sky, I told Violetta that I called it Haljesta's Moon because it had risen just hours after I discovered the first evidence of the temple. She found that so romantic. Haljesta has been our very own deity ever since,' Dorothy said. 'We just wish we could taste some of her beer.'

She went on to talk about the ancient Egyptians and their reverence for beer. Many different styles were brewed, each with their own poetic name. Historians were already familiar with Beautiful and Heavenly, Beer of Eternity, and others, but Beer of Ecstasy was a new one.

Archaeobotanists had analysed residue on the inside of clay pots that they suspected had stored beer, and discovered it contained cereal, fruit — possibly dates — and the root of the mandragora plant, popularly known as mandrake, which was associated with love and fertility and known as 'the phallus of the field'.

'Mandragora was thought to be an aphrodisiac. Haljesta's priestesses brewed Beer of Ecstasy in the temple for disciples to binge on during her festival. That's why the statue in our temple hall has the body of a shapely woman and instead of a human head, a representation of the plant's leaves and berries. It's a reconstruction of what I discovered in Egypt.'

'Oh, we do have to try it. The Weasel is a brew pub. We could recreate the beer if you want us to. Would you work on it with Daisy, our brewer?' Cordelia asked.

'What a super plan. I have an incantation that I found on the wall of Haljesta's temple. Beer of Ecstasy brewers would have chanted it as they brewed, beseeching her spirit to enter the beer. I'll do that too, and we can serve it at this year's Jubilation then we'll be able to test whether it really does have magical properties!'

++++++++

It was late afternoon when Cordelia returned home from Heartwood and she popped into The Weasel to see Oscar.

'Morning, gorgeous,' he said smiling at her. 'Cup of tea?'

'Would love to but I have a couple of sketches I need to do quickly. Will you be here in an hour? There's something riveting I want to discuss with you, Rivington.'

'Any clues to tease me with?'

'Aphrodisiac beer. That is all I shall say,' she replied tantalisingly.

Oscar's eyes narrowed. 'You minx. How can you leave me hanging on?'

'*Ciao*,' she replied kissing her hand at him, and whistling the closing music of TV's most popular soap opera.

+++++

Oscar loved the idea of Haljesta's beer so much he decided to get up in the morning and join Doroletta on brew day. Daisy was excited about the challenge and read up on ancient beers, what they might have contained and how they would have tasted. As she explained to Dorothy, she had to make substitutions because contemporary brewing ingredients differed from those the Egyptians had access to.

'They used a type of wheat called emmer, and in place of hops, which did not grow in that region, herbs and spices. An extra source of fermentable sugar was necessary, and you said that Beer of Ecstasy likely included dates so I will too. As for yeast, back then wild microflora would have fermented the brew giving it a sour tang. I can replicate that by adding lactobacillus, but the beer will be fermented with our cultured house yeast.'

Brew day was a blast. Oscar wheeled the pub's upright piano into the brewhouse and Violetta played a medley of popular drinking songs as the others belted out the lyrics. Cordelia made sure there was plenty of cake to eat referring to the quotation from *Twelfth Night* when Sir Toby Belch says to Malvolio, 'Dost thou think, because thou art virtuous, there shall be no more cakes and ale?' In her opinion a person could never have enough cake, virtuous or not.

When it came to adding the crucial element, mandragora root, there was reverential silence as Dorothy sprinkled it into the brewing kettle and repeatedly chanted, 'Haljesta, the lady who fills us with blissfulness, may your essence enter this beer.'

After a couple of hours when the brew was cooled sufficiently, Daisy asked Violetta if she wanted to pitch the yeast, and then handed her a bucket.

'How long before the beer is ready to be consumed, dear?' she queried.

'In about ten days, just in time for your party. You'll have to drink it all though because without hops, and being lowish in alcohol, it won't keep and will quickly turn into vinegar suitable only for salad dressing.'

'There's no chance whatsoever of leftovers,' Violetta replied laughing.

'Our guests are always thirsty and will be even more-so when they know they are guinea pigs to test if Beer of Ecstasy has supernatural effects!'

++++++++++

'Did you know Doroletta have a thing for you?' Cordelia said to Oscar on the way to Jubilation. 'They want you to move in with them and be their prized ornament.'

'What an offer! I shall consider it thoroughly. So, do you think Beer of Ecstasy will turn the party into saucy central?'

'From what they've told me of previous gatherings, sauce has always been one of the condiments,' she replied with a chortle.

It was Midsummer's Day, the sun had got its hat on and Cordelia was looking forward to this *fête champêtre*. Doroletta hadn't revealed any details but insisted they must both be on time. 'You won't want to miss a minute of it!'

'It's odd seeing you up so early,' Cordelia said.

Oscar had set three alarms and asked her to come and tickle his nose to make sure he woke up on time at midday.

'Be careful you don't turn to ashes in the daylight,' she joked.

'I won't make a habit of getting up at such an hour. My body is in shock.'

When they arrived outside Heartwood, Cordelia felt the happiness she did each time she walked through the gate into a world where mainstream society did not intrude. Their hosts greeted them.

'There you are, dear Cordelia, and with our number one man. We're all assembling by the temple,' Dorothy said.

On the stroke of 3 p.m., a procession of musicians wove in between the temple columns rhythmically beating goblet drums, jingling sistrums, and shaking menits. They dance-walked towards the dais where Haljesta's statue stood.

That day, in addition to the stone representation, there was a living version, a young woman in sandy coloured robes, with a headdress made of real mandragora leaves and berries. The mesmeric music suddenly ceased as the living Haljesta stretched out her arms in welcome, and from a small basket threw mandragora flowers to the audience where they were eagerly grabbed. Whoever caught one was guaranteed good fortune. Then two Egyptian shenebs, long straight trumpet-like instruments, sounded a shrill call to action and the party officially started with the crowd chanting, 'Good times, revels and tolerance', as they scattered throughout the garden.

According to Cordelia's creed, all social gatherings should include singing and dancing, and Jubilation had an abundance of both. At the centre of the lawn was a maypole in the shape of Haljesta's statue, bedecked with lotus flowers, and instead of colourful ribbons, long plaited palm leaves descended from the crown for dancers to weave into patterns as they skipped round. Some drag queens were so tall their wigs got caught up which took some unknotting so that halted the action for a while.

In the temple's main hall, a crowd gathered to sing, '*Vivat Bacchus! Bacchus lebe!*' and other operatic drinking songs. Over on the dancefloor, a gypsy-jazz band performed impossible-not-to-twirl-to melodies and freestyle moves included polkas, reels, and dosey-does. A conga line meandered around the garden; the participants nibbling on fresh dates dipped in edible gold leaf placed by each sculpture. Those not dancing stood drinking and talking and were encouraged to tap the floating balloons bearing Haljesta's image to keep them in the air. Whoever let them touch the ground, had to kiss a stranger.

'So, when am I going to meet the legendary Elodie? Rex mentions her all the time. Is he in love?' Oscar asked Cordelia.

'Only from the nose up. And he's very partial to the gift wrapping because she's so stylish. It's all very pure. He woke up the morning after they first met unsure if he'd conjured her up in his imagination. Says that spending time with her is like being enveloped in a fragrant mist of gorgeousness. I've never known him to react to a woman like this. It's so darling.

'Actually, she reminds me of you in some ways. Unaware of her gigantic charm, gives full attention when someone is talking and makes them feel as though they are the most fascinating person alive. And she's very playful. Always chooses mischief over the mundane, although on first sight, her *soignée* demeanour gives nothing of that away.'

'Should I be jealous?'

'Never, it's impossible to have negative emotions with her. She's completely adorable and sees the positive in everything despite, through her charity work, witnessing what the worst of humanity can inflict.'

'Maybe I'll fall in love too.'

'Everyone else does, so you'll be in good company. It's as though Oberon has sent Puck ahead of her to sprinkle enchanted dust in people's eyes.'

'What, even Celestine? She usually has the measure of a person and can see through any façade.'

'Charm cannot be faked — a person either has it or they don't. Cel calls her "honorary precious jewel". She's smitten like the rest of the planet.'

'Then perhaps I should never meet her at all. The expectation might be too high and what if I'm disappointed? That would never do. I'm all for keeping the extraordinary on a pedestal.'

'Aren't you lovely?' Cordelia said, putting her arm around his waist.

'Who's that with Violetta?' Oscar asked.

It was Drag King Wenceslas in the garb of a 1960s Latin lover with black hair greased back, a pencil thin moustache, tight jeans, and a patterned shirt unbuttoned to the navel, displaying ripped abs. Violetta introduced them.

Wenceslas greedily eyed up Oscar, swaggeringly fist bumped him, and said, '*Hola* Weasel Man!' Then, not in character, 'If I could live anywhere I wanted, it would be in your pleasure gardens. I've had some brilliant times there. If you ever want to collaborate, please call me. And Cordelia, great to see you again. I didn't have chance last time we met to say what a fan I am of Shoeseum. Love the Pope Joan exhibit. How about a Monkey Business Ministries field trip there one Sunday?'

'Yes with a capital yes to a visit! And thank you, I too really like what we did with Joan. She was one spirited lass, and despite some academics claiming that her story is a legend, it isn't. It's true. Her shoes told me so.'

'Are you always looking to add to your collection 'cos, this sounds a bit random, but I was in a kebab shop in Green Lanes last week and I heard the owner talking about his cousin's neighbour in Istanbul who deals in antiquities and has shoes that belonged to the Queen of Sheba.'

Cordelia's eyes lit up. Elodie had been searching for the Queen of Sheba's shoes for ages. She had even hired an international investigator to discreetly sound out dealers and collectors.

'Most definitely. Thanks for telling me. Do you know the name of the takeaway? I shall go and talk to the owner about falafel and footwear.'

'She's very convincing,' Oscar said after Wenceslas had walked away. 'And the abs on that fake chest were very impressive.'

'Not as impressive as yours,' Cordelia replied putting her hands to his. 'Actually, I take that back,' she said tittering. 'Do you want to come with me to Monkey Business Ministries sometime? It's a hoot. Wenceslas is the *compère*. Very droll. First time I went, she looked like the Chancellor of the Exchequer circa 1950, that ultra-City gent look: Savile Row double-breasted navy blue suit, black Oxford lace-ups, trilby, furled umbrella. Dresses as a different male archetype for each performance. Taught us how to throw an insult like a Shakespearean character.'

'Go on then, Falstaff, offend me.'

'For sooth. Thou art a beslubbering plume-plucked vile canker-blossom.'

'Such useful life skills. What else happens?'

'All sorts, it varies. There's a loose format based on a traditional mass, which they call "sass". Readings from amusing writers, a homily that is anything but sermonising — usually a polemic on some daft subject. The "hymns" have racy lyrics and are sung in gospel choir style. If it's not irreverent, it's not included.'

'Sold. When are we going?'

'There's more. Communion is composed of a different bread delicacy each week, matched with the perfect drink — blinis with fizz, bruschetta and Chianti. Then it finishes with a game called Cocktail Cabinet and we are issued with a card like at bingo. Wenceslas shouts out the names of spirits, mixers and garnishes, and we tick them off. Whoever gets a full house has to mix that particular concoction for the others to sup. There are five rounds and I never remember much after that. It's so liberating because I don't have to be on my best behaviour.'

'You're never on your best behaviour anywhere,' Oscar replied incredulously.

'I am, lots of times. What about when I first met your parents and was so quiet they thought I must be an impersonator because I did not fit your description of me? And don't you remember us meeting the archbishop at Sylvester and Ravi's wedding? Absolute best behaviour.'

Cordelia had said to the archbishop that the only church she would ever consider joining was one where the men wore beautiful frocks like he did. He chuckled and said that if she only designed swish men's shoes, he would buy some to wear with his liturgical robes. So, Cordelia created a pair of tapestry slip-ons decorated with mitres especially for him. In his effusive thank you letter, he revealed that his ratings on Prayer Circle were much better when he wore them.

'Oscar, my dear, we dare you to take the first sip of Beer of Ecstasy,' Dorothy said approaching him and Cordelia.

As was the manner in many beer drinking cultures of antiquity, Haljesta's acolytes would have consumed the divine nectar in a communal manner with two or three at a time gathered round a large clay jar, sucking the liquid through hollow reed stalks to avoid any floating cereal husks and other solids. They were nascent drinking straws and high-status personages had their own, adorned in lapis lazuli and other precious materials.

Dorothy handed Oscar a long slim tube resplendent with tiny coloured glass beads and said, 'May the spirit of Haljesta be with you and take up residence.'

He took a mouthful, nodded his head, smiling in approval, and stood aside for her to sample it.

'I expect to be gazing yonderly within an hour,' she said leaning over the jar and sipping. 'Here, there's room for you to dip in as well Cordelia. Oscar, have some more.'

Daisy's interpretation of the beer was brown and cloudy with flavours of caramel and honey. Just a smattering of mandrake root had been added as a little went a long way, and in high doses it could cause headaches, vomiting and rapid heart rate. That would never do because it was the opposite of the beer's intention to be hypnotic, mildly hallucinogenic and to test its reputed aphrodisiacal properties. She had brewed several gallons and on the day of the party, it was decanted into capacious clay amphorae. Guests were invited to gather round them so they could drink like an aristocratic Egyptian through an ornamented straw. In ancient Egypt and other Middle Eastern cultures, there was no shame in being sloshed at festivals to honour the deities, in fact it was mandatory, so at Jubilation, 'when in Cairo do as the Cairenes do' edict was a given.

Dorothy had waited until the party had been sparky for a while before serving Beer of Ecstasy so she could observe the before and after conduct. As it turned out, the combination of mandrake, alcohol and jollity was potent. Soon it was quite apparent that this was no ordinary beer, not least because no one bothered to keep the balloons aloft, and when they touched the ground, rather than pay the forfeit with a chaste peck to a stranger, there were full-on snogs.

On the dancefloor, it was less of the two-step and more of a tango, and during musical chairs, when the music stopped, players ignored the empty seat and landed instead on the nearest lap then didn't get up immediately when it started again. With all the flirting and coquettish looks, it was as though pheromones had been pumped into the atmosphere generating an urgency and sense of anticipation. The crowd broke up into couples standing close together and the soundscape changed — voices at a lower pitch, and a different speech rhythm with shorter sentences, no rambling conversations, or long jokes.

Cordelia had wandered off and was having a quiet moment sitting under a tree, far removed and dreamy, picturing Lancelot in her head.

'Blimey, the beer. It's incredible,' Oscar said as he walked by, snapping her out of the reverie. 'And you should see what they're up to in the temple!'

She stood up and gazed into his eyes — dilated pupils. Hers were too. Where did Lancelot end and Oscar begin? He touched her arm. Electricity. There was no doubt, Beer of Ecstasy lived up to its billing.

'Home?' she said to him as they walked out of the party hand in hand.

Chapter Eight

Cordelia stretched out on the sofa in Rex's office. 'What's Call Me Rich up to and how many times today has he claimed that holograms cause cancer?'

'Are you sure you want to know?'

'No, not really. I just want more reasons to hate him.'

'Look at this then, it will add to your haul.' Rex showed her a grainy image shot with a telephoto lens showing a chubby bloke on a large yacht, no top on, hairy chest and back, and pendulous belly hanging over the briefest barely-there swimming trunks. It was hard to make out the details of his face but if the rest of him was anything to go by, she was relieved.

'Yuck, is that him? Where is he?'

'The Caribbean, where he spends most of his time. Lives on the boat. He's British and his company is registered in the Cayman Islands. Tax dodger.'

Cordelia looked again at the photo. 'That could be you if you let yourself go and stuck a shagpile carpet on your chest and back,' she teased.

'No, it blooming well could not! I'm gorgeous and he's a minger.'

'I wonder if he has any female company. Some oddments like a furry manatee. Urgh. What's wrong with me? I'm becoming obsessed with this repugnant man. Is there any footage or close-up photos? I want a good look at Jill's nemesis. And then I will immediately need hypnosis to erase him from my mind.'

Rex laughed. 'Can you take any more hating?'

'A smidge,' she responded, shivering in anticipation.

'Says the reason he never does video and avoids photos is so the husbands of the dolly-birds (his words) who visit the yacht don't know what he looks like so they can't biff him on the nose.'

'Stop! Nobody really talks like that, do they? As for girlfriends, I bet the only women on that boat are inflatable.'

'And he has a new technique in his Footloose battle — the guilt trip. He's been posting footage of crying Filipino children. The subtitles suggest their parents worked in his shoe factories but are now unemployed. He's threatening to sue Jill Mitchell personally, not Footloose, saying she has a moral duty to those families and he's demanding she pays reparations.'

Cordelia sighed. 'I'm guilty every day of my life about all this. What can we do to make it better?'

'I have an idea. You'll want to say no but hear me out.'

'Go on,' she replied cautiously.

'How about offering to collaborate with Call Me Rich by designing a special collection for his company? You, rather than HoT. For the world's greatest shoe designer to take this action with a range of inexpensive collectors' items would employ his workforce again, then maybe he'll halt his assault on Footloose. And it might persuade the public to start supporting other shoe brands. What do you reckon?'

Cordelia thought for a minute. Although the idea of any association with Nailer was abhorrent, the challenge and lure of the limelight was irresistible.

'Genius strategy. I'll do it so long as I never have to communicate directly with him.'

'I wouldn't inflict him on an enemy, let alone you. I'll do the deal and the logistics. You just develop something incredible like you always do.'

'On it! I'll take Blanche for a walk to stir up my creativity. I've missed designing real shoes.'

Blanche was very pleased to be outside and pulled on her lead in the direction of the common.

'Good choice, Waggy,' Cordelia said realising her dog's intention. As they walked, ideas came into her head. She stopped to scribble 'toothbrush and bottle tops' in her notepad. Not the title of a melancholy country and western ballad, but the theme of the collection with Nailer. 'He's too much of a prat to get it, but he'd be an idiot to refuse.'

'WHAT? JUST BECAUSE SOME PEOPLE CAN ONLY AFFORD MY TYPE OF SHOES, THEY DESERVE TO WEAR TRASH?' was his screeching response through email when Rex sent Cordelia's proposal.

'Says the man whose entire fortune was built on cheap rubbish that falls apart after only a couple of outings. Is he even familiar with the word irony or does he think it's a metal like coppery?' Cordelia replied heatedly. She was not used to her virtuosity being criticised, particularly by a potato stuffed into tiny bathing trunks. 'I haven't seen any other inspired solution to the billions of toothbrushes, plastic bottle tops and carrier bags discarded annually.

'If it was up to me, I would add a returnable deposit to the purchase price as an incentive to collect them for recycling. That solves a major landfill problem and reduces the production of new plastic. Melt them all down, weave the bags into raffia for decoration, and use it all to make shoes. It will be called the Sustainable Shoe Collection,' she said loftily from the saddle of her high horse.

'He's such a dunderhead. I went back to him and said that the media is guaranteed to be all over this range, that it's bound to win product design and innovation awards, and the shoes will sell by the shipping container load. I threatened to go to the Major Shoe Corporation if he's not interested. They're his competitors so that swiftly shut him up.'

'Could we just go with Major anyway? He's so vile and does not warrant the plaudits he'll earn by involvement with me.'

'I know,' said Rex sighing, 'Complete nightmare to deal with, but because he's so shouty on soshe, the media picks up on his rants and amplifies whatever he writes. Once the news is out, it might inspire other top designers to do something similar and that will help kickstart shoe manufacturing. Then we'll have no more remorse.'

'All right then. Even though he's been abominable about Jill. If we can use his gobbiness to repair the damage, let's go with him.'

'It's the most strategic option,' Rex assured her.

Richard Nailer eventually agreed to a partnership with Cordelia, having been convinced the connection with her was platinum plated. He insisted on being the first to announce it. Any interviews would be done through email to keep his voice and face unrecognisable by 'failures': his description for the men he claimed were cuckolds.

Cordelia had no such coyness about appearing on TV, and being a polished interviewee, she would willingly talk about her innovative concept. Predictably, the tabloid media took the sex angle when the Nailer/Cordelia alliance was announced.

'So, are you one of Rich's bitches then?' Vance Dorkin asked her when she appeared on 'It's Breakfast'. 'How come posh totty like you has got into business bed with a diamond geezer like him? Have you run out of money and need to sell yourself to the king of the business jungle?'

Dorkin had been hostile to Cordelia ever since he had told her at a party that she would be more attractive were she not so self-assured. Cordelia had responded to say that having worked non-stop for everything she had achieved, she refused to be shy about it and would not be taking lessons in humility from the man who had threatened to defect to the opposition if his bosses did not name the new TV centre after him. They had declined, leaked the demand, and public opinion had excoriated his arrogance. Being full of hot air and no action, he had not flounced off as threatened and instead remained in his well-paid job.

'Vance, you're embarrassing our guest, just stop. It's an interview not an inquisition. Sorry, Cordelia, tell us more about the Sustainable Shoe Collection, and when and where it is available,' said co-host Miranda Jenkall, staring disdainfully at him.

Cordelia was adept at playing the media game and only ever answered questions she wanted to, ignoring silly comments and deftly changing the subject to her benefit if required. Even though viewing figures were probably not as large as Vance's salary, 'It's Breakfast' was a show where the content was plundered by other broadcasters, print and online outlets. An appearance on that show was worth it for the publicity gained through other media. She felt sorry for Miranda having to sit next to him and apologise for his frequent inappropriate comments.

Vapid Vance thinks he's edgy, when really he's just thick and uncouth, Cordelia thought as she walked out of the studios. As usual, she had come out on top, shown the design artwork for the new collection and had promised to send Miranda a pair of espadrilles for her to wear on vacation. Social media was immediately busy, and so was her voicemail with interview requests.

'I think we're onto something with SusSho. I'm doing a couple of interviews tomorrow. No doubt Call Me Rich will claim it was all his idea so I'll get in first,' she said to Rex sliding onto the bench seat opposite him at Antonio's café. 'Are we ordering lunch?'

'You betcha. I fancy the shepherd's pie, but only if it contains real shepherds,' he replied looking at the menu.

'In that case, I shall have Welsh rarebit, extra rare, and with a bit on the side.'

'Talking of bit on the side, how's Lancelot?'

'Beautiful, fragrant and flirtatious,' she replied with a sigh. 'I saw him last night at a party hosted by the Prince Regent who was everything bad I'd read about. Gluttonous too. There were thirteen puddings on the dinner table. Most guests just had a spoonful of one or two of them. He had a dish of each. No wonder he had gout.'

Rex was envious of his sister's extra-sensory skills and the fact she could magic up a fancy man whenever she wanted, with no commitments and none of the annoying things about a relationship. He changed the subject and said in a low voice, 'Email from Call Me Rich to say he doesn't know when production on SusSho will begin because it takes a while to un-mothball the factories. But let's keep on with the publicity. You did brilliantly this morning. Hype is what we need and I know it will have the effect we want.'

'We've become such accomplished dissemblers. We're really good at it and it worries me that perhaps underneath we are scoundrels,' she whispered plaintively. 'If anybody discovered we were so bare faced, no one would ever trust us. What if Celestine was aware of what we'd done? I mentioned Jill the other day with a comment as though we are acquainted, and Sebastian asked if I'd ever met her. I'm losing track of what is real and what is not. Which sounds implausible given that I have an imaginary boyfriend.'

'It's only short-term,' he assured her. 'When shoe factories reopen, we'll assess everything and return to LBL.'

'LBL?'

'Life Before Lies.'

+++++++++

Six weeks later, Rex had news about Richard Nailer. 'Call Me Rich says his backing of the Best Foot Forward campaign made it so successful that shoe sales are increasing and he's reopened the factories. He also suggested that you might want to stick the Sustainable Shoe Collection up your jumper,' he told Cordelia fully expecting, but not receiving, a volley of vulgarities.

'Excellent news. I'll be so relieved never to hear from that man again. But didn't he sign an agreement with us?'

'Yes, and he suggested that I stick that up *my* jumper. So, I will, with pleasure.'

'I do like the idea of sustainable shoes though. Could we produce them elsewhere?'

'Yes, we'll contract the manufacturing to somewhere that was damaged by shoe-mageddon. It'll take a while to get it organised but I promise you it will be a priority.'

Gearing up for production and rehiring laid-off employees took some time before the Sustainable Shoe Collection was all-go. It was a gratifying confirmation of Cordelia and Rex's brilliance that their Midas touch continued when the first shipment of sneakers and casual sandals instantly sold out. Repeat orders were immediately placed. All profits went to development charities meaning the shoes were sustainable *and* sustaining.

'Thank goodness we're making amends,' Cordelia said over coffee in Rex's office.

'Me too. And, joy of joys, Call Me Rich seems to have forgotten how to use social media. Haven't heard anything from him for ages.'

'Maybe he's died of nastitis.'

There was a knock on the door and Sebastian came in. 'Letter for you, Rex.'

'What a treat, letters are so rare now,' he said opening the envelope from the student retained to redirect correspondence from the rented post office box in Luton that was the recipient of anything forwarded from Footloose HQ, aka a post office box in Zurich. It was like unwrapping the layers in Pass the Parcel because inside was another envelope but of higher quality stationery and addressed to Jill Mitchell.

He read the contents and said, 'Wow. The plot thickens. It's from the Government Honours and Appointments Secretariat. Jill has been nominated as a Dame Commander of the Order of the British Empire for services to computer innovation.'

Cordelia looked astonished. 'She deserves it! We deserve it! How does she accept? Letter? Phone call?'

The fact Jill Mitchell did not exist was a minor hiccup and they had an animated chat about which member of the royal family would be pinning the insignia.

'If I dress up as Jill, would I be able to fake it convincingly?'

'Well, no one knows what she looks like in real life, but the question is, can you do bland?'

That day just so happened to be one of Cordelia's screen goddess venerations and she was dressed as Rita Hayworth in *Gilda*, a cascading mane of auburn wavy hair beyond her shoulders, silver grey satin halterneck top, matching palazzo pants, and chainmail cummerbund.

She raised an eyebrow at him. 'I'm sorry, what was that word? Of course, *I* can't do bland but Jill can. I'll just have to practise. We could role play it. You can be the royal.'

'I'm not called Rex for nothing, thank you very much. Do dames get touched on the shoulder with a sword? I'd be rather good at administering that.'

'I don't know but have a go anyway. You're adept at waggling a cutlass. Let's do it at yours so I'm not seen in the hideously dull outfit Jill is going to wear.'

A few weeks after Rex had written to accept on behalf of Jill, the official announcement about the latest tranche of honours was released to the media. Cordelia burst into his office holding a newspaper.

'Have you seen this? Call Me Rich has been nominated for a knighthood! A knighthood. That contemptible, vulgar cretin,' she cried incredulously. 'It's for services to business and enterprise. What enterprise? The blooming Starship? His factories are all overseas, and his company and profits are off-shore. Bet he donated to the government's election fund. It's how they reward political donors. He's bought this award.' She paused, with a look of concern. 'You know what this means. If his investiture is on the same day as Jill's, they might meet at the palace. He'll be rude to her and I won't be able to prevent Jill from telling him to take a hike.'

'Hopefully they won't recognise each other. She's so wishy-washy and there are no close-up photos of him so you've never seen his face, but if you see a slob in a suit and suspect it's him, you can exit stage left.'

'He better not spoil Jill's big day because knowing what I do of her, she's never going to have anything more major than this happen.'

Chapter Nine

'Now you can open them,' Cordelia said to Elodie who was about to see for the first time how her collection was displayed in Shoeseum.

Celestine had created a room within a room, a grotto with a rough stone-like surface rendered in papier-mâché, and painted gold to resemble iron pyrite ore. The shoes were inside small individual glass and chrome pyramids hanging from the ceiling, giving them a mystical ambiance.

'*Oh là là*! Perfection. Celestine is a virtuoso.'

'I knew you'd worship it. Me too. And I want everybody to know that it's yours. Should we call it "L'Archambeau Bequest"?'

'What a privilege. Yes please. I can't wait to learn all their psy-comm secrets. When will you do it?'

Cordelia had been pondering psychomatricks and whether she could be a conduit for someone else to experience what she did. That someone being Elodie. They had so much in common and her lifeforce made Cordelia think that of anybody, she might have the capability.

'I've been wondering about whether you have the gift too. Do you want to try? I'll explain what to do.'

'Yes, yes, yes. Should I be nervous? Will it hurt?' she replied excitedly.

'No pain, but it does tingle, and the brain releases neurochemicals which are delicious and always make me high. That's one reason I get such a kick from doing it. And being nosy about other's lives. Do you want to try now?'

Elodie chose a pair of black leather knee-length boots from the nineteenth century. 'They belonged to an Englishwoman called Lady Runcible but that's all I know about her.'

'Let's see if it works when you do it alone. I suggest you hold the left boot with your left hand. Us lefties have magic in our fingers.'

Elodie held on to it, closed her eyes and concentrated the way she had seen Cordelia do when they first met in Los Angeles. Nothing. 'Oh, I'm so disappointed.'

'Now we'll try it as a double act and see what happens. Here, take my left hand, palm to palm, and we'll interlock our fingers. Put your right one on the boot. I will too. Now breathe slowly and deeply as though you are meditating.'

Suddenly, two high-energy beams travelling close to the speed of light fired through their nervous systems, and in that moment, the Large Hadron Collider was relegated to being the world's second most powerful particle accelerator. They opened their eyes in disbelief unlinking hands and breaking the circuit.

'Are we still here on Earth? It was as if we were taking off into space!' Elodie said breathlessly.

'I've never known anything like it,' Cordelia said, shaking her head. 'It's as if we created a forcefield. We should sell it into the National Grid as renewable electricity.'

They started again, with the same effect, but this time they maintained the circuit, kept calm and meditated. Images of Lady Runcible appeared in their mind's eye and her boots were bounteous in revelations including that her name was only ever whispered, and then solely by men of a certain predilection amongst whom she was a legend.

Lady Runcible, the boots disclosed, was a handsome twenty-eight-year-old who earnt a substantial living with a very specific type of performance. Men, hidden behind screens, paid to observe her as she quietly went about life at home, eating lunch, doing needlepoint and writing letters, innocently hiking up her floor-length skirt each time she sat down to reveal calf-hugging boots with intricate tight lacing and kitten heels. That fleeting glimpse was what stirred them.

The Lady, as her devotees referred to her, charged extra for clients to watch as she ascended the stairs, because then they had a longer flash with the dress swishing around her ankles. Those with bulging wallets paid a premium to enter her dressing room and gaze as her maid unlaced the boots. They never saw anything more than that. It was the thrill of concealment that they craved. Titillation *par excellence* because the hidden was forbidden.

Only one man at a time was permitted in the house. The Lady never interacted with them, carrying on in silence as though they were not there. She never spoke as that would have shattered the illusion, because rather than speaking in aristocratic tones as her title suggested, she had an East London accent, being from the Isle of Dogs. As a child, her dad Albert Runcible, a porter at Millwall Dock, had nicknamed her Lady.

Lady had realised that voyeurism could be monetised when she observed men on the streets waiting for females to cross the road and lift their skirts slightly as they mounted the kerb. That hint of what was underneath was enough to make them quiver. Easy money-making options for a person of her class were limited. Hard scrabble drudgery was the norm and Lady was an exception in escaping that fate. So, with her younger sister Queenie to play the role of maid, and brother Abdy as doorman and security, they went on the road travelling to British cities where they could be anonymous, and taking short rentals in fine houses. In each new location, they placed an advertisement in the local newspaper and waited for callers: 'Lady Runcible at Home for Discerning Gentleman. Relishment for Daring Connoisseurs.'

Lady didn't sell her body, she sold fantasies and they appealed as much to men who could not describe what stirred them, as to foot fetishists and individuals with a penchant for a dominatrix. Her perfectly legal wealth creation scheme was like no other, but no one apart from her siblings were aware of the income source. Lady told their parents they were touring performers and Mum and Dad never questioned it, grateful for the money that had supported them ever since a work accident left Albert disabled. For a woman with no formal education, Lady's success was even more impressive.

+++++++

When Cordelia and Elodie emerged from their trance, there was a momentary silence as they came to. Discussing what had occurred, they described the identical scenario so it was apparent that Elodie had definitely psychometrised.

'This is mind-blowing. I'm so relieved you are able to do it too because I don't think anyone believes I can see and hear the characters. They think it's just my imagination,' Cordelia said.

'I cannot describe how astonishing that was, but you can probably sense my feelings. Rather than devaluing the experience by using trite language, I shall not say anything, and instead talk about Lady Runcible. What an entrepreneur! She supported her whole family with only a pair of lace-up boots, and the ability to keep a straight face.' Elodie continued, on a roll as she talked about her area of expertise. 'It was rare in that era of long dresses for a man to see a woman's ankle, never mind anything else. Men had limited opportunities to gaze at the female form unless they paid for it or had a wife. Of course, they could go to a museum to see art. Manet sexualised nudity in his painting of Olympia because she is wearing mules and that means she is naked rather than nude, a vital distinction, and she looks straight at the viewer and challenges their voyeurism.'

'I think Shoeseum should have an exhibition about the connection between shoes and sex, with a lecture from you, also available online. You would have global interest and could attempt a world record for the largest congregation of foot fetishists.'

'We need a collective noun to describe them. What about a fumble?'

'Good word, She-She. I'm sending it to the Oxford English Dictionary for inclusion in the next edition. Now, are you weary? I am. A brain workout that generated more power than nuclear fission is tiring. We can psy-comm the others later. I need a cup of tea and something to eat. Do you fancy lunch?'

Sebastian had booked The Islander, the lunchtime only bistro owned by star chef Willamina Dorrington. As its name suggested, the restaurant was on an island in the middle of a lake in Myrtle Park. Diners reached it in a small wooden cable ferry propelled across the water by ropes. It was a temporary summer project with only five tables so securing a reservation was a feat, but Cordelia had priority treatment because of Willamina's frequent residencies at The Weasel Pleasure Gardens.

Willamina was one of a rarefied group of chefs awarded three Disherama rosettes and was now a member of an even more rarefied group who had returned the accolades because of the restrictions they imposed on how they cooked.

With the burden of the rosettes, The Islander would have been impossible because the idea was to reduce, recycle and reclaim. That applied to the building itself, constructed of used wine and beer bottles in a mosaic of green, brown and clear glass, with upcycled furniture inside.

The food was surplus stock from growers and retailers and likely to be dumped. She had no idea from day-to-day what her ingredients would be and that was the challenge: to create scrumptious dishes with no prior planning. There could be no theme or focus on a particular cuisine and the question, 'what type of food is served at The Islander?' could only be answered by saying 'a hodge-podge'. Each day there was a three-course set menu and diners ate what they were offered — no choices, no substitutions. Simple but stunning.

'I have some news,' Elodie said as they savoured their aperitifs. 'Now that my collection and lab are here with you, I intend to stay more often.

I'm in love with that black glass building we saw on your mirthday and am in the process of buying it to be my London residence. Do you think Celestine would work on refurbishing it? She has an exquisite eye.'

'Oh She-She, utter joy all around in Clan Tan! Rex will attempt a cool exterior but inside he'll be melting. Can you imagine how Blanche will react? She'll wear out her tail.'

After eating smoky calamari, creamy courgette and spinach souffle, followed by bread and butter pudding with spiced nectarines, Cordelia suggested they go to The Weasel for a look round the Minoan Lair so Elodie could check if it was a suitable venue for her lecture.

They sat in the stalls and Cordelia pointed out that the numerous plaster cast figures of putti were the pre-Renaissance versions, secular symbols of fertility and erotic passion, not the winged cherubs hijacked by Christianity as representations of God's omnipotence.

'This is perfect. With all the red velvet, it resembles a bordello, and devilish Dionysus encouraging his disciples to misbehave is just the backdrop this presentation requires,' Elodie said looking around and nodding in satisfaction.

'It will be brilliant and you will be brilliant. If Cédric could contact Sebastian and coordinate our diaries, we'll set a date. Let's go and have a drink and think of the most appropriate audience to fill the theatre and hang onto every word you utter.'

As they went back out into the pub, it happened — a brace of heavenly bodies came face to face as Oscar walked by.

'Vulpy come and say hello to Elodie,' Cordelia said, trying not to be anxious that two of the most important people in her life were meeting for the first time. What if, by some as yet undiscovered law of physics, they both faded in each other's company? That would never do.

'Oscar, I can't believe it's taken such a time for us to meet. I've longed for this moment. And now I understand why you are so precious to our darling Coeurdelia. You are magnificent!'

'Oh stop,' he said bashfully, 'Actually, don't stop. Carry on, I like it.'

His face was aglow with something Cordelia had never seen on him before. He was blushing.

Oscar recovered quickly. 'Elodie, I'm so pleased you're here and that I'm no longer the only one in our family who is not under your spell.'

They stood gazing at each other with smiles for miles and Cordelia breathed easy observing that her two charm titans remained high on their columns illuminating the universe and had not cancelled each other out.

'Do you have time for me to show you Weasel world? Me and Cordelia have created an epicentre of entertainment that combines the things we love: food, drink, theatre, music, art, dancing, singing and games. We also encourage naughtiness because there isn't enough of it these days. That's why we have the pleasure gardens.'

Elodie, typically, was full of enthusiasm for everything she saw, from the design of the rotunda, to the layout of the actual garden.

'A wildflower meadow. How beautiful. And hives on the roof. Are you an apiarist?'

'Yes, we have two hives. The queens are named after Aretha Franklin, and Boudicca, vanquisher of Roman invaders.'

'You visit your bees every day and converse with them, don't you, Vulpy?' Cordelia said.

'I certainly do. It's tradition to tell them the news of what's going on at home. They respond with excitable buzzing if they like what they hear. I'll let them know I met you. They'll be happy. Would you like to see them sometime? You can help me collect the honey and then taste its London terroir. We use it to brew small batches of mead.'

Elodie nodded excitedly and said, 'Everything here is enchantment. It's a magical realm with delight at its core. I never want to leave.'

'What a gorgeous thing to say, thank you. This is mostly Oscar's doing though. I just give him support and whole-heartedly enjoy whatever he does. And we have top parties. We must plan one with an extra-special theme for you,'

Next on the VIP tour was a stop in the pub cellar.

'We make our own ale and have a house yeast. It's the most precious thing we possess and is unique to The Weasel giving the beers an aromatic and flavour profile like no others. Yeast cells are female, and I call ours Lizzie, after my vivacious grandmother who was such a character and so full of humour,' Oscar explained. 'These barrels contain cask conditioned ale. That means the yeast is still live and goes through a secondary fermentation so it needs lots of care and attention and optimum conditions to coax it into readiness for serving. I talk to the yeast and play music to keep it happy.'

'What music do you play?' Elodie said, intrigued, and as always full of intellectual curiosity.

'Italian opera because fermentation is such a dramatic phenomenon. It depends on the beer style but I've noticed that heavier, darker beers prefer Verdi, beers in shades of brown are partial to Rossini, and for pale ales it has to be Donizetti, principally *The Elixir of Love*. Would you like to pull your own pint?' he asked, leading them up to the bar.

Oscar demonstrated how to do it, handing the full glass to Cordelia and then said to Elodie, 'Your turn. Hold the glass at a slight angle and pull the hand pump towards you. That draws the beer through a pipe from the cask, then return the handle to the original position and pull again. There should be just under a pint and if you do some slow topping up, it will create a lovely foamy head.'

'It's harder than it looks,' said Elodie concentrating on the task and then presenting a textbook example.

'Impressed! That's for you to drink. It's brown ale.'

She took a sip. '*Délicieuse*. I like English ales. Just by the taste I think it listened to *The Barber of Seville*. I'm enthralled and want to entertain Lizzie. Do you think she would like to hear my piano accordion?'

'Definitely! What tunes do you play, so I can think about the beer style that will enjoy it the most.'

'Always happy and upbeat, never anything miserable. My fingers move quickly over the keys as though they are dancing.'

'Well, in that case, it has to be a sessionable strength India pale ale made with an English hop called Jester. I'll ask Daisy to brew it the day before you are next here and then will you come and play as fermentation is revving up?' Oscar replied pouring himself a pint and sitting down. 'Have a look at the Champagne section,' he said passing Elodie the drinks list. 'Bonheur. It's Rex's favourite fizz and our customers love it too. So many venues have that ubiquitous you know what from Epernay. Give me Reims any day.'

'For that, you deserve the freedom of the city. Would you both like to come to *la Maison de Champagne Bonheur* so you can taste it at the source and see our underground caves? Thousands of bottles sit there quietly maturing. Rex must join us too. I inherited a château not far away in the Marne valley. Come and stay.'

'How could we resist?' Cordelia said. 'But be careful because once we are there, we may never leave.'

'What a happy thought. Château Beausoleil will be our own personal holiday camp. It has a ballroom and karaoke machine, so that means dancing and singing for us two, and a card parlour for Rex. We need something for you too, dear Oscar.'

'All of the above, thank you.'

'Let's go for a weekend that is so long it extends into a week!' Elodie said, then changed the subject, 'And now I must go and get ready for a formal occasion although I'd rather stay here at The Weasel with you.'

'I wish you didn't have to leave. Where are you going?' Oscar asked, a disappointed expression crossing his face.

'For a dinner at Buckingham Palace to honour the state visit of the President of France.'

'What are you wearing? I hope the ensemble includes cowbike boots,' Cordelia said.

'Of course. Jade patent leather. Divine. The gown is ankle-length with a V-neck and a V-back, draped from the waist and made of emerald metallic *fils coupé*. I hope the heating is on at the palace. Monsieur le President asked me to escort him.

'He's very grand, has emperor ambitions, and rarely smiles but each time we meet, I manage to make him laugh because I beg him to tell me the secrets of other world leaders. "Doctor l'Archambeau, that would be like kissing and telling and a gentleman never does that," he says. So I reply, "Promise me you are saving it for a tell-all memoir when you are out of office and may I have the first signed copy please?" And he says, "I do not intend to be out of office," then laughs,' Elodie said mimicking the president's imperious manner of speaking.

'You'll probably have one of the princes sitting on your other side at dinner. I've always wanted to know if, with so many rooms in the palace, they play hide and seek. You might be able to score an invitation for us to go for a game. And while you're at it, could you ask him for the key to the wine cellar? I hear the royal collection is very special so I would conceal myself in there with a corkscrew and hope not to be discovered for a while,' Cordelia said.

'He probably needs some respite from being princely so I'll invite him to join me on Nike as I try to do the fastest lap possible of the M25.'

'If you're stopped for speeding, the police will not issue a ticket because you'll have a member of the royal family on the back. And when you're at the palace, please send photos of your boots contrasted against the red carpet so I can gaze longingly at them.'

+++++

After Elodie left, Cordelia said to Oscar, 'So, opinion?'

'Fabulous and makes everything feel right, like an opiate does. You did try to prepare me but I thought you were exaggerating. I could feel myself blushing which I never normally do. And where did those tinkling wind chimes come from when we were introduced?'

'That was just in your head, darling. We've all had our first-moment-with-Elodie reaction. Mine was the world in slow motion and shimmering golden light, and Rex had a full orchestra playing the most exquisite music ever composed.'

'Well, I'm captivated and her goodbye kisses felt as though my cheeks were being caressed by velvet. I'd get up in time for lunch every day with her!' he replied laughing as Cordelia tweaked his nose.

'That's lovely. We'll all be best friends. Rex is having a deck of playing cards printed with pictures of us as the suits. Elodie as hearts, him as diamonds, in honour of Shirley Bassey, me as clubs because I like dancing, and you as spades. Not because you are sloppy seconds, but because you have charisma in spades. What a happy family we are,' she said sighing and relaxing into the sofa, then jumping as her phone vibrated. It was a message from Elodie.

'I adore him. So engaging. And how beautiful with his green eyes and perfect chin. I can't believe you two are divorced, you're so sympatico.'

Cordelia looked at Oscar mentally agreeing with Elodie's comments but certain of the decision they had mutually made to end the marriage.

'Elodie has texted to say how wonderful you are and that she can't understand why you're no longer Mr Tanner.'

'It's hard for those who see us together to get it. If only they knew how impossible it is with our out-of-sync body clocks to sustain the marriage we deserve. Our relationship is different now but I cherish it, my mistress of the morning. And with our private times when circumstances align, we're not exactly brother and sister.'

'I believe an alignment of circumstances is overdue,' Cordelia said with a wink.

Oscar moved his head close to hers, gazed into her eyes and said in a low voice, 'You smell of beer.'

'So do you. Irresistible!'

Chapter Ten

Shady, Cordelia thought, surveying the man sitting opposite who was manspreading wider than the Dardanelles Straits. Average height, wearing a rayon-blend grey suit that gave it a metallic sheen effect, grey shirt with a stain where he had spilled breakfast, no tie, chunky Breitling watch (fake), sweaty forehead, and spray-on hair to cover his bald patch. He resembled a confidence trickster who plays the shell game in tourist areas gathering a group together and, while all attention is on the sleight of hand, an associate picks their pockets.

A few weeks after Drag King Wenceslas had mentioned the Queen of Sheba shoes, Cordelia and Elodie were in the conference room of a faceless London hotel in Cromwell Road to meet the man who claimed to have the footwear and was willing to sell. Cordelia could tell by looking at him and hearing his hard to pinpoint Black Sea/Caucasus accent that Robert Milton was an assumed name, chosen to sound Anglo. He described himself as an art-dealer-importer-exporter which was a euphemism for 'really dodgy bloke'.

Milton was the type who drank Cognac and smoked cigars in hotel bars around the world doing deals with other men. He was also the type who did not take women seriously. That included Cordelia and Elodie who had given false names so Milton did not know he was with a leading designer and a world-renowned surgeon-academic, but could tell from their well-groomed appearances, dashing outfits, and handmade boots they were wealthy. In his head, he tripled the asking price for the Sheba shoes.

'So, you two lovely ladies collect shoes. That's a nice hobby. What do your husbands do?'

'I keep mine locked up in the basement of our house so he's not doing anything at present,' Cordelia said, then laughed.

Milton wasn't aware that women could have a sense of humour having never had a meaningful conversation with one so he was not sure how to react.

'Can we see the shoes please?' said Elodie eagerly. Unlike worldly Cordelia who was already suspicious, she was optimistic that he might have the footwear she'd been searching for.

He placed a box on the table and opened it. 'These are so rare that I keep them close and hold them regularly just to confirm they are real,' he said, taking out a pair of brown leather flipflops with coloured glass baubles on the straps. Even without Cordelia handling the goods, it was obvious they were fakes. His ineffective attempt to scrub away the Really Truly Holy Shoe Corporation logo stamped into the leather sole was a clue.

'Darling, tell Robert what you read about the Queen of Sheba's visit to King Solomon,' Cordelia said.

He turned to Elodie who explained that the queen was said to have brought spices, incense and precious stones as gifts for Solomon. 'Only a handful of regions had all three commodities, so academics believe that the land of Sheba was either in the Horn of Africa or the southern Arabian Peninsula.'

'I suppose you have plenty of time to flick through magazines and learn stuff like that when you're at the beauty parlour,' he said dismissively.

This distraction gave Cordelia the chance to psychometrise the shoes and she was able to determine that Milton was indeed dodgy and most antiques he handled were looted from museums in war zones and failed states, then sold on to private collectors. Being fluent in Arabic, English and Russian meant Milton could communicate with suppliers and potential clients worldwide.

'We'd like to think about the shoes please,' she said when he had finished treating Elodie like a half-wit.

'Of course. I will give you one week to make a decision but I do have other interested collectors so the price might increase.'

'I'm not surprised. They are priceless,' she replied, trying to keep a straight face.

By now, Milton was even more convinced he was dealing with numpties so he said, 'I have another pair of shoes you might be interested in,' and placed a cloth bag on the table. 'These belonged to Mary Magdalene,' he said, untying it and pulling out a pair of large-sized Roman soldier sandals purchased from a fancy dress shop then distressed to make them look old. Cordelia and Elodie struggled not to snigger.

'What big feet you have, Grandmama.'

'Mary Magdalene was very tall,' Milton replied, not understanding Cordelia's sardonic remark.

'May I photograph the shoes to make a decision alone?'

'No photos allowed. I am sure you will remember the appearance of such unique shoes.'

'Fair enough. We'll be in touch.'

When they were alone and laughing about Milton's amateur attempts to antiquify the shoes, Elodie asked what Cordelia had discovered about him.

'He handles stolen property and deals with some disagreeable characters. If he tries to scam all his clients like he did with us, he'll end up as mincemeat fed to stray cats. But I did discover something very interesting. Do you remember the Degas painting that went missing from the Lenter Museum a couple of months ago? He has it. I have the details of where it's stored. The insurers will be keen on this intel and when you two were talking, I sneaked a swift photo of him so they will know who to look out for.'

'Will they believe you?'

'Good point. They definitely won't have heard of psychomatricks, seeing as I made up the name, so I'll mention remote viewing instead because that's quite a well-known concept. A couple of USA intelligence agencies used it with some success during the Cold War. I once met the man who had been in charge of the programme. Top secret status had expired so he could divulge previously classified information.

'He told me about his greatest hits, including revealing the existence of the Soviet Union's new class of nuclear submarine and where it was being constructed. If I describe myself as a remote viewer, then they might be more likely to consider it.'

'And if they don't believe you, should we go and rescue the painting? Milton would think we were just there to buy his worthless shoes.'

'Yes, you could divert him by discussing a magazine feature that he'd assume you'd read at the hairdresser's and treat you with the "there, there, little lady" attitude. Meanwhile, I'd be rummaging round in his garage and retrieving the goods, before we scarpered on Nike with the painting slung around my back.'

'We would be cultural vigilantes. What a good title to have on a business card. Although I do know someone who works at Globo-Pol. I can call Manon. She'll send someone to investigate Milton.'

'Let's go straight to Globo-Pol then. Much more effective than desk jockeys in insurance offices. Good contact to have. What does she do there?'

'Secretary General.'

++++++++

Several weeks later, Manon contacted Elodie to say that, following Cordelia's tip, the Istanbul police had raided the address she supplied and arrested Milton, recovering the Degas painting and many more stolen items. The neophyte sleuths were gratified the painting had been reunited with its rightful owner, but they were a bit disappointed their reverse heist had not been necessary.

'We should start Elodelia's Detective Agency,' Elodie said after hearing the news. 'With psychomatricks, we would be unstoppable!'

++++++++

'Look, it's the Dog House,' Rex said, nudging Cordelia as the bus they were on passed the cemetery where Pauline Westwich's nocturnal fundraising activities had been revealed through her lost slingback. 'Wonder if it's located in the K9 grid on the A–Z map?'

They were heading to Hackney Empire for the first night of a new play about the nineteenth century music hall star Nessie Litherton who had found fame after being booked for a US tour by an impresario who thought she was Bessie Bitherton, noted Shakespearean tragedian. When Nessie arrived in Philadelphia from Liverpool and the mistake was revealed, the promoter had a conniption, but Nessie promised to turn tragedy into triumph reading from Hamlet, Othello and King Lear in a comedic manner, playing different characters but always in her own accent: Scouse. The crowd loved it, in particular the asides and impromptu jokes. Nessie was an instant hit.

'So, tell me more about your mirthday,' Cordelia said.

'Flawless. When you told me beforehand that Elodelightful would organise something beyond, I didn't realise just how beyond.'

They had started with breakfast at the cabman's shelter in Masters' Square meaning Rex had achieved one of his aims in life. It was worth the wait.

'How did She-She manage that? Actually, that's a stupid question because she manages everything and nowhere is off-limits.'

'We were with Serena Taxi Driver. Her aunt Brenda runs the shelter and made an exemption to let us in even though we're not cabbies,' he replied. 'She told us all sorts about the original concept of the shelters. They date from around 1875 and could be no wider than a horse and cart because they were built on public highways and should not obstruct traffic. Ours seated ten around a U-shaped table and we managed to squeeze into the last spaces.'

'What did you eat?'

'Fried egg sandwich just how I like it, flipped over and not too runny, served with strong tea. That set me up perfectly for a mid-morning aperitif and game of blackjack, two player variant, at the top of the former Post Office Tower.' He smiled at the memory.

'This used to be a revolving restaurant, but it's been closed to the public for years,' Rex had said, 'Too much of a security target. I've longed to visit and now, here we are. Aren't you clever to make it happen!' He sipped a French 75 and took in the London panorama from the vantage point of what was, until 1980, the tallest building in the UK.

'I thought we deserved to see inside so I made a few calls and eventually found the person who could say yes. Should we play?' Elodie said shuffling the cards.

'Yes please. But first, let us raise a toast to Dolly Parton, patron saint of big hair. Bottoms up!'

Rex continued describing the day to Cordelia. 'After we called a truce at cards, we went to the Bank of England for lunch with the chief cashier. She showed us the original design for the Alan Turing fifty pound note. It's packed with imagery. Ticker tape printed with his birth date in binary code, technical drawings for the machine used to break the Enigma code, and other symbolic designs. Fascinating.'

'And how was bingo? Was that old battle-axe who sucks her teeth at us there?' Cordelia asked, grimacing at the thought of the woman who always gave them prolonged evil looks.

When it came to bingo, Rex was the equivalent of the super recognisers employed by police forces to spot persons of interest in crowds, except he recalled numbers rather than faces. Which meant he could play more than one sheet at once and cancel them within a nano-second of the numbers being called. He won more often than other players making him an enemy to the daily regulars. That and the fact he shouted 'Bingo' rather than 'House' which caused them to be irrationally angry, and not least because he visibly enjoyed himself. Overt jollity was not allowed.

'You mean Gwendoline. Me and E are great pals with her now, you know. She was at the table next to us, scowling in my direction as usual. Elodie smiled at her, said good afternoon, and that was it, they were chatting like old friends.

'Gwendoline admired her bracelet which, it turns out, is made from mahjong tiles once thrown at her by gangsters in Shanghai frustrated when she won game after game. Then Gwenders asked about the woman's portrait on Elodie's ring so she explained who Apolline was and promised to send her a bottle of Bonheur.' But there was one thing Rex did not tell Cordelia. It was so touching he wanted to keep it for himself.

Gwendoline had asked Elodie if Rex was her husband and she had replied, 'Oh no, he's much more significant. He is the twin brother of my closest friend and that makes him profoundly special to me.'

'Do you think Scary G will revert to type and glare when it's just us two?' Cordelia asked.

'I expect so.'

'How about taking a hologram of She-She to sit at our table like a bodyguard protecting us from cantankerous old biddies.'

'Urgh, don't mention holograms. The word makes me think of The Predicament and I just want to revel in the glorious memories of my day out.'

'Did any cake pass your lips?'

Rex sighed dramatically. 'I hardly have the words. Well, I do but I need to put them in order.' He paused, gathering himself. 'Mont Blanc with Bonheur rosé served on Gloriana, the royal row barge. There's nothing like being conveyed downriver by eighteen oarswomen in a twenty-seven-metre long scarlet and gilded gold leaf wooden craft!'

If Rex thought the day could not be any more memorable, then he had underestimated Elodie. They alighted the barge at Embankment Pier and walked up past St. Martin-in-the-Fields and the statue of Nurse Edith Cavell, and into The Symphony pub.

'Splenny-d. They have Kingston Black, my fave apple variety.'

They ordered drinks.

'Here try this,' he said offering her the cider, 'Acidity and tannins — that'll perk up your palate!'

'So good. Do you want some of my beer? I've never tasted a stingo before. *Délicieuse.* '

'I love this pub. It's like the National Portrait Gallery but with better booze.'

The walls were hung with a collection of pictures of public figures mostly by amateurs, and though not intending to be abstract, it was often hard to tell who they were meant to portray.

'Look at that one. It could be me,' said Rex pointing at an accomplished pencil drawing. He peered closely and cried in surprise, 'It *is* me!'

Elodie beamed at him. 'I know Riona and told her about you and your mirthday. She also loves Dolly Parton so when I asked her to do the drawing, she put aside all her other work *et voila!*'

Riona O'Keefe was the most in-demand portraitist with a waiting list of many years.

'She did it from a photo I took of you when we first met. The Wynterburne Gallery in New York has asked to display it in a retrospective of her work. Will you be able to spare it?'

'Botticelli!' he exclaimed with joy.

'Riona perfectly caught your happy facial expression, so it deserves to be the centre of the exhibition. She asked if you would go to the private view and wear that same beautiful suit.'

'Are you sure that you really exist or have I dreamt up the most fabulous person who makes the best things in life happen?'

Elodie smiled, waggled his earlobes and said, 'If you can feel that, I'm real. Promise.' They finished their drinks. 'And now, I want us to prove the answer to something that has intrigued me ever since I first set eyes on it. Only you can help me.'

Having been brought up by Celestine and Cordelia, Rex liked it when women were in charge so he happily followed Elodie out of the pub and around the corner into the empty Imperial Theatre, through the lavish Baroque foyer, and up the imposing marble staircase to the dress circle.

'See those statues? Do you think they have six-packs?' she said pointing to the Roman charioteers that flanked each side of the proscenium arch. 'Let's learn the truth.'

She led him up to the balcony level, along a corridor and through a tiny door that opened behind a charioteer dozens of metres above the stage.

'Reach your hand around to his torso and have a feel.'

They both had a grope then looked at each other and laughed.

'It's more like an eight-pack! But I'd better just double check,' Rex exclaimed, going in for the second course.

'Excellent core strength,' said Elodie joining him.

Back in the dress circle, they sat in the front row.

'I saw the most divine *La Traviata* here,' said Rex, 'Almost dehydrated myself weeping at the letter scene. I sat in that box over there and watched the conductor working. Her interpretation of the score was lush. It made me long to conduct a full-size orchestra.'

Elodie looked at him. 'Then you shall, *mon chéri*. I have a surprise.' She opened her bag and took out an official Imperial Theatre programme. He read with amazement the words, 'Rex Tanner conducts the London Symphamonia Orchestra with vocalist Elodie l'Archambeau.'

'You will be conducting me too. I'll sing torch songs but please be kind and don't shout "ah no" to my soprano if I hit some bad notes. Here's my repertoire. And this is for you,' she said, handing him a long narrow purple leather case. Inside was a baton the length of his forearm, fashioned out of rosewood. 'It belonged to Leonard Bernstein.'

Rex was stunned and momentarily speechless so he squeezed her hands with all the gratitude he could communicate and looked at the song list. They were all familiar.

'Darling Elodelightful, this is the most monumental thing anyone has ever done for me. And please don't be mad at me if you hear some bad notes because of my conducting. Although if I do, only you and the orchestra will know,' he said, pulling himself together.

'But how could you think we would celebrate your debut with an empty theatre? It will be full and everyone will adore you!'

A full house was 2,350, making the Imperial London's largest theatre. Some individuals might have panicked at the thought of 4,700 ears witnessing a maiden performance but not Rex — the Tanners had confidence printed indelibly on every cell in their bodies.

Ninety minutes later, he was attired in classic black tails, white shirt and white tie, waiting for the orchestra to finish tuning up. As he walked towards the podium and heard the applause to welcome him, the reality hit. Rex bowed to acknowledge it then gulped as he turned round and saw dozens of professional musicians all waiting for his command. He stood up straight, raised his arms, indicated a preparatory tempo beat with the baton and the musicians began.

Elodie had chosen an overture of tunes by First Choice because of their sultry Salsoul orchestration. As she walked on stage, shining in a gold satin ankle-length sheath cut on the bias, with a Super Trouper spotlight following her, the orchestra's string section dialled up their luscious-o-meter and played 'Doctor Love'.

Rex had an out-of-body experience. He could see himself, the orchestra and Elodie, aware of how magnificent it all was and cognisant of how the musicians did not really need him to direct them but were respectful and gave full attention to his visual instructions.

Elodie's set was a combination of standards from the bossa nova, pop, jazz and lounge catalogue. 'Can't Take My Eyes Off You', 'The More I See You', 'Stairway to Paradise', 'Desifinado' and more, sung in a smoky, lyrical Julie London meets Dusty Springfield style with such come hither that it beckoned with each finger. Every single person was convinced she was singing the lyrics to them alone especially the line from 'The Look of Love' about sealing the lover's vow with a kiss.

Never had a seasoned karaoke singer performed on such a grand scale and with such glamour. And never had there been a more rapturous audience, recruited from the Royal Society of Pub Singalongsters and the Sisterhood of the Hairbrush Microphone.

When Elodie finished and left the stage, they stamped their feet and wolf whistled until the building shook so much that glasses fell from behind the bars. The applause went on and on until the auditorium, by now blacked out, was suddenly illuminated with white strobe lights creating a trippy effect as Elodie drove slowly onstage astride Nike with Cordelia sitting side-saddle behind her. As they dismounted, the orchestra started playing the opening notes to 'Kinky Boots' and there were screams of delight at Cordelia's thigh-high boots, only finished by her workshop that afternoon, decorated in black crystals and gold feathers leading from the ankle up the calf. She wore them with black sequin hot pants, a gold lurex bolero jacket and a golden feathered headdress.

Elodie had matched silver suede cowbike boots with a mirrored 1920s knee-length cocktail dress fringed on the hem. When they started singing 'These Boots Are Made for Walking', the vocals could barely be heard above the crowd who was singing along and wildly dancing.

Everyone was delirious when Elodie took her solo bow and called Rex up on to the stage. In a dreamlike state, he grabbed Cordelia's hand

and pulled her from the wings to share the ovation. He could see it all clearly, and felt that the decibel level was soaring, but all was silent in his head. Euphoria.

Elodie drew them close in a hug and forever after Rex would remember the scent of her perfume, and the sensation of Cordelia's feathers tickling his forehead.

Chapter Eleven

The evening before Jill Mitchell's investiture, Cordelia checked into an anonymous hotel in St. James' carrying a garment bag and wheeling a small suitcase. She'd disguised herself as Jill in a public loo on the way, entering the cubicle in a moss green trouser suit and exiting as someone else — light brown neck-length bob, spectacles and casual separates.

At the hotel, she ordered Jill-ish room service — glass of Chardonnay (New World) and a Club sandwich. *Poor lass, if she wasn't so uptight, she could have gone to the pub and had a pie and pint of Porter. But I must get into character,* so she drank the wine. *Too much oak influence,* she thought, and ran through the lines, body language and posture rehearsed over and over at Rex's.

'Can I get away with bending my knees so I'm not as tall and don't stand out amongst the crowd?' she had asked him during one run-through.

'Depends on the hem length of the frock. It would have to skim the ankles to conceal your contortions.'

When Cordelia tried it, Rex snorted with laughter at her clumsy attempt to look shorter.

'Stop, I have a stitch,' he said holding his stomach as she picked her way across the room. 'You're moving like a flamingo.'

'Maybe I shouldn't try it when walking, just do it when I stand.'

'But you'll think "flamingo" and then guffaw. Best not do it at all, birdy.'

Next morning after her ablutions and room service breakfast (plain yoghurt and blueberries for Jill even though Cordelia fancied a full

163

English), she applied a little makeup, just mascara and coral pink lipstick which was Jill's, not her, shade, and got dressed. She'd gone shopping in a high street chain store to buy inconspicuous clothing and had chosen a cream dress printed with tiny blue flowers, matched with a cappuccino coloured peplum jacket, head topped with a small fascinator. It was the definition of discreet and she could have been going to a friend's second wedding in the registry office of a provincial town. She took a photo of herself in the mirror and sent it to Rex along with the red-tailed prawn emoji because it always made him smirk having thought it was a croissant holding a boxing glove when he first saw it.

He replied, 'Who?'

I wish he was here. He'll miss the performance of my lifetime. And peeps will think I am Jilly No-Mates when I turn up alone. Or maybe it's better he's not. He'd give me that look and I'd snigger, Cordelia thought as she strolled the short distance to Buckingham Palace. Looking so average no one she passed seemed to notice her. *It's as though Jill is invisible. Perfect.*

Cordelia realised there was no going back on this jape when she started walking up the red carpet of the palace's grand staircase, which in its upper reach was a two-pronged structure of polished hardwood bannisters, curlicues, urns and Tudor roses, lined with full-length portraits of Queen Victoria's family including her grandmother, Queen Charlotte.

Look at the shoes. Wonder if they're in a museum collection anywhere. She was unable to stop and scrutinize the painting because of the crowd behind her heading to the reception room for the briefing on details of what to do during the investiture. Most people looked nervous, out of place and not comfortable in their newly purchased finery. In their day-to-day life, they were dinner ladies, lollipop men and women, charity fund-raisers and youth workers; all worthy nominees for the honours they were about to receive in recognition of their tireless work in the community.

How awful if Call Me Rich is here. What has he done to be worthy of an award? At least Jill is behind something truly innovative. All he's responsible for is blisters from the ill-fitting footwear he churns out. Cordelia frowned and felt bad tempered about him so she did some breathing exercises, pulled herself up to her full height, head held high, shoulders back, until she remembered Jill had rounded shoulders and a stooped posture. *I'm so glad I'm not her. Completely unremarkable. Apart from the damehood which, as it happens, is actually mine.*

Right on schedule, the honourees were ushered into the ballroom to take their seat on a straight-backed gilt wooden chair with red cushion. The room was the epitome of nineteenth century bling: endless gold leaf and lit by vast crystal chandeliers. Its focal point was two thrones, originally used for the coronation ceremony of King Edward VII and Queen Alexandra, sheltered under a red velvet canopy enclosed by a triumphal arch flanked by sphinxes and statues of winged figures symbolising history and fame. *If Rex was here, he'd start with a migraine,* Cordelia thought contemplating the décor.

Then the ceremony began. Everybody stood for the National Anthem as the Prince of Wales entered the room accompanied by the Yeomen of the Guard in scarlet and gold tunics, knee breeches, red stockings and black headwear. The Lord Chamberlain called forward the investees one-by-one announcing their name and title of the honour they were to receive.

'My name is Jill Mitchell,' Cordelia repeated over and over in her head so when she heard that moniker along with, 'Dame Commander of the Order of the British Empire for services to computer innovation', she responded by walking forward, curtseying (purposely inelegantly because Jill would not know how to do it properly) and gave a respectful closed-lip smile as the Prince of Wales pinned on the insignia, congratulating her for the success of such a pioneering concept as Footloose. He laughed as she pointed to the cream suede court shoes hologram she was 'wearing' and admitted, in Jill's higher pitched voice than her own, that underneath them she had on her comfy loafers.

They shook hands, she bobbed down again and was led away back to her seat just in time to hear the words, 'Richard Nailer, Knight Commander of the Order of the British Empire for services to business and enterprise'.

Cordelia shivered at his name and craned to see him. From her seat half-way down the room, it was hard to get a good look but she could make out that he was tall, podgy and with an unconvincing comb-over. The Prince of Wales recoiled when Nailer high-fived him and there was an audible tut from others in the room.

Urgh, that man has no decorum, Cordelia thought fingering her new badge. *And I need to think what to say if we meet afterwards. Don't forget, I'm Jill and he despises me.*

Down in the quadrangle after the ceremony, Cordelia looked around at the excited awardees. It seemed as if all of them, apart from her, had booked the official photography and video package as a souvenir of their day. *Sensible not to have Jill's pixelated face out there to be poured over*, she had thought when the option was offered.

Then to her horror, she saw a large man in a gangster-like black and white pinstripe suit strutting towards her. Richard Nailer. He was more unappealing in real life than she could have imagined. Mirrored sunglasses, the chunky moustache of a 1980s TV private eye, top button of his shirt unfastened and tie loosened so dark hair poked out. Worst of all, he had on cheap brown shoes with Velcro fastening and was blocking the exit so she would have to engage with him on the way out.

All the malicious things he had said about Footloose repeated loudly on a loop in her memory. So did all the retaliatory comments she had rehearsed over and over.

Nailer bowed to her then said in Estuary English, 'Dame Jill, let me kiss yer 'and.'

Cordelia instinctively pulled away but he had a tight hold. Unwillingly, she looked at the man whose lips touched her skin and then burst out laughing before hastily composing herself. It was Rex.

'You sneaky sod,' she uttered through her teeth in case any lip readers were around.

He put his arm around her shoulder, then leant in and whispered, 'That's Sir Sneaky Sod to you.'

Jill had better be polite, she thought in case anyone was looking at the two known enemies, and said, 'Congratulations, Sir Richard,' with an unreadable expression on her face.

'No 'ard feelings, Jill. You stuffed me good and propa, but us billionaires always bounce back, and I 'ave.'

Cordelia stifled a laugh. *Where did he get that unconvincing accent from? Eliza Doolittle?* she thought, then said, 'Congratulations on that too. Goodbye.' She walked past him managing to keep her face straight until she was out of the palace grounds and able to laugh uncontrollably, knees weak with mirth.

As she did so, her phone buzzed with a text from Rex. 'And the Academy Award goes to… you. And me. I'll explain. Need to change from my mafia gear though. Drinkie in an hour at The Constellation?'

Cordelia could not wait to leave Jill in the garment bag and discover how and why Rex had so convincingly deceived her. She was mightily impressed and just a tiny bit miffed. There must have been a business reason for the deception.

'Yes, sir! You get 'em in,' she texted back.

Rex was first to the pub. He ordered two pints of stout and took a table in an alcove trying to look casual for when Cordelia arrived. The fact was he felt nervous that she would be upset at his double-crossing.

'I know, I'm a rotter. But I can't bear it if you're mad with me. I did it for us,' he blurted out as she sat down.

'I'm not mad. I'm not. Just thankful that Nailer doesn't really exist.

Poor Jill. Did you see how he tried to lick her hand? No wonder she flinched. Honestly, it's fine. But why did you do it? And where did you get such revolting shoes?'

'Advert in the back pages of a Sunday newspaper magazine where I could also have ordered slacks in several shades of blue, a revolutionary hearing aid and a greenhouse,' Rex said, reassured she was not angry.

He started to justify his actions, telling her he'd conceived the idea when global shoe sales collapsed, and dreamt up an acutely unattractive character who needed to be relentlessly obnoxious and aggressive towards Footloose so the consumer media rather than just the financial pages would cover the story. If the public constantly heard from Richard Nailer about how negatively Footloose had impacted the sector, related companies and employee livelihoods, it might make them start buying shoes again.

Just as Rex had done with Jill Mitchell by inventing a backstory and online existence, so he did for Nailer, seeding the Internet with evidence of business-life, social media accounts and long-lens photos of real men on yachts that were grainy enough not to be identifiable.

'Do you recall that you asked me selectively to inform you about what he was saying so you did not have to look yourself? Well, I censored most of it. He was much worse than you knew. Such fun to develop his dastardly actions though. Completely out-of-control. A pantomime villain who deserved all the boos. And by the way, the denial-of-service attack never happened. I made it up for extra jeopardy.'

'But why didn't you let on about what you were doing?'

'Because you abhor cruelty and would have asked me not to be so unpleasant to Jill Mitchell. Call Me Rich had to be detestable but you might have tried to persuade me that someone so atrocious wouldn't exist in real life, and that he was unbelievable as a character.'

'Was he based on a real person?'

'Every bastard businessman with a boat,' Rex said emphatically.

'Chiefly that one who nicked the staff pension funds.'

'How did you get him and Westwich together?'

'Money. Call Me Rich contacted her and said he'd fund the Best Foot Forward campaign. She didn't take any persuading. Agreed immediately.'

'You're not still paying her, are you?' Cordelia asked, aghast.

'No, just after we agreed the Sustainable Shoe Collection deal, he emailed Westwich and said that, because his factories were reopening, there was no further need for his participation with her crusade. On the surface, she was polite in her reply, despite him not saying thanks for all the effort in advocating for shoes, but I could tell she had dipped the keyboard in poison.'

'Scum. That's what he is,' Cordelia said, then laughed. 'It's going to take a while to remember he's not real. How did you wangle the knighthood?'

'Like you said, he bought it. I bunged a few grand to the party central office with the promise of more, and lo and behold, months later, arise Sir Richard Nailer. They repay donations from businessmen with a trip to the palace.

'I was shocked when the Honours Committee letter was forwarded to our post office box in Luton though. It was a risk to accept in case we ran into each other at the palace but the caper was too tempting to refuse. I checked to see where to buy a hairy chest with large belly costume before RSVPing. If you ever need one in the future, I recommend Fat-Hairy-MF.com.'

'What are we going to do with our insignias? They're so distinctive that we can't ever show them off. I loved wearing mine even for that short time.'

'Me too. Even though it was slightly lost amongst the pinstripes on Call Me Rich's dodgy suit.'

'I know, how about we have a party á deux each year on this date and invent a cocktail to memorialise the wheeze? We'll dress up as our alter egos. Jill will have consulted a stylist by then and she will wear a

Footloose extravaganza that resembles the imperial state crown as the upper with the sceptre for heels. And if she reverts to dullsville and you see any shades of beige creeping into her outfit, call the fashion police!'

They sat quietly sipping their drinks then Cordelia said, 'Has he dumped us now? Please say yes.'

Rex was circumspect. 'He's useful to have in reserve, don't you think? How about we keep him moored in quiet waters and when needed, we'll prod him to set his ire on fire.'

++++

'Darling, after all you have done for British cordwaining, it's a travesty that Jill Mitchell is damed and you are ignored. It's not as if she had any artistic or technical input, she just signed the cheques.' Celestine was looking at a newspaper gossip column. 'I've a good mind to have a word with the Prime Minister. She's invited me to Number 10 to play backgammon. I think she wants to discuss the role of Creative Industries' czar, so she's mixing a social occasion with work.'

'Or czarina. Maybe she's auditioning you!' Cordelia replied.

Celestine read on further. 'I thought Richard Nailer and Jill Mitchell were adversaries. It says here they were spotted canoodling at the palace after their investitures.'

'Can I look?' said Cordelia with slight hysteria in her voice.

As it was Sunday morning, Cordelia was at Celestine's for breakfast and to read the newspapers together as they did most weeks. She skimmed the brief diary piece. *Why did Rex draw attention to us like that? I wish he hadn't. Twit,* she thought.

Fortunately, there was no photo but whoever had written it must have seen Nailer with his arm round Jill and whispering in her ear just after Cordelia had realised it was Rex. She tried to recollect the details. Yes, he had kissed her hand, but she barely engaged with him and had left almost immediately. Typically, the tabloid press had baked a crumb into a loaf of lies.

'Will you be in Number 10 itself or at the PM's private flat?' Cordelia said, quickly changing the conversation.

'Verity said the flat is a bit pokey so she prefers to host downstairs in Number 10. You know, I will say something about deserving an honour for everything you do for British design.'

'If that would make you proud, then yes please, put a word in. You'll be my date to the palace.'

Celestine smiled. 'Or how about a seat the in the House of Lords? Baroness Tanner of High Heelopolis. I can't wait to see the shoes you design to match your ermine and velvet robe!'

++++++

If Cordelia thought the report of Richard Nailer and Jill Mitchell getting cosy would soon be yesterday's news, she was wrong. It prompted discussions in online chat rooms about why a woman in her position would even entertain the attentions of a man who had humiliated and bullied her. The subject was then picked up for a popular daytime TV show where the panel dissect a topic in the news. When the studio audience was asked to vote on whether Jill was a loser for consorting with a man who had trashed her reputation, the overwhelming response was yes. This led to an opinion piece on the radio show of Dan Bull, a notoriously opinionated windbag, who claimed he had been to parties on Nailer's yacht, and that because his friend was a victor at everything, there was no way he would choose a no-hoper as a girlfriend so there couldn't be anything going on. And even if Sir Richard and Dame Jill had been hobnobbing, it was just a dalliance because he had large appetites for everything and did not know the meaning of monogamy.

Social media went into overdrive making up stories about Jill, claiming she had approached Sir Richard at the palace, propositioned him and then nibbled his earlobe in full view of the Prince of Wales.

A common theme was that she had no money, was not a successful investor because no women ever were and Nailer was the real owner of Footloose. There was more than a whiff of misogyny.

'Who are these oddities and why are they fixated on a stranger?' Cordelia said as she and Rex scrolled through the posts.

'Jilldos,' Rex said. 'Look at this one. It says she blackmailed him into installing her as the ostensible proprietor.' He continued scrolling. 'This one suggests they were in cahoots and all his attacks were contrived to make people angry and support Footloose even more. If only they knew how close that is to the truth!'

'It makes her sound rather Lady Machiabethy with all this scheming. She should be in government. But seriously, this attention on them might encourage investigation by the press. Dangerous. Time for Call Me Rich to leave the stage and never be heard of again.'

Rex nodded. 'Die?'

'Yes, and let's make it grisly. That'll serve him right for being so foul.'

'He jinxing well deserves it. What's his fate to be? We need something where the body is never found. He lives on a yacht. It sinks in a hurricane down to the bottom of Davy Jones' Locker,' he pondered, tapping his lips with the end of a pencil.

'Ghastly man. Could his end be ghastly too?' she said shivering at the thought of punishing him.

'Let's make a list of horrid endings and vote on them. We need to get rid of Jill too. How should we do that?'

Cordelia had been waiting for this moment. 'Jill decides to sell Footloose, retire and zoom off to Zurich, never to be seen again. HoT is her preferred choice of buyer. We purchase it, turn it into a charitable foundation to support workers affected by shoe-maggedon, feel all warm and altruistic and then sleep at night. Everyone's a winner, baby!'

+++++++

In order to get maximum media reach, timing was critical for the final stages of Jill Mitchell and Richard Nailer's connection with Footloose and the Sustainable Shoe Collection, so Rex waited for viral videos of ballet dancing cats and the newly born baby whose cry sounded like the 'Queen of the Night' aria because her mother had listened non-stop to *The Magic Flute* during pregnancy to peak before they broke the news about Footloose becoming a part of House of Tanner. The transfer of ownership story received extensive coverage but there was no mention of Jill Mitchell. She was only interesting to the media in the context of Nailer and as he was not involved in this transaction, they did not care about her.

'I'm so relieved she's gone. One less fiction to remember the details of,' Cordelia said to Rex as they took Blanche for a walk the day after.

'I can't believe we managed to pull it all off. Now it's just Call Me Rich to see the back of. We need to decide how his days will end.'

They sat down on the Victorian band stand in the park. 'I wish these were used more often for music,' she said admiring the green and red wrought iron railings. 'Let's sponsor a concert with a brass band that plays rock-a-billy requests!'

Rex pulled out the list of pitiless endings they had compiled for Nailer. Slipping on sun-tan oil spilled on the deck of the yacht, cracking open his skull rendering him unconscious and bleeding to death while the crew, who could not stand him, watched his life fade away was a contender. So was being garrotted by pirates who attempted to hijack the boat. A crossbow arrow fired into his chest by cocaine traffickers was also a possibility. They eagerly discussed all the methods but decided he needed a more lingering and horrifying death.

'We're colluding in an unspeakable end for a loathsome individual,' Rex said to Blanche stroking her ears. Blanche smiled, tail wagging as usual. 'You approve, do you, my treasure?'

'I have it!' Cordelia said, then described her idea. 'Is it do-able?'

'Probably. But it will take me a while to arrange. I'm on it though.'

'I like this game. We should play it regularly. It's similar to Cluedo but with added evil overlord omnipotence.'

'Do you want me to tell you when it's about to drop or would you prefer to be surprised?'

'Surprise me then I can be genuinely shocked if it's mentioned at work.'

++++++++

For the next few weeks, Cordelia focused on the House of Tanner incorporation of Footloose. She was looking forward to announcing that the app would no longer be a for-profit business and instead operate as a social enterprise that supported a variety of charities. The intention was to feature designs from young people in developing countries whose creativity deserved celebration and compensation.

'We already have established designers creating content for Footloose but I also want it to be a showcase to encourage and support talent that might otherwise struggle to be seen, and provide a channel to jumpstart their careers,' her statement read when the press release was sent out.

If admiration could be measured in football results, then the Footloose Foundation put Cordelia at the top of the Premier League. Doing something positive made her content and she was so busy selecting from thousands of submitted designs that she forgot about Richard Nailer until Rex's text reminded her.

'Look at soshe. Call Me Rich is trending,' it read with a link to a video.

How the flipping heck has he managed that? She thought in disbelief as it played. It was shaky and slightly out of focus but showed a flabby, hairy-chested man on a yacht flaunting his fishing tackle then pouring chum from a bucket into the ocean. He pointed towards dark shapes in the water and, as he turned again to face the camera and gave two thumbs up, he slipped and accidentally fell overboard. The footage showed numerous black fins fast approaching the boat and then the unforgettable image of a tiger shark's head rearing out of the water; its voracious mocking grin directly to camera. Nailer was nowhere to be seen in the middle of a feeding frenzy of man-eaters. Mercifully, there was no audio.

'Don't move,' Cordelia texted him back, then rushed from her studio to his office and cried with glee, 'It's a bloody masterpiece!'

'It turned out better than I expected. The annoying thing is that only you and I can know I'm the auteur,' Rex replied with the look of someone who had been promised a giant Toblerone but only received a miniature.

He explained that it was a combination of game fishing video lifted from the Internet, close-ups from nature documentaries and scenes borrowed from films, all photoshopped, and cleverly edited. 'Providing it was a bit bleary, I realised it would look like a home video.'

As far as viewers were aware, it had been shot on an old camcorder by the yacht's captain who went by the name of Skipper. The only way of reaching him would have been to leave a comment on the video sharing site but that facility was disabled for that particular work. He refused to do interviews but made it known that what was depicted in the footage was no less a fate than Richard Nailer warranted because he was truly reprehensible. No one would mourn his death.

Unsurprisingly, shark bait begat clickbait. The video was dynamite and went viral with millions of hits. Skipper, being the copyright holder, had licensed it to an agency on a pay-per-view basis with all fees donated to the Footloose Foundation.

'Richard Nailer was unremittingly hostile about Footloose and now the charity will benefit from his demise. He would have hated that,' the accompanying message stated.

When Cordelia was asked by a journalist how she felt about the foundation receiving so much funding from what was basically a snuff movie, she had her answer already prepared.

'I understand why you are asking me and yes, he had a frightful death. But what's worse, benefitting a charity helping to improve lives, or media outlets earning a fortune from companies that have clamoured for advertising to exploit the video's notoriety? I know for a fact they are not donating any of their profits.'

Considering that almost every media outlet in the world showed it, anybody trying to shame her was not standing on moral high ground and no one asked the question again.

As Skipper had predicted, Richard Nailer's death was unmourned apart from the treasurer of Britain's governing party who was expecting more money. In the absence of a body and as the video appeared to show it was an accident in international waters, the conclusion was that it was death by misadventure.

+++++++++

'We're free, Rexicles!' Cordelia said when the mania over Nailer's dramatic end abated. 'No more of that abhorrent man and his boorish behaviour. But I would like to raise a toast to Skipper's hungry shark porn because it has generously endowed the Footloose Foundation.'

'I wonder if Call Me Rich will become a pub quiz question — name the man who was devoured by tiger sharks when he fell off his yacht.'

'Natural justice if it encourages views and clocks up more funds for our charity. What will you do with the hairy chest wig?'

'If the central heating ever fails, I will put it on to keep warm. And Blanche could wear it and go as a black bear to The Weasel's next costume party.'

'And how about the crime against humanity known as Call Me Rich's hideous Velcro-fastened shoes?'

'I'm keeping those and they will appear from time-to-time when you are least expecting them — the Slip-ons of Damocles.'

'Careful, or I will haunt your nightmares dressed only in that awful peplum jacket Jill Mitchell wore to the palace, her cream court shoes and absolutely nothing else. That'll traumatise you for life.'

'Oh do, I might enjoy it.'

++++++

In the months following the end of the Mitchell and Nailer duplicity, Cordelia and Rex both noticed how serene they felt. Calm prevailed even though House of Tanner was busier than ever with clients returning to the luxury of bespoke shoes after the ruckus caused by the Foot Freedom Liberation Front. Sitting with Rex in The Weasel, Cordelia admitted that she liked the peace of mind in some ways but missed the adrenaline of the disrupter period.

'I've had an idea for other applications of our incredible Footloose technology. How about this? TattYou — virtual tattoos for needle-phobes, the indecisive and women on hen parties who wake up with a hangover and the name of their childhood pet permanent inked on their forehead.'

'Interesting,' said Rex taking a sip of his gimlet.

'Actually, there are two ideas. Hair Raising: virtual hair. Users could change their style and shade throughout the day. Bald or thinning pates would be festooned with luxurious tresses. How about if someone needs an elegant up-do for a formal event but can't get to the hairdresser in time? And just the thing when in need of a quick disguise.'

'I like it, but I'm having a flashback to shoe-maggedon. It would cause massive collateral damage for crimpers, colourists and hair product manufacturers. They'd all be after us. I like my barber and don't want him to hate me. He gives the finest head massages.'

'Is that a no then?' asked Cordelia, disappointed.

'Not now, no. We'll think it through and weigh up the ramifications. I can see it working for those who lose their hair through chemo. That way we would be providing a useful service. It's just that I still feel traumatised when I think of what kicked off with Footloose.'

'I don't want to stop having ideas so I'll write them in a notepad titled "Might Have Unintended Consequences and Make Me Very Unpopular." I'm going to concentrate instead on finessing my psy-comm capability and finding some more practical uses for it.'

'If you do, please work out a way to take me on some of your psychic jaunts. I want to meet Lancelot and if he's as swoon-worthy as you describe, I might stay a while.'

Chapter Twelve

'Have you heard from Doctor Love?' Rex asked expectantly as he did every morning when Cordelia came into his office for the daily business update.

'Not a word,' she replied.

They both sighed. It was weeks since Elodie had last been in touch to say she was off on a mission and might be incommunicado for a while. She meant it — there had been no communication at all. Even during her absences for medical work, she managed to send occasional photos and video messages to their group chat, and was always a keen player of Cryptic Diptych. That was a game they had concocted where they sent phrases connected with two artists or composers and the others had to guess the link. To date, Deaf and the Maiden, where she united Beethoven and Schubert, had been her finest hour.

'I didn't think I could miss someone so much,' Rex said forlornly.

'Me too, so so much. She's our sister from another mister. Imagine if you'd disappeared, that's almost how bad I feel.'

That day was their real birthday, Elodie's too, but neither could be bothered to celebrate.

'Life is so gloomy without her. Not even winning at bingo yesterday and Gwendoline congratulating me has improved my down-in-the-dumpserism,' Rex said.

'Even Blanche is looking glum and Oscar is sighing a lot which he never normally does. Come on, let's go to The Weasel for Snappy Families and a cuppa. That might cheer us up.'

They played and laughed for an hour but it was a temporary lightening of their moods.

'Rightio, Rexicles. I'm off to sketch something for next season's collection. That card of la Marquesa de Caradonna in her Spanish lace has inspired me.'

'I'll stay here for a while longer. The thought of work is not tempting at all.'

Cordelia walked into the lobby of House of Tanner then stopped and sniffed the air. Rose, honey, citrus — Elodie's perfume! The aromas crept through her limbic system to the corner of her brain related to memory and emotion, and tears welled as she recalled the good times with her best friend. *Just my imagination.*

But as she climbed the staircase, the scent became stronger and her pulse raced as she followed it into Shoeseum towards L'Archambeau Bequest. Her heart juddered at the sight of Elodie, glowing in a golden moiré taffeta trench coat, chestnut linen bell-bottoms and chocolate snakeskin cowbike boots, sitting at a table under a tree with a bottle of Bonheur and two glasses.

'She-She, you're here!' Cordelia cried out overjoyed, tightly embracing her friend. 'Where have you been? Everyone missed you so very much. Everyone. Blanche's tail has barely wagged since you left. Neither has Rex's.'

'*Mon coeur.* How I missed you and being here with my English family. I didn't expect to be away for so long. I'm so sorry for being out of contact but I was in such a remote area of the Amazon and my solar phone charger stopped working. I should have called on Tuesday when I arrived in Lima but I wanted to surprise you and be here for our birthday. It's been a great adventure and if only you could have been there too but I was hunting for something very special and it had to be clandestine.'

She handed Cordelia a boulle-work rosewood box decorated with arabesque patterned tortoiseshell inlay. Inside was the carved model of a tree with tiny shoes hanging from the branches.

'I was looking for the Shoe Tree as a gift to you and found it! It's growing in the rainforest so, of course, I left it there. This is a representation made by Ascensión, one of my guides.'

Explorers had talked for years about Amazonia's fabled Shoe Tree. Some thought it was a legend, others that it was a mistranslation of the name of the sheetri bush, an essential food source for the green iguana. Elodie had read about the Shoe Tree during her PhD studies and when Cordelia introduced her to the fairy tale domain of Shoeseum, she was determined to prove it existed. She commissioned a small plane to fly over the Uncontacted Frontier, a vast area of rainforest that straddles the borders of Bolivia, Peru and Brazil, home to more uncontacted tribes than anywhere else on Earth.

After much searching, the pilot spotted men and women, their bodies daubed with red ochre, gathered around a tree in a clearing as though they were conducting a ritual. Camera footage was inconclusive but Elodie had an instinct about it and that was enough for her to go on the quest. She hired local guides and, with the GPS coordinates, set off for a hot and sticky expedition; first by boat up-river, then on foot, cutting through thick undergrowth, in and out of ravines, clambering over slippery rocks and wading across countless streams. It took weeks of dodging bullet ants, mosquitoes and jaguars, sleepless nights, and miniscule rations, until they arrived at the clearing. And there it was — the mythical Shoe Tree.

To understand its meaning, they had to communicate with the leader of the Kyaa-lani but being protective of the tribe's non-contacted status, Elodie and Ascensión stayed hidden while the Peruvian, Tey, who was a forest native and spoke a similar language, conversed with the chief.

He discovered that the Kyaa-lani believe a person's soul is in their feet. When a family member dies, their relatives create hand woven grass slip-ons to place on the feet of the departed for the soul to infuse the shoe. These are then packed with seeds and hung from the Shoe Tree. Birds that eat the seeds ingest the soul and thereafter when they sing, the bereaved hear their deceased loved ones talking and are able to converse with them.

'They learn how to translate birdsong by consuming the hallucinogenic leaves of the chacruhana bush to expand their mind. I smuggled some back for us to try amongst the trees of Shoeseum,' Elodie said excitedly.

'You went to all that effort for me? It's precious beyond words. I'm overcome,' Cordelia said choking up, then, recovering, smiled and said, 'What a time you've had. And as usual, you're making light of any peril you might have been in.'

'Nothing bad ever happens to me, so please never worry.'

They sipped their Champagne and Elodie showed Cordelia photos of the Shoe Tree. It was approximately three metres tall with a narrow trunk and thin branches from which fern-like leaves drooped. Hanging from the branches were numerous shoes with birds clinging to them, feasting on the seeds.

'It makes me feel quite emoshiony when I think of the poignant ritual. Should we recreate the tree here in Shoeseum and explain the meaning and how you located it?'

'What a superb idea. But at some point, you must see the real tree with your eyes and feel it in your heart in order to communicate how soulful it is.'

Cordelia sighed and looked again at the photos. *I must include woven grass as a material for the Sustainable Shoe Collection,* she thought, then said, 'What are your plans for today?'

'Celebrating our birthday together! Oh, I've I missed you and Rex. Being here feels like home now.'

'It *is* your home, darling. When Blanche sees you, she won't let you leave. Do you want to join us for lunch at Antonio's? We're helping with his new menu development. But first, I'll call Rex to see where he is. I left him in The Weasel.'

Rex was still at the pub. 'I wasn't in the mood to do any work so me and Effie have been playing Snappy Families. You should see what she did with a group of sixteenth century manly aristocrats in their pumpkin breeches and stockings. She called it There Goes the Hose.'

'Stay there, babe. All your dreams are about to come true.'

As Cordelia and Elodie walked towards The Weasel, they could hear Blanche yelping in excitement and when the door opened, she launched at Elodie, standing up on her hindlegs, front paws hugging her waist and tail wagging in overdrive.

Rex's face was pure joy when he looked up and saw Elodie. 'Beloved, what a vision you are! Come into these arms for the biggest hug of your life,' he exclaimed.

'*Ma colombe*, how is it possible that you're more handsome than when we last met?' she replied, kissing him. '*Bon anniversaire*! I have a gift for you.' She handed him an antique japanned box that contained a small wooden bird. 'It's a purple winged dove that lives in the Amazon. Even though it's an endangered species and there are so few left in the wild, I saw one. Ascensión, my wonderful forest guide, is very talented and made this for you.'

His eyes filled with tears. 'It's immaculate, thank you. Oh, how we've missed you. Please don't ever disappear again. Our hearts will not survive.' He put his arms around Elodie and Cordelia's waists, kissed both on their cheeks then said, 'Who's ready for lunch?'

++++++

Antonio, fourth generation British Italian, ran Bonnati's: the most perfect traditional café with unshowy comfort food served in large quantities, and where a noisy coffee machine competed with the shouts of staff passing orders into the kitchen.

Bonnati's was much valued by customers. It was the type of place where cramped shared tables were likely to include boxers, poets, road sweepers and *flâneurs*; strangers to begin with, but not by the end of the meal. Antonio needed to entice a younger demographic because his aging black pudding loving regular customers would not be there forever. He was planning a number of additions to the menu to modernise it, hence inviting Cordelia and Rex to taste test.

'This is a breakfast dish. Bloody Mary on Toast,' he said as he placed the plates on the table. 'With toast cut in the shape of a Martini glass.' It was composed of tinned tomatoes over which vodka was liberally poured.

'Tasty but how about fresh horseradish grated on top to zing it up?' Rex said.

'Yes, I agree. And maybe a little lime juice and Worcestershire sauce?' Cordelia added.

Antonio took notes. 'Good suggestions. Now, how about this for a vegan option? French Fries Risotto.'

'I'm all for carbs-on-carbs,' Rex commented looking at the dish of beige food where the chopped fries blended with the rice. 'And will you encourage customers to add ketchup for a little colour?'

'That or brown sauce,' Antonio replied, ignoring Rex's sarcasm.

Elodie was keenly tucking in. 'I ate so little when I was in the rainforest because we lost most of our supplies after the boat overturned in rapids on the return journey. We survived by catching red-belly piranha and grilling them over a fire. They are salty, bony and I'll happily never eat them again. At night, I dreamt of Véronique's cooking, but if I had known about Bonnati's, then my dreams would have been of this instead.'

'Say hello to Sausage Henge,' Antonio said proudly introducing the meaty model which did in fact resemble Salisbury Plain's World Heritage site. 'It's aimed at druids and kids. I'll also be doing a bangers and mash version of the Millennium Dome.'

'If I'd ever had children, I would have encouraged them to play with their food and become champions at it,' Cordelia said admiring the way

Antonio had secured the lintels over the uprights with the aid of wooden toothpicks.

'And finally, dessert. I call it Cocorella — a combination of chocolate puffed rice and creamy hazelnut spread. What's better as a base: bread or toast?' Antonio asked handing them versions of both.

'Bread works for me. It adds to the combination of textures — crunch, smooth and clag. Builder's tea to wash it down,' Cordelia said.

'How about a premium version with raspberry syrup? You could call it Cocorella Royale,' Elodie suggested.

'Nonna would have a conniption at these dishes,' Antonio said making a sign of the cross and kissing his fingers towards heaven.

'But once she tasted Cocorella Royale, all would be forgiven,' Cordelia said, laughing.

Rex had to leave them soon after they finished eating. 'Dull, dull, dull, and I don't want to go but I have a meeting which I cannot delay. Elodelightful, so wonderful that you are back where you belong. Birthday drinks tonight if you're free? And can we play piquet together soon please?'

After he had left, Elodie said to Cordelia, 'Do you have to work this afternoon or should we free our minds?'

'I choose freedom! Actually, I was planning to scrutinise Shoeseum to see what needs refreshing so it's closed to the public. Your timing is impeccable for an excursion to the other side,' she answered.

Back in Shoeseum, they decided the best place to sit for post-luncheon psychedelics was on the moss amongst the trees because that gave the impression of being in woodland. If the Kyaa-lani were surrounded by forest then Cordelia and Elodie would be too, even though theirs was more of a copse.

Elodie opened a bottle of Bonheur, they toasted each other and the unknown voyage they were about to embark on, chewed a handful of chacruhana leaves and waited. All was calm for a few minutes then wham! Vision became focused on countless multicoloured lights forming symmetrical shapes and falling the way they do in a child's kaleidoscope toy. Then the lights were tossed into the air like lava from a volcanic crater alternately strobing and shimmering. It felt as though they were being catapulted through a mirrored tunnel, tumbling, spinning, and accelerating at top speed under intense G-force.

Immediately ahead of them, leading the way, were rotating brushes similar to those found in a car wash as their psyche was polished.

Suddenly, with a mighty jolt and sonic boom, they broke through a solid wall that liberated their mental hard-drive and then all was calm. They were euphoric, floating in air, surrounded by white light and every receptor was transmitting a feeling of ecstasy.

Emerging from the trip, they were not sure if they had been gone for seconds or hours. However long it was, their brains had been rewired and their consciousness reset.

Silence. Spoken words were inadequate to describe the experience. They were clear headed and felt lighter as though the constraint of gravity was no longer so tyrannical. Later, they would realise their personalities were unchanged but now they looked at life with even more wonderment. Anybody who knew them probably would not have noticed any difference in their behaviour because it was all interior.

Cordelia did mention in passing to Rex and Oscar that she and Elodie had chacruhana-ed but did not go into detail because there are few things as yawn-inducing as listening to somebody recount a psychedelic trip.

Chapter Thirteen

'This is what I've always wanted The Weasel to be: a place where unexpected friendships are formed,' Oscar said grinning at Rex as they both relished the sight of the tall, bearded man clad in nothing but a studded posing pouch and black latex workboots covered in silver spikes, talking animatedly to the fully dressed short balding professor of Freudian psychology.

'Do you think the "Back in One Hour" sign has gone up in the door of all the fetish shops of London? Everyone who works in them seems to be here!'

Oscar and Rex were in the pub where almost everyone who had been at Elodie's lecture was having a drink — academics, design students, bondage club members, lifestyle journalists and local office workers who thought a lunchtime talk on sex and shoes would make a change from the usual classical music recital at the local church.

'I liked the way Elodie and D'Rug interviewed each other so it was not the traditional lecture format but more of a chat. And how fabulous did they both look newly booted and suited?' Rex continued.

Elodie's presentation had been most enlightening, and attendees learnt a plethora of facts, including:

▶ Tactile and sensory information, such as touch, pleasure and pain, is registered in the somatosensory cortex of the brain. Feet and genitals occupy an adjacent area so, in some people, there may be some neural crossover that leads them to fetishise feet and footwear.

▶ The narrow spike of a stiletto heel is an object of power

that could cause damage, explaining its association with dominatrices.

► High-heeled boots elongate the calf for a longer legged appearance which is generally considered to be sexually attractive.

► The tropes of fetish footwear design — thigh-high boots, tight lacing and buttoning, towering heels — persevere regardless of changing fashions.

Cordelia sidled up to Rex and Oscar and said, 'Have you seen She-She surrounded by her new devotees? Maria Callas superfans. They almost passed out when she mentioned taking singing lessons from the granddaughter of Callas' vocal coach.'

The others looked over to see Elodie standing with a group of men, all music students, who, although young in years, were the old fogey type. Each was holding a glass slipper into which she was pouring Bonheur.

'What's the connection with Callas, shoe fetishism and slippers?' Rex queried.

'None. They just happened to hear about the lecture and were fascinated by the subject. The glass slipper is the symbol of their cabal and connected with Callas' lead role of Aida in Mexico City in 1951 when she sang a top E flat in the triumphal scene. It's one of the most legendary moments in opera history. She was wearing slipper type footwear as part of the costume.'

'Look at them. So cute, they're like her pets. I'm going to listen in to what she's saying,' Rex said.

After a few minutes, he came back. 'This is the first time they've drunk from the slipper. Elodie suggested they did it, telling them how drinking from footwear is a cross-cultural activity that dates back centuries. The intention is to bring good fortune or show devotion to a lover.'

'Vulpy, how come you never did that for me when we were dating?' Cordelia asked Oscar.

'Because I was too busy worshipping your mind.'

'Is the right answer,' Cordelia interjected.

'And I must congratulate you on your calm response when that lass accused you of supporting the patriarchy by designing high heels,' he continued.

A blogger had demanded to know why, in her words, Cordelia exploited females by selling symbols of subordination that kept them subservient to men. Cordelia had defended herself saying that her clients, including President of the Global Bank, General Secretary of Our Planet United and Chief Executive of the World Football Association, would disagree. She also suggested that it was patronising to imply that women could not make their own choices of what to wear.

'Thanks, love. When I saw the evils she fired my way, I thought she might kick off so it was a relief when Elodie changed the subject and quoted from that poem.' She was referring to the erotic writing of ancient Greek poet Philostratus which included the earliest recorded examples of foot fetishism in literature.

The pub started to empty as people drifted back to work and Rex said, 'What are you and Elodelicious doing after her admirers have departed the building?'

'Having a jaunt back in time to 1799, I hope. We have some psy-comming to do.'

'So envious. I have a spreadsheet to gaze at.'

'Babe, I know you'd rather be fiddling with formulas in House of Hypatia than consorting with eighteenth century aristocrats in need of a visit to the dentist.'

++++++++

Shoeseum was busy when Cordelia and Elodie popped in so they decided to do the psychomatricks in the laboratory.

'Sorry, we have to remove this pair temporarily,' Cordelia said to a customer looking at the displays in L'Archambeau Bequest. She picked up the Duchess de Roches-Villeroy's shoes, took them upstairs and placed them on the lab bench. They sat down, each held the left shoe, linked hands, closed their eyes, slowed down their breathing and concentrated.

Unlike the first time they did it jointly and such immense power was transmitted between them, what they felt this time was a slight sensation in the fingertips as they pictured themselves being gently propelled on a gondola through a tunnel lined with iridescent mother-of-pearl.

Then, seamlessly, they were in Tellering Hall's octagonal-shaped room with duck-egg blue walls on which eight antique busts of Greek poets and philosophers were positioned on gilded brackets. The ceiling was covered in a painting that depicted mythological characters including Mercury, patron of travellers, thieves and tricksters; the latter of which was most appropriate given the considerable amount of gambling that happened beneath it.

They sat down at a card table with Joséphine, a lively woman in her mid-seventies, and Earl Billingford, a solid man of about thirty-five who resembled a toad. The duchess was like no one else in her appearance, clad in an A-line gown of white muslin with a waistline just under the bust, and a padded hem embroidered with Egyptian lotus flowers; a look that would not become the fashion for another twenty years. As usual, she was an innovator.

One of the pink and white tapestry Pompadour shoes owned by Elodie was pinned in her simply coiffed hair. What made that shoe style singular were the three inch high-waisted heels bent in sensuous lines under the instep. The vamps were high cut and buckles of red garnet caught the eye.

Joséphine glanced across the room to where Lord Dennington was sitting and said conspiratorially, 'He is involved in *une affaire de coeur* with Lady Hampton. I have just seen her holding a closed fan to her bosom and then opening it and using it to cover her left ear. She's so young and must be unaware that we are all fluent in the secret language of fans!' She tittered as she shuffled the cards and cut the deck to play faro.

Lady Hampton had signalled to Dennington that he had won her love and begged him not to divulge her confession.

'I'm not surprised she's dallying. After all, her aged husband is hardly Lord Humpton and a young filly like her needs a thoroughbred,' the earl replied staring lasciviously at Cordelia and Elodie and licking his lips. The duchess laughed; she enjoyed an intrigue and a gossip.

Cordelia whispered to Elodie, 'This is different to the other times I've psy-commed. It's as though they know we are here. I've only previously been a spectator, never actually in the action. Incredible.'

It turns out that chacruhana had clicked a switch in their brains and inexplicably given them the ability to interact with characters in the scene. No one seemed to notice they were in twenty-first century garb, or that Cordelia, who could just about manage to play snap with Rex, was completely clueless about faro.

Elodie made up for that however and, because it was a pacey game, she played with abandon, as was usual for her, betting on four cards at once so she soon acquired a pile of chips; a contrast to the earl's distinct lack of winnings. He was not having a good day.

After an hour of concentrated play, the whole party took a break for refreshments. Typically for a gathering at Joséphine's, guests did not just gamble on cards, they took a punt on anything, and the men started playing Bouche Ball, a game she had devised, where her monogrammed bon-bons were flicked high into the air and players lunged to catch them in their mouth, often clashing heads in the rush. Wagers were placed on the person to succeed, and even on the one who ended up with a cracked skull. Viscount Cholmondeley being tall and with an extra wide mouth had the advantage, won several rounds and was declared overall winner.

Earl Billingford, betting on his friend, was relieved to recoup some faro losses.

Cordelia, standing with Joséphine, said, 'Your headdress is stunning.'

Her host replied, '*Merci beaucoup*. You probably know this as the Pompadour shoe, but it should be called the Joséphine shoe because I invented the style when I was younger. I have big feet and the placement of the heel makes them appear smaller. They are very difficult to walk in, but who cares if they look good.

'Madame de Pompadour always admired my dress sense and often copied what I wore. Her status as mistress of the king meant that ladies at court emulated her clothing and my design became associated with Madame. Now I have a carriage in the shape of my shoe so at least I can be acknowledged for that innovation!' What Joséphine did not know was that in the twentieth century, the carriage would become the inspiration for the sleigh that conveyed snow queens in motion picture films.

'How unfair for someone else to have the credit for your genius,' Cordelia replied.

'It also happened with the Duchess of Devonshire who is very dear to me, but the English believe she is responsible for ostrich plumes in the hair and soaring wigs decorated with tiny models of ships. I did it first. Georgiana admired the embellishments when we met during her visit to Versailles to see Marie Antoinette.'

That's a wrong we can make right at Shoeseum, Cordelia thought. *I'll ask She-She if she wants Joséphine to have the 'If the Shoe Fits' treatment so visitors know about her originality of style.*

'That would be the recognition she deserves,' Elodie replied, nodding. 'I wish she knew now how future generations would celebrate her.'

'Hang on,' Cordelia said to Elodie. 'You didn't move your lips but you responded to my thought.'

'I heard you say something about Joséphine and If the Shoe Fits.'

'I was having a conversation in my head and didn't say it out loud but you replied to it.'

'Does this mean we have become telepathic?'

Before they could discuss it further, Joséphine made an announcement. 'And now it is time for the Tellering Dash. My friends, are you ready to place your bets?'

There was a commotion as everyone rushed outside to see the line-up and back their favoured runner. The Tellering Dash was the legendary chase where able-bodied males raced piggyback for a perimeter of the serpentine lake. Prize money was generous and the winner took all. Lots were drawn to choose runners and riders so there was every chance of handicaps when portly chaps who gorged on Stilton cheese were paired as the rider with a will-o-the-wisp tasked with carrying them.

That day there were five couples and on Joséphine's signal, they set off to stagger through the course, impeded by the generous volume of wine they had guzzled during cards. It was less of a dash and more of a dawdle as all but one team collapsed without finishing.

The victor was Charles Addenbrook, youthful rising star of Whig politics whose sturdy legs kept him upright, with James Boothman, the satirical cartoonist and scourge of high society, as jockey.

As the party began to break up, Earl Billingford addressed Cordelia and Elodie in his oily manner. 'Will you be attending Lady Bentley's ball?'

'We haven't been invited,' Cordelia responded, suspecting he would consider them *persona non grata*. How right she was. He turned his back and removed himself from their company as though responding to an electric shock.

'What a relief he's gone,' Cordelia said to Elodie. 'His leching was about as subtle as a stag party on the Stella. I'd like to think he was gazing at your spectacular boots but I may have mispronounced that word.'

Elodie, who happened to be wearing Cordelia's caduceus-decorated gift, did not understand the sarcastic comment and replied, 'I wouldn't blame him if he was looking at my beautiful boots. Nothing compares to them.'

'Each time I see them, I feel like the proud mother with her favourite child. Of everything I've designed, those are the ones I love most,' Cordelia said sighing. 'Now, are you ready to return to HoT?'

In the lab, they took their hands off Joséphine's shoe and were immediately back in the twenty-first century.

'Wow, brain 2.0 is giving all the gifts! What an exhilarating development if we are able to communicate telepathically in the real world. It'll be very handy in noisy places and for when we are confronted with scamps like Robert Milton. We won't need to roll our eyes at each other to signal our opinion.'

'Let's test it now,' Elodie suggested, then in her mind she said, 'I'm imagining a well-known artwork.' It was *The Birth of Venus*. 'Who was the artist?'

Cordelia, without speaking replied, 'Botticelli!'

They both laughed and threw a double-handed high five, although their version had great panache and perfect manicures.

'I wonder if it works when we are not in proximity,' Cordelia mused. 'I'll walk down the corridor and try.'

She left the room and concentrated on thinking, *I wish someone would put the kettle on, I'm dying for a cuppa.* Then went back in and asked, 'Anything?'

Elodie shook her head.

'What a shame, 'cos we could save so much time by sending a telepathic message instead of typing a text.'

'It's probably a good thing. Just think if I was performing critical surgery on a patient and started giggling when a conversation from you appeared in my head.'

They chatted excitedly about what had happened and decided their capability of communicating by telepathy should never prevent them from speaking unless there was a good reason not to.

'I don't want to lose the capacity to talk, and besides, I like the sound of my own voice, as you've probably noticed,' Cordelia declared.

Elodie giggled. 'I like it too. Go on, say *le prestidigitateur*. Your pronunciation is adorable.'

Cordelia did as requested with extra r rolling then said, 'I wonder if when I psy-comm alone, I'll be able to communicate with others in the setting, like we did at Joséphine's.'

'I hope so then you can have a conversation with Lancelot. And maybe more!' Elodie said with a wink and nudge.

'I was thinking the same. I shall do a test run with some shoes I bought recently. They belonged to a party-boy called Lord Maximus and I want to see for myself if he is the rascal that history portrays him as, and whether he can speak to a female without hitting on her.'

'And another time, can we visit Pulcinelli? I long to hear his singing voice. We might be lucky and see him perform. Ideally, I would have the chance to be alone with him but as you and me are conjoined when we psy-comm, that's not possible so instead I'll dream of his allure.'

'Yes, let's. And we'll dress up as though we are going to a recital, with Champagne cocktails and opera cake beforehand.'

+++++++++

Lord Maximus was an infamous rake who had returned to England from France when King Charles II was restored to the throne in 1660. This ushered in an atmosphere of merriment as the years of Puritan restrictions ceased. Cordelia owned a pair of Maximus' fashionable black leather square toed high-heeled shoes tied at the ankle with a large satin bow. Judging by the poor condition they were in, with scuffs and worn-down heels, he'd taken little care when he wore them.

Cordelia took one in her hands and started to psychometrise. She saw he was with a group of drunken friends in a Covent Garden tavern, standing on a table and reciting a poem he had written about female conquests. He was hardly Poet Laureate, more Poet Notalot with the terrible quality of his verse, including rhyming 'maidenhead' with 'laid on bed'. She sniggered because the scenario reminded her of inebriated nights as an art student and a word game called Blue Movie Artist. Cordelia was a legend for coming up with 'Modiglipunani' and 'He Works Hard for the Monet'.

Well, that's a let-down, she thought trying but failing to engage with Maximus. He, like the others in the tavern, was unaware of her.

Chatting with Elodie on a video call the following day, Cordelia said, 'I tested to see whether I could converse with people if I psy-comm alone, and I can't, I'm just a voyeur. So, thanks to our magnificently harmonised chacka-lacka-ed brains, it only works when we do it together.'

'I'm so disappointed for you because Lancelot will never know how amusing and intelligent you are or appreciate your physical beauty.'

'Actually, I'm a bit relieved. I've had a crush on him for so long and if we had a conversation, it might destroy the fantasy. Maybe the perfect lover is the one who exists only in the imagination!'

+++++

Cordelia was meant to be concentrating on designs for the new season House of Tanner collection but it felt like a chore and all she wanted to think about were the advances in her psychomatricks proficiency.

I wonder if I need to be holding an actual object to make it work or would placing hands over the surface of something a person had touched be enough? she thought, half-heartedly sketching a pair of mules covered in grape leaves.

The next morning, she tested the theory in Antonio's café by sitting down at a table just vacated by a bus driver, stretching her arms over the surface and concentrating. No result. *It needs a full capacity super-charged power circuit,* she concluded and picked up her phone to send a text to Elodie.

'Solo Psy-Commer Seeks Support. Uber Oomph Requested *Tout De Suite*. I'm plotting. When are you next here?'

'Not for two weeks,' Elodie replied. 'I have news. Don't plot without me!'

+++++++++

As promised, Elodie was back at House of Tanner a fortnight later and showing Cordelia her new acquisition. It was a pair of Hessian boots originally owned by Antonin Carême, the world's first celebrity chef who was credited with inventing haute cuisine.

'Carême's pastries were exceptional, and often fashioned in the shape of architectural structures. I saw them via psy-comm for a dinner that Lancelot attended. We all oooh-ed at the Temple of Artemis built with meringue columns, raspberries for capitals and cemented in place by almond paste,' Cordelia said.

They both admired and stroked the knee-high polished calfskin boots named after German mercenaries from Hesse who fought with the British Army in the American War of Independence. Like many military fashions, they became popular with civilians.

'That era for men's style makes my knees weak. Those cutaway tail coats! Those cravats! And especially those tight breeches!' Cordelia said enthusiastically.

Elodie nodded in agreement. 'Now, Coeurdelia, do you want to know what my news is? It involves adventures and art.'

'I like it already. Fancy going to The Weasel for a cup of tea? Blanche will want to hear all about it too.'

Blanche was indeed very interested, cosying up with Elodie as she explained.

'It was after your discovery of the missing Degas. We joked about taking back the painting from that nasty man. He would not be expecting two women to be on such a mission. Anyway, that is the daydream, but the reality is your psychic prowess. In the right circumstances, you can uncover things that law enforcement cannot. Manon has been in touch to say how intrigued she is by what you did and asked if you are willing to psy-comm with objects at Globo-Pol to verify that finding the painting was no fluke.'

'Thrilling! How could I refuse? You must come too. Psy-comming is so much more effective with the two of us. But are you willing to risk your reputation by being associated with something that has no scientific basis?'

'Please don't be offended if I'm undercover for anyone other than Manon. With my academic work, it would be less of a problem but if my medical peers knew, they might send me to an asylum. I really want to do this and I know Manon will be discreet about my participation. And just think of the fun we can have when we are away.'

'Please send a very big yes to Manon. I'm all in. So, do you want to hear my plot? I've been thinking about whether the quintessence that surrounds humans might be readable through psy-comm. Maybe individuals leave in their wake their lifeforce when they touch hard objects.

'I tried a reading at Ant's by sitting in the seat of a just departed customer. It didn't work with me alone, but if we do it together, your added potency might give us the capability. Want to try even though we are venturing far along Supernatural Strasse?'

'Absolutely. We need to investigate all aspects of your gift,' Elodie replied. 'That's the scientist in me talking. As for the non-scientist, I would like a holiday home on Supernatural Strasse.'

Cordelia suggested going into Shoeseum and seeing what they could learn about anyone who had recently been in a pod. They chose the one featuring Angus Meldrum, Mary Queen of Scots' preferred partner for the sports she excelled at: archery, hawking and none more so than golf, which she had learnt as a youth growing up in France.

Angus' display shoes, black leather brogues, revealed he had placed a substitute ball on the fairway after the queen's own disappeared into the water when she sliced a shot. She had noticed his advantageous move and chided him saying she wanted to compete equally and only win by earning it.

After the pod door closed, Cordelia said, 'Let's try two things. First, we'll test the air by lifting up our left hands as though we are taking an oath in court, at the same time as holding each other's right hand. Second, we'll place left hands on the door handle in case the visitor touched it and keep the circuit closed with our other hand. Then we'll meditate and see what we generate.'

For the first experiment, they felt an intermittent crackle as though their power was buffering. They were able to make out hazy images of a young man in contemporary clothing but nothing to identify him. For the second, they had a clear view of his face and a suggestion of his name. When they were out of the trance, Cordelia did a sketch of him and asked Elodie to describe everything she had seen. It was identical.

'I wonder if the person we are describing is the man in the pod?' Cordelia said. 'Let's see if we can confirm.'

She asked the receptionist to play the CCTV camera recording and very quickly spotted him. He resembled the drawing.

'Could we see the names of recent bookings?' then as an aside to Elodie said, 'We're like private investigators.'

The details matched exactly what they had both noted down.

'This is colossal,' Cordelia said in her most excited voice.

They were both silent for a couple of minutes as they contemplated the developments then Elodie said, 'You know, I've been thinking about how chacka-lacka opened our minds and if we have another dose, it might expand them even more. Who knows what that would add to our psy-comm abilities. I have some left over. We didn't take it all the first time.'

'You have the best ideas. Let's go up to the Heath tomorrow at sunrise and sit amongst the trees to do it. We'll pretend it's the Amazon.'

'Chacruhana is why the Kyaa-lani can understand birdsong. Maybe we will too!'

'That would be so trippy. Then if we are ever in Trafalgar Square, we can listen in to what the pigeons are on about. I guarantee it won't be pretty.'

'Do you think they swear at tourists?'

'Undoubtedly. And as for evil gulls in coastal towns that scope targets, dive bomb to nick their chips and then laugh disdainfully, they are probably saying, "You deserved that for being common and eating in the street".'

+++++

Early the next morning, a cab pulled up outside House of Tanner. Elodie got out and handed Cordelia a cup of coffee.

'I asked the driver to drop us near to thick tree growth and then leave us. We don't know how long our trip will be. It could be hours.'

'Hope so,' Cordelia said cheerfully. 'Thanks for the caffeine.'

The taxi drove them to the top of Hampstead Heath and stopped opposite a popular pub originally built as a tollgate in 1553.

'That place does such a good Sunday lunch. Rex loves their roast potatoes,' Cordelia said.

'So, you two are *des rosbifs* after all.'

'*Mea culpa, ma grenouille*, but totally rare breed.'

They walked from the road deep into woodland. As it was late summer and the birds were not breeding, there was no attention-seeking singing going on, and instead they sat, unheard by humans, amongst the branches.

Elodie pointed to an ancient oak with multiple trunks. 'I like this one. Do you want to chacka-lacka here? The canopy reminds me of Medusa's hair and looks other-worldly, which is where we want to be,' she said pulling from her bag a bottle of Bonheur and the binoculars case containing glasses.

'Sparkles for breakfast. Every day should start like this. And pink too, delish. I have an elderly friend called Gloria who describes rosé as being "neither nowt nor summert". It's slang that roughly means it isn't one thing or another. I'm with her because I would never drink still rosé wine but give me the fizzy version and it's impossible to resist.'

'How many should we have?' Elodie asked opening the container of chacruhana leaves and counting them out.

'Whatever we did last time, let's double it,' Cordelia said chinking glasses and taking a sip.

They sat under the tree, chewed the leaves, linked the other's little left finger and waited. All of a sudden, intense light filled their vision and a sensation like the caress of a lover suddenly took physical form in a wisp of smoke that stroked their fingertips, went up their nose, and into the eyes, ears and mouths, but not in an alarming manner, rather as the most exquisite feeling of being cared for. A pea-souper fog lifted in their awareness and clarity reigned.

Next, they were floating in a lake of Champagne, laughing hysterically as they bumped into life-size bubbles and heading them to each other as though they were balloons. And then they heard it. Bird chatter. The chacruhana had worked and they were fluent in Avianish.

Listening in, it was apparent that the subjects of conversation were multitudinous. They included:

'These early starts are killing me. Why can't it be called the mid-morning chorus?'

'I recommend the worms that live under that beech tree over there. Very tasty.'

'How does such a svelte little number as you belt out such a big song?'

'You don't want to get off with him, he's a weakling and all the eggs he fertilises are small and feeble.'

'Excuse me, but what sort of *declassé* accent is that? This is Hampstead not Hemel Hempstead!'

'Parakeets, so vulgar with that bright plumage and tuneless squawk.'

'Look at the two drunks down there necking Champagne for breakfast and then slumping on the ground. Have they no dignity?' a robin said.

A nearby mistle thrush responded with, 'Well, aren't you a judgmental one? How do you know they haven't just finished a night shift and this is their post-work drink? Anyway, I think they look fun. Have you seen how much they smile?'

Cordelia and Elodie were lying under the tree laughing at all the twitter, particularly the comments about them. Suddenly, a dog ran up and said, 'Will you throw my stick please, missus?'

Cordelia sat up and looked at Elodie in astonishment. 'Did she just ask me to throw it?'

'I heard that too but thought it was my imagination.'

'Crikey, we can understand dog lingo!'

The dog barked and nudged the stick but they were unable to translate.

'It only works when our hands are linked. That's a relief because I don't want to know what Blanche is saying. It would be like spying on her.'

'Whatever she says will be happy and positive. Now, do you have the munchies? I do. Is there anywhere nearby for breakfast?'

'Yes, a place called Sacred Grove about a fifteen-minute walk down there,' Cordelia said standing up, pointing south and hugging the trunk of the tree. 'I recently listened to a nature documentary on the radio and learnt that, when required, trees transfer nutrients to a neighbours' root system through a network of fungi buried in the soil. They can communicate with each other about their needs. The scientist who made the discovery described it as forest wisdom.'

'Treemendous!'

Cordelia laughed and said, 'Do you know how I know that you meant to say that as a pun rather than it just be your pronunciation? It's because you had an almost imperceptible cheeky expression in your eyes, with a slight raise of an eyebrow. I've noticed it before. It's your tell.'

'Oh no! As a card player, I cannot be careless and give away my intentions. How about this? Treemendous.' This time she was inscrutable.

'That's a very convincing resting Ice Queen face. I'm a bit scared.'

They set off for Sacred Grove and strolled through deciduous woods rich with earthiness, leaf mould, moss, and the scents of foxes, squirrels and dormice.

'I can really notice my sense of smell today as if my nose is working at full power,' said Elodie.

'Me too. Mine is so super-charged I could sniff out wild truffles.'

'In that case, let's go to the Piedmont in autumn to search for the Truffle of the White Madonna. It is incredibly rare. Without a dog, the truffle hunters will think we are just walking in the woods and wonder why their hounds are so interested in our bulging pockets.'

'Top plan. Oh good, there's no queue at the café. Normally it's a long wait for a table,' Cordelia said, suddenly realising she could see from a much longer distance than before.

'Where are you looking?'

'Through the trees, down there,' she said pointing towards a thatched round house constructed of wattle and daub and situated in a woodland glade.

'Yes, I see it. So rustic.'

Five minutes later they were sitting outside it drinking coffee. Sacred Grove specialised in dishes made from foraged foods, ingredients that imparted beneficial health effects and those with mythological association.

'Look, they explain the symbolism of the ingredients,' Cordelia said glancing at the menu. 'Hawthorne was used by ancient Romans for wedding bouquets. They believed the leaves counteracted evil spirits.'

'Someone is talking about us, can you hear it?' Elodie said, looking around to see who was speaking. There was no one there.

'Have you seen that totty outside? I'd give 'em one. Actually, I'd give 'em two,' came the voice and then laughter.

A second voice followed saying, 'What, buy one get one free?' followed by cackling.

'The first voice sounds like the lad who showed us to the table. We've scored, She-She,' Cordelia said chortling.

'They're inside but we can hear them clearly out here. Is it all thanks to our exceptional Amazonian botanical?' Elodie whispered.

'What if chacka-lacka has enhanced our senses? Did you notice how much further than normal we could see earlier? And our noses were more sensitive to aromas.'

'I think we might be experiencing neuroplasticity and our brains are being modified very swiftly. It's a scientific fact that the brain continues to evolve in response to life experiences, but I have never heard of the senses being altered so dramatically.'

'How extraordinary. We are like real-time medical experiments. Our smell, sight and hearing appear to have transformed, and now we can test whether our sense of taste has changed too. What do you fancy?'

'Scrambled eggs with sautéed nettles. According to the menu, nettles are detoxifying, anti-inflammatory, and the Romans used them for urtication, lashing the stems against skin to treat arthritis.'

'Ouch, that must have 'urt.'

'What masochistic dish will you have?'

'No pain for me. I'm all about living forever so I'm having the "Pair of Pears" with yoghurt and honey. According to this, the ancient Chinese considered the pear to be a symbol of immortality. And in Roman mythology, they were sacred to three deities: Juno, Venus and Pomona, so if they have goddess seal of approval, they are on my plate, thank you very much.' Cordelia sipped her coffee and continued looking at the menu then said, 'Do you think we'd be friends if you were not a gastronome? I can't imagine wanting to spend time with an individual who did not take such pleasure in absolutely everything the way you do.'

'Impossible. I don't believe in the statement that opposites attract unless we are talking about magnets. A person who experiences no bliss in eating and drinking, two of the fundamental human motivators, cannot fully appreciate life. Just think if I swooned at what was in front of me and you just glared. Horrible.'

Cordelia had a flashback to Café Majestic when Pauline Westwich sat with a glass of tap water, scowling at her as she tucked into sandwiches, cake, tea and sparkling wine.

'I forgot to tell you I bought a self-portrait by Angelika Kauffman. This is a photo,' Elodie said, passing her phone to Cordelia.

The painting from 1773 portrayed a brown haired, dark eyed woman in her early thirties, holding paintbrushes and palette and looking at the viewer.

'I'm going to hang it next to one of my other favourites *Dans le Blue* by Amelie Beaury Saurel.'

Cordelia looked at the image of a *fin de siècle* woman drinking coffee and puffing on a cigarette.

'It inspired me as a teenager because the subject was unrepentantly enjoying her vice,' Elodie explained, 'I used to copy her by sitting in the exact pose and smoking Gauloises that I rolled myself. If I had continued with that rough black tobacco, I fear that my singing voice would now be mistaken for Louis Armstrong.'

'I love that you collect female artists. Have you heard of the island of Libertas near Naples? A hive for art produced by women.'

'I was there for my twenty-third birthday! What a place. It was during my time at medical school and I needed sun and beauty.'

'What an incredible coincidence. I was there for my twenty-third birthday too. Why didn't we meet? Were you doing the deluxe version as I did the no-frills?'

'I don't believe it. We were breathing the same air. We might have walked past each other and never known that we would become such friends. I stayed in a suite in the hotel and could see Vesuvius from the window.'

'I was in one of the shared lodges, a bit like a youth hostel. From my room, I could see the volcano too. What were you doing on our actual birthday?'

'Sitting in the casino at the baccarat table as the muses chose the winning cards for me. They wouldn't let me leave for hours but I didn't argue.'

'I spent the evening with some other budget students on a treasure hunt searching for clues dotted about the woods. Each time we found one, the rule was to do a shot of grappa, which is why I found myself swimming in the sea at 3 a.m. and trying not to think of the opening scene in Jaws. If you had seen us careening around the island, you might have thought we were feral beasts.'

'I would have joined you if my muses had allowed it. But honestly, chérie, although half of me wishes we had known each other since that night, the other half is glad we met when we did and not before. We are the people now that we are meant to be as friends. Meeting earlier might have torn a hole in the curtain of destiny, made our lives take a different direction and not led us to where we are now.

'That means I would not have one of my favourite memories of you standing on the bar of The Blue Moon saloon, dressed in your double helix suit, the barman's cowboy hat on your head, explaining how Rosalind Franklin was robbed of a Nobel Prize, then playing pool and beating everyone who challenged you.'

'That was such a good night. We were already friends by then but when I realised you are partial to a bit of Patsy Cline, it was upgraded to bestie status.'

When their food came, they ate with gusto but could not work out if their sense of taste was magnified or if they were just hungry and enjoying everything about the morning so far.

'I have an idea. We'll buy something really bland and eat it with nothing added. It should have virtually no flavour but if we detect anything then we'll know we have turned into supertasters,' Elodie said.

After breakfast, they stopped at a grocer's on the way back to House of Tanner and bought plain tofu and white pita bread.

'Here's the test — taupe food. We better not tell Willamina. She might ban us from her life for willingly eating it,' Cordelia said as they sat down in her studio.

They chewed what they suspected would be almost flavourless and were surprised to register the tofu's nuttiness, and a honeyed note from the bread.

'It's subtle but I do get something,' said Cordelia. 'Is it our taste receptors that are elevated or are we more aware of our senses now and everything is amplified?'

'We need to do more research on this one. Lots of food and drink testing, but only if that never includes naked tofu again. Unless Véronique prepares it. She makes all food taste like the finest banquet. Even dust would be delicious if she cooked it.'

'I may appear to be rather casually accepting that our favourite hallucinogenic has changed how we respond to stimulus. I'm not complacent in the slightest but it's because I'm wondering if we are still tripping, and all these discoveries are not real after all and just in our heads. Or maybe chacruhana has not altered us physically but just our perception of the world around us.'

'Perhaps we'll never know, and this is our reality forever. I would be happy with that. The fact that both of us are having the identical experience suggests that it's real. I suppose we could become philosophical and ask, "what is reality?" but I don't wish to question it. What we have is so special and I want it to continue.'

'You're right. I'm not going to interrogate it. Just celebrate the revelations our mind is giving us. Let's see if we can have a perfect score by checking how our sense of touch has advanced. Time for the fingerprint finale. I was thinking that we could ask the production team individually to handle pieces of paper to transfer their prints onto, then we'll try and identify which is which.'

Sebastian was tasked with collecting them. He handed Cordelia an envelope containing five sheets of plain white paper and chuckled as he said, 'The rozzers probably already have these prints on file.'

After he left the room, she laid the papers randomly on the table. 'I think we should just hover our hands over each one as though we are doing non-contact reiki,' she said to Elodie.

They did so, eyes closed, and saw unformed human images.

'This one reminds me of George Braque's *Man with a Guitar* if I had worn a blindfold and painted it with my right hand.'

'Now, let's interlock right hands without psy-comming, but still meditating.'

They moved their left hand over the sheets of paper, felt a prickle in their fingers and clearly pictured members of the production team in their mind eye.

'Did you see them? I did!' Cordelia cried. 'It's unbelievable what has happened to us. I'm running out of superlatives. If there was such a thing as the Sensory Olympics, we would be permanently on the podium. Interesting to note that it is most effective, with or without psy-comm, when we do it in tandem though.'

'It must be the force of our combined energy but I'm glad we need the two of us for optimum results because I wouldn't want my senses permanently in overdrive. Although it would be useful to switch the superpowers on and off at will.'

'That would be handy. You could use them to change traffic lights so they are always green when we're on Nike. But we must make a pledge not to abuse our awesome ability by using it to give us an advantage over other people without good cause. Fortunately, we can only do it when we are together so that is the equivalent of the nuclear missile option where authorisation from two officers is required to launch. Let's choose a code word to use as a check and balance before we start being omnipotent.'

'How about "Blanche"? She's so innocent and her name will be a reminder only ever to use our power for positive reasons.'

'Beloved Waggy. Yes, invoking her name and picturing that gorgeous smile will prevent us from becoming Big Sister. And now we have value-added brains, the next development is to become the subjects of a comic book,' Cordelia replied, doodling scenes that illustrated the arrest of Robert Milton.

'And what follows a successful comic book, but a film franchise. Who will play us in the films?'

'We will. No one else could do us justice. Besides, we'll be executive producers so we can cast who we want. Cel can design the sets.' Cordelia stifled a yawn. 'This psychic work-out is exhausting. I must get fainting couches for us to recline on after our next psy-comm. But in the meantime, Rex has a sofa in House of Hypatia. Do you want to go for a lounge?'

'What is a fainting couch?'

'Similar to a chaise longue but with armrests. Perfect for when languidity strikes. What shade of upholstery do you want yours in?'

'Thinking of colour symbolism and being a medic, I will go for green. It's associated with health and revitalises the body and mind. Plus, it's lucky. How about you?'

'Mine has to be purple, the colour of fantasy, magic and creativity. And not least because of its association with royalty. I am queen of clubs after all.'

That evening when Cordelia was alone, she reflected on the remarkable and agreeable transformations that chacruhana had activated.

Things started to change when I met Elodie. With her, my psychomatricks is off the scale, she introduced me to chackalacka and now, as a duo, we have sensory superpowers. It's unreal. But perhaps Rex is right and she's just in our imagination like a fictitious friend. I'm used to that with Lancelot. She's so enigmatic, comes and goes all the time and has a mysterious life away from us. If we did conjure her up, then what a brilliant job we made of creating a perfect being. Cordelia pictured the joyous reactions of people, including her own, on meeting Elodie for the first time. *Anyway, she better really had exist because this new aspect of my life is mindboggling. It's like being a character in a magical realism novel, only more stupendous.*

Chapter Fourteen

A week later, Cordelia and Elodie were sitting in the conference room of Globo-Pol's Marseille headquarters.

'This is between the three of us,' Manon said. 'Police officers deal in actuality, not unproven psychic phenomena. However, I was very impressed with the Istanbul arrest. I hope you can repeat the success because, if it works, your technique of locating stolen goods is superb. We have an innovation division and what you offer could be a tool it can use. But we need to test and test again to confirm that the Degas recovery was not a lucky accident.'

As the most senior official in the organisation, Manon could not risk being accused of indulging in snake oil prospecting so the testing was to be done covertly. She led them to a blacked-out room and handed over three items: a single shoe and two envelopes. In the dark, they could not check them for visual clues to aid educated guesses.

'I shall go away so you can work. Call me when you finish,' she said, closing the door and leaving them in darkness.

'Want to do the shoe first?' Cordelia asked. It was a trainer, large, possibly belonging to a man. 'Are you ready?' she said, holding it in her left hand and linking her right with Elodie's.

They meditated and felt intense discomfort as though they were hurtling down a chute lined with spikes. It was so different to the placid deliverance when they psychometrised Joséphine's shoe.

'Wow, this is severe. I wonder if it's because the temperament of the owner comes out through the shoe and we can feel it,' Cordelia said telepathically to Elodie.

'If that's the case, I don't want to spend any time with them. Whoever this is makes me think of a bad-tempered crocodile with toothache.'

With a violent thump, they landed inside a derelict warehouse. In the middle of the floor was the incongruous site of a pink garden shed decorated with Hello Kitty motifs. They walked towards it and Elodie opened the door. Inside was a single-person camping tent.

'Get away right now unless you're here to let me go. And don't bring any more of that inedible slop you call food,' a man's voice bellowed from inside the tent, the sound of clanking chains accompanying his roar.

'Who is he? Let's go deeper into a trance and find out,' Cordelia telepathed. More concentration and slow breathing and soon the answers they wanted came to them. The voice belonged to Haadoman, the nickname of a Japanese crime boss, who for years had been a target of arrest by police forces across Asia and Europe. He was also a target for competing gangs and had been kidnapped during his morning walk and imprisoned in the tent. His value as a hostage was immense, not just in money but for the message it sent to other gangsters that he was no longer invincible.

His bodyguards had been paid to offer no resistance, so Haadoman was easily taken without guns being discharged and just a little pistol whipping to show who the boss was, and it was not him. During the mêlée, he had lost a trainer which the local police picked up as evidence and checked for DNA to prove it belonged to their most wanted. As his crimes were cross-border, and his kidnap a major development in mafia turf wars, Manon had requested the shoe for Cordelia and Elodie to work on.

'Are you going to talk or not, you scum?' he screamed at them from the tent. He was speaking Japanese but thanks to chacruhana they were able to understand all languages.

'Are we?' Elodie telepathed.

'What a bad-mannered bully but let's hear his reaction when he discovers that his location is not scout camp.'

Haadoman's adversaries certainly knew how to pick a secure site. The warehouse was inside the abandoned Shirobishi power station still dangerously radioactive years after an accident caused the nuclear reactor to meltdown. If he called for help, there was no chance of being heard.

Cordelia spoke to him and said, 'We can contact the police to come and rescue you.'

'No police. Give me a phone now. And get me some tea.'

'You are being held in Shirobishi power station. No one is going to walk by and hear you calling, so we are your only option and there is no possibility of being liberated unless you mind your manners. What's the magic word?'

'A comedian, are you?' he replied. 'Get my tea and give me your phone.'

'Such *shitsurei*. We gave him a chance to be less discourteous and he refused, so should we leave him to it?' Cordelia said to Elodie making sure Haadoman heard.

He started swearing loudly and thrashing about in his tent but the psychomatrices did not hear because they had returned to the room at Globo-Pol.

'Oof, that was unpleasant. It's made my head ache. But I have numbers and letters in my mind. Do you? I think they might be the GPS coordinates of where he's on holiday,' Cordelia said scribbling them on a piece of paper. She also drew what she thought Haadoman looked like even though he had been hidden in the tent.

'What a horrible man,' Elodie said, as she jotted down a group of numbers and letters that corresponded with Cordelia's.

Their virtual outing to Shirobishi had tired them, so they waited a while to work on the remaining two tasks, both of which were in envelopes. They chose the larger of the two first. It contained a fifteen-by-twenty-centimetre sheet with a ribbed texture. Unable to see it in the darkness and by touch alone, Cordelia said, 'It's laid paper, the type used by artists for working in charcoal or chalk.'

Compared to the psychomatricks session with the gangster, this one was subtle and took more effort to 'read'. It was a red chalk drawing depicting a nightmarish vision of what looked to be swaddled shapes on the floor, possibly humans, and a central spectral figure in rags.

'I've seen a drawing similar to this at the Museo del Prado. It reminds me of Goya's *The Beds of Death*,' Elodie telepathed.

'I think you're right, but this is not an original. I can see a modern-looking fella working on it but I'm not reading much more. I wonder if it's because, unlike a shoe in which a person's essence is impregnated, the energy left on a sheet of paper is ephemeral.'

This was a low wattage episode with no artist interaction so it was a struggle to glean information but together they learnt his name, Eduardo Benitez, plus a visual description including that he was missing the little finger on his right hand. They identified the street address of his swish Madrid apartment block from where he ran an art forgery business. His clients included newly minted billionaires who proudly showed off their 'original' Goya to associates, unaware that the drawing they had purchased was not authentic.

'He's so adorable when he watches soap operas with his elderly mother,' Elodie said when they were out of the trance. 'I feel guilty that we'll reveal his name and address to Globo-Pol. His *maman* might be upset to know what her son is up to.'

'I'm afraid I must disagree with you and I have no guilt about reporting him. Forgery makes me really mad because he's stealing someone else's creativity and making money from it. It happens with HoT. A shoe company in China uses one of our trademarked features in their completely rubbish shoes and has the temerity to call their brand House of T'Anna. They are squatting on mine and Rex's intellectual property and exploiting it and we can't stop them. In the case of Eduardo, we do need to report him and prove to Manon that psy-comm works.'

'You're right. But could we tell the police not to go mid-afternoon? That's when they watch their favourite TV shows.'

'You're such a softie. Go on then, we'll say that they are bound to find Eduardo at home at 1600 hours on weekdays. Now, do you have enough vigour to work on a third item?'

Cordelia put her hand into the envelope and pulled out what felt like paper bank notes. They both held them and concentrated. This too needed much effort, even more so than with Eduardo's drawing.

'I'm not getting anything from this, how about you?'

'Me neither. We're tired. How about a break for tea and a cake? There's a café round the corner.'

Two cups of tea, and a shared rum baba and mille feuille, restored them. Re-energised, they returned to continue the task and discerned that the bank notes were forged Euros. Although the images they saw were a little vague, they could make out a couple of men loading boxes into a van parked outside an unmarked archway under a North London railway line. The vehicle registration number was visible, as was the name and contact details of the neighbouring panel beating business. They sensed that the currency was being printed there.

'I don't think we'll get much more from this scenario but we have clues to the location. Can you recall the phone numbers of the company in the next door arch?' Cordelia telepathed.

'Yes, I wrote them down, and the number plate too,' her partner in crime-fighting replied.

As always, they compared details of the encounter and as always, they matched. When they submitted their findings, Manon thanked them and said she would be in touch. Two weeks later, she emailed to schedule a conference call.

'Your conclusions are impressive. In each case, you supplied intelligence that traditional policing would have struggled to provide, certainly in the timeframe you did. Thanks to you, officers from London Metropolitan Police have arrested the gang of currency counterfeiters, and as you requested, Eduardo Benitez was visited at home after the soap opera had finished.

'The most difficult case was Haadoman. I can confirm that he has been apprehended but it was complicated. The police sent a drone carrying a thermal imaging camera into the warehouse and it registered a living being inside the shed as you described. Specialists in hazmat suits went in to arrest him. He screamed at them and demanded tea, then swore repeatedly and said he would rather stay shackled in his tent than go with them. He is now in custody in solitary confinement with only a Geiger counter for company.'

Even though Cordelia and Elodie were confident in the accuracy of their discoveries, to have it confirmed and learn that the police had acted with such success was staggering. Manon was thoroughly convinced and asked to work with them on future cases.

'We must keep this private so the criminals do not know we have a new method of solving crime.'

Naturally, they both agreed and could barely keep from jumping on the table and cheering at the news.

'I wish I could go back in time to the ten-year-old me who devoured adventure novels and tell her that, as an adult, she'd partner with a motorbike-riding surgeon to create a new way of investigating international skulduggery. If I could measure my excitement in this moment on the Richter scale, it would be magnitude 9.5 which is the biggest earthquake ever recorded.'

'If I was to measure mine in Champagne bottle sizes, it would be a Melchizedek, the largest, which holds two hundred and forty standard glasses. And my excitement is so immense, it's a whole crate!'

Cordelia felt a nervous flutter in her stomach when Elodie uttered a name which she associated with The Predicament. It was a reminder of the hullabaloo her and Rex had unwittingly sparked. *Blooming nightmare,* she thought, then said, 'I plan to make changes to how Sebastian manages my diary. He's like a tyrant, but that's my fault for packing too much in. I've decided on a less-is-more approach to my life — but not in my dress sense and design sensibility — and start delegating work. I want to concentrate on psy-comm sleuthing escapades with you.'

'We will make it happen. One of the benefits of being our own boss is choosing how we spend our time. My only commitment, which is non-negotiable, is Rebâtir, but I always know well ahead what the dates are. Actually, I leave next Monday for a couple of weeks in Cambodia.'

'You are so saintly. I'm frivolous in comparison. Of all Apolline's descendants, I'm sure you are the one she would be most proud of.'

'That's lovely of you to say, but it is my duty as someone with such fortunate circumstances to help if I can. I wish we could psy-comm with Apolline to tell her what a difference her bequest has made, and also congratulate her on creating the world's most popular brand of Champagne.'

'But what would happen if we visited Apolline and you discovered that she was a plonker?'

'I don't know what a plonker is but by the tone of your voice it does not sound good, so definitely no to a psy-comm then. I want to maintain her as a noble figure in my head. As a substitute, let's visit her portrait at the museum in Reims and give a message to the painting.'

'And I will do a drawing of you standing there as you deliver it, so you have a souvenir.'

'Wonderful, I shall wear your favourite footwear child in the guise of the caduceus boots.'

Chapter Fifteen

Cordelia looked around the Majolica Room where she and Rex were having a drink. It was her favourite area of The Weasel, a refuge lined in turquoise, green and purple Minton glazed earthenware tiles in peacock tail patterns — appropriate for a woman who never failed to put on a show of style.

'Wonder where I can find a cloak adorned with real peacock feathers like the one Hedy Lamarr wears in *Samson and Delilah*,' she mused.

Rex returned from the bar. 'Look, Daisy's new braggot. I got you one,' he said, handing her a pint and taking a sip of his. 'Oh, that's 'licious. Now then, we need to think. What are we doing for the glorious second anniversary of our inaugural threesome with Doctor Love?' Rex was referring to his first meeting with Elodie when the three of them had dined together in that very room.

'Don't forget Blanche. She was there too, so that makes it a pawsome.'

'How could I forget you, my treasured morsel?' Rex said, stroking the dog's head. 'Let's plan a jollification in the pleasure gardens with games and gorgeousness.'

'Botticelli! I'll ask Willamina to cook a feast. I wonder if Celestine would create an outdoor dining room for us?'

'Let's have afternoon tea as well as dinner. We'll need hours together and ample sustenance.'

'No day is complete without afternoon tea. It should be the law. I'm calling Willamina right now to beseech her. You ask Cel if she'll design an elegant setting.'

'Does the festivity have a name or a theme?' Celestine asked when Rex explained what him and Cordelia were planning.

'It's called Whole-ly Trinity and the theme is the three of us and what heaven it is to spend time together.'

'What a delightful notion. I have ideas already.'

++++++

Elodie was unaware of any details of the jamboree apart from her instructions to choose a poem, verse from a play, or a quotation and be prepared to recite it, and to bring ingredients for a film cocktail and any related props.

On the day of the party, she arrived at The Weasel in a taxi with a case of Bonheur. Cordelia, Rex and Blanche were at the door to greet her.

'Always one of my favourite sights,' Rex said pointing to the box of Champagne.

'This is not just any Bonheur. It dates from the year of our birth! It is a tradition that whenever a female member of the family is born, *la maison* stores hundreds of bottles of that year's vintage for the child to drink for special occasions throughout her adult life. I think this is a very special occasion and the best reason for a celebration. And it's already chilled.'

'Then let us sit down and toast ourselves,' said Cordelia leading the way into the gardens to a table set up by the fountain of youth, as Oscar had nicknamed the sculptural feature that fed water from the underground spring.

'I have something else for us,' Elodie said passing them a large heart-shaped cardboard box. Inside, macaroons were laid out in the colours and shape of the House of Tanner bird of paradise logo. 'They are made in Paris by Madame Pelletier, my favourite *pâtissier*. She started working when she was fifteen and is still creating edible art at ninety-three.'

'Divine,' Cordelia and Rex said in unison, both sighing.

'Others might say the array is too splendid to eat, but that isn't me.

And although they are beyond beautiful, I want Madame Pelletier to know that we could not resist them. May I?' Rex said.

'Please do. But you have to guess the flavours by tasting them and cannot look to see which you chose. Here, wear these,' said Elodie passing them both eye-shades.

Rex unknowingly chose a lilac coloured macaroon from the bird's tail and nibbled it. 'Glorioso!' he exclaimed savouring the sweet treat. 'It tastes of violets.'

Cordelia took one that was an intense shade of scarlet and flavoured with rose which she guessed correctly.

'I asked Madame Pelletier to use floral flavours because you both love flowers. She's so clever.'

'Good challenge, She-She. Mmm, this one is nutty but I don't know what it is,' Cordelia said nibbling on one with an emerald hue and a hint of dahlia.

'Let's try to guess them all before we start with the other games. They are irresistible,' Rex said biting into a yellow one. 'Honey?'

'Can you be more specific?' Elodie asked and when he could not, she revealed it was honeysuckle.

'Oh yes, now I taste the nectar. Scrumpchy,' Rex replied.

'What a top game. Let's go on a pilgrimage to see Madame Pelletier so I can worship at her altar of almond,' Cordelia said.

'Are we all ready for the entertainments?' Rex asked.

They started with 'Easter Island' which entailed standing statue-like with an unfathomable facial expression like the stone heads on that eponymous Pacific territory, while the other two said or did daft things to elicit a laugh. No touching was allowed; it had to be words or actions only. Whoever lasted the longest without breaking into laughter was the winner. Rex triumphed because of his years of poker playing and being able to keep a straight face despite Cordelia reciting a rude limerick about his most recent ex.

Next was Holler Hoop where the player spun a hula hoop around a nominated body part all the while performing their choice of song, poem or prose. Elodie went first and span the hoop insouciantly around her left index finger while reciting Baudelaire's poem 'Le Vin des Amants' with a glass of fizz in her other hand, sipping while she did it. When she had finished and was bowing to the applause, Blanche ran up, grabbed the hoop and lay down with it between her front paws.

'I wonder if she can make it hula around her tail as it's wagging?' Cordelia said.

'Try it!' replied Elodie, then called to Blanche, 'Come here, *ma belle*.'

The attempt failed because, instead of standing, the dog sat down next to her looking so adorable that sustained stroking was the only option.

'Now me,' Cordelia said, taking the hoop. She recited 'Anarchy in the UK' by the Sex Pistols, spoken poetically in an ultra-RP accent. Her technique was to hold her arm straight out, hooping around the elbow and flicking the Vs as her arm moved in a clockwise circular motion.

Rex took his turn. Within seconds, the others were crying with laughter. They voted him the undisputed champion for his performance of Portia's 'Quality of Mercy' speech from *The Merchant of Venice*. Speaking verse in iambic pentameter whilst hula hooping around the neck was the epitome of multi-tasking. He graciously accepted the appreciation by performing an encore but this time reciting the lines in a geezer gangster London East End accent.

'Now, who's ready for afternoon tea?' Cordelia said.

'Yes please. It's the most civilised of refreshments. I salute the person who invented it,' Elodie replied.

'We should all curtsey to Anna Maria Russell, Duchess of Bedford. She's credited with starting the ritual because of her habit of eating bread and butter then cake with a cup of tea when she was peckish between lunch and dinner. Whoever upped the game with cucumber sandwiches has my vote.'

After their tea, Rex stood up and said, 'Now, settle in for my Rex Talk on the Rule of Three. Numbers are beautiful and three is the most symbolic. And don't give me that look, D'Rug. When you hear what I have to say, you will be captivated just like I am.'

Cordelia's countenance was just as it had been during every mathematics lesson at school — a mixture of horror and bafflement. Her brain cells failed to fire with that particular discipline, and she'd had to re-sit her basic examination three (coincidentally) times before scraping a pass and was still unable to do long division.

'I won't need that sort of knowledge where I'm heading,' she had said to the teacher.

'Maths underpins everything, Cordelia. It's how the world operates,' the teacher had replied.

'Well, I'm fascinated to hear all about it, especially the symbolism. I wonder if the fact that our birthday is on the third is noteworthy,' Elodie said giving him rapt attention.

Rex was on top form as he discussed his favourite number explaining how it was significant in:

- ▶ Nature (domains: land, sea and air)
- ▶ Literature (three points of view: first, second and third person)
- ▶ Mythology (Three Graces, Three Fates, Three Furies)
- ▶ Fairy tales (Three Little Pigs, Goldilocks and the Three Bears)
- ▶ Religion (Christianity, Hinduism and Buddhism all focus on trinities)
- ▶ Physics (Newton's Three Laws of Motion)
- ▶ Chemistry (states of matter: solid, liquid and gas)
- ▶ Architecture (orders of columns: Ionic, Doric and Corinthian)
- ▶ Time (birth, life and death; past, present and future; beginning, middle and end)

'Pythagoras considered it to be a perfect number. He divided the universe into three parts, which he called the Supreme World, the Superior World and the Inferior World.'

'He was obviously thinking of The Weasel with the Supreme World,' Cordelia interjected. 'Anyway, as you were, Rexicles, I'm gripped.'

'Thought you would be. I've almost finished but there's just a little more. Numerology. Three is all about communication, unique thinking, creative expression, having fun and expressing love and joy.'

'That describes us,' Elodie exclaimed. 'Three is now my favourite number too.'

'Babe, you've enlightened me and now I'm going to be looking around for examples of threes.'

'They're everywhere. "Third time lucky", "third time's the charm". It's the number of good fortune.'

'And of being a lady: once, twice, three times,' Cordelia said tittering. 'Who fancies pre-dinner cocktails? All of us. Excellent. Then let's play Big Screen Booze. She-She, do you want to go first again?'

Elodie pulled a hot water bottle from her bag, slugged in bourbon and sweet vermouth and shook it before pouring the contents into glasses.

'Does anyone have maraschino cherries?' she asked in an American accent acting out the scene where Sugar Kane mixed Manhattans during the illicit sleeper carriage party in *Some Like It Hot.*

'Definite hint of rubber on the nose but I could get to like it. Cheers!' said Cordelia taking a sip.

For Rex's entry, he rustled up a Martini using gin and dry vermouth and as he popped a mini pickled onion into the glass said, in his finest theatrical voice, some of the lines spoken by the character Addison de Witt. The Gibson cocktail gave it away and both Cordelia and Elodie guessed he was quoting from *All About Eve.*

Then, cheersing them, he said, as himself, 'If it weren't for that film, you two would not have met, and I would never have had a midnight feast amongst the vines of the ultimate Champagne house and then laid looking up at the stars with my two best women. So, I'd like to raise a toast to fastening seatbelts and bumpy nights.'

Finally, it was Cordelia's turn. She poured Cognac into a glass, took a large glug, then acting as though she had been disturbed by someone walking into the room, pulled a bottle of cologne from her pocket and gargled with it.

With a look of disgust, she said in her own voice, 'Frankly, that is the first and last time I shall drink a brandy and eau de cologne cocktail,' having copied the scenario in *Gone with the Wind* where Scarlett O'Hara is rumbled by Rhett Butler as she boredom-drinks.

Just then, a waiter approached the table and said, 'Would you like to take your seats for dinner?'

They followed him to the dining room: a temporary structure amongst the trees that was, unsurprisingly for a Celestine project, stunningly effective. A number of long white chiffon panels were suspended from a circular frame surrounding a round dining table and they moved with the breeze. Navy blue muslin formed a ceiling that was dotted with LED lights to represent the Milky Way with planets, constellations, and as August-born babies, the sun, their astrological ruler, at the centre. Flares outside created an ethereal shimmering effect.

'It's magical. Did you design this?' Elodie asked Cordelia.

'No, we asked Cel to create something but had no idea what it would be. It's a revelation to us too. She can never do anything less than dazzling.'

'This is so simple and effective. I can see that with the pared down aesthetic, Rex approves. And Courdelia is looking for all the grandeur and gilding but not seeing it,' Elodie commented. 'I love being surprised. It's rare for me because I'm usually the one with the plan. Not knowing anything other than it will be *magnifique* is most pleasurable. I should do it more often.'

'No, sorry, you're not allowed to. We love your plans and the way you choose activities that are completely suited to the one you are with. What you organised for my mirthday is worthy of the Pulitzer Prize for Party Planning,' Rex said.

'Dinner should also be amazamenty,' Cordelia said. 'Willamina has prepared something clever. We have no clue what it will be.'

The superstar chef had created what she described as Frenglish fusion with a starter of wild Scottish smoked salmon tartare, followed by roast beef bourguignon with Yorkshire pudding, and then tarte tartin crumble and custard. Oscar had paired each course with a perfectly matched drink, starting with Bonheur, then imperial stout, and finally mead, the latter two brewed by Daisy.

'That was the best Yorkshire pudding. What's the secret to such fluffiness?' Elodie asked.

Cordelia looked at her with a bemused expression. 'Don't cook, won't cook and never step foot in a kitchen unless under duress, so I'm not the person to answer that. Let's see if Willamina will explain.'

Cordelia video called her and said, 'We're all genuflecting to you and your scrumptious meal. Thank you! Elodie wanted to know how your pud is so good.'

'It's a secret ingredient that I'll reveal if you promise not to divulge it to a soul,' she replied.

'Lips sealed,' Cordelia assured her as the others drew a forefinger across their mouth.

'Two tablespoons of water from the Yorkshire Dales. It's the best in the world, and I'm a trained water sommelier, so that's not just me talking rubbish. I use it in all my cooking and have it shipped here by tanker. If only someone would build a pipeline to London, I would be happy. So glad you enjoyed it.'

After dinner, the waiter ushered them to an anteroom lit by dozens of candles where squashy armchairs in a small circle waited for them to sink into. A pot of peppermint tea and porcelain teacup and saucer were on each of the three occasional tables.

'Our Celestine thinks of everything,' Cordelia said with a contented sigh as she sat down.

'Now, my darling Elodie, don't go anywhere because me and Cordelia have something to say,' Rex said.

'That sounds serious. Should I be nervous?' she said apprehensively.

'Don't worry, it's just us being grown-up for a couple of minutes,' he replied, then stood and began. 'When you were in the Amazon and out of contact, it was the worst period of our lives, missing you, thinking something terrible had happened and that you might never return to us.

'You and me had an immediate rapport the moment we met and by spending such delightful times together, I've realised our bond is more familial than friendship. I've only ever felt like that with Cordelia. You'll know the feeling if you and she really were twins in a previous life. I do hope that's the case because I can't bear to think of her being alone without the comfort of the one who loves her the most.' He paused as his voice choked. 'Oh dear, I didn't mean to be so emotional.'

Cordelia stood up, squeezed Rex's shoulder and continued. 'It's true. When you were out of contact in the rainforest, there was such a void in our lives. You are more than a friend, so we'd like to propose that you become our official sister. Adult adoption is possible in some countries, but who needs legalities when we know the truth in our hearts?'

Elodie's eyes filled with tears and there were several seconds of silence as she gathered herself. Rex and Cordelia looked at each other in alarm, as if to say, 'What if it's a no?' They need not have worried.

'What an exquisite idea. I always longed for a sister and brother. When the three of us were together for the first time, I felt so comfortable, as though we were a family. And that sentiment becomes more powerful each time I see you. If there were adoption papers in front of me right now, I'd sign immediately with all my soul.'

Blanche, who was snoozing by Elodie's chair looked up. Cordelia noticed and said, 'Rexicles, we never consulted the most important being in this proposal before we made the decision. Blanche, sweetheart, me and Rex want to adopt Elodie as our sister. Do you approve?'

The dog leapt up and, with tail madly wagging, jumped, barked and ran around the room before pushing Elodie to stand, nudging her towards the other two. Laughing, they all linked arms. Blanche sat down, grinning, and Rex said, 'That's a yes then.'

'You know what this means, She-She. You'll no longer be Celestine's honorary precious jewel,' Cordelia said.

'Why? I love being called that. Will she disapprove of me joining the family?'

'On the contrary, she'll be so happy with the news, you'll be upgraded to full membership of precious jewelry.'

'We must have a spectacular party to celebrate,' Rex said excitedly. 'Which, of course, means I'll need a new suit.'

Suddenly the opening notes of the 'Ode to Joy' segment from Beethoven's Ninth Symphony filtered in from outside.

'Show time!' Rex said and led the way into the garden where the London Symphamonia Orchestra, headed by its principal conductor Octavia Forrester, was assembled with the rotunda as an exotic backdrop. A chorus of dozens of men and women attired in formal wear sang the choral passages with such verve that tingles catapulted high into the sky, floated down and landed on everybody within hearing distance.

When the music ceased, there was a momentary hush as no one wanted to break the spell but the sound of cheers and whistles drifted in from pedestrians listening from outside on the street as they demonstrated their appreciation.

'Heavenly,' Cordelia said. 'Our turn now.'

She and Rex went up on stage, stood behind microphones and, accompanied by the orchestra, sang the ditty 'Bring Me Sunshine'. It was such a jolly song and always made Cordelia happy as she recalled Celestine singing it to them at bedtime when they were children, so she begged Octavia to let them perform it again. Her wish was granted. Their audience of one (and a dog) cheered appreciatively shouting 'encore!'

which was rewarded by another reprise.

'Now, are you ready to sing for your supper, Elodelicious?' Rex said when they had finished their duet, pointing to her piano accordion as it was carried on stage.

Elodie looked stunned. 'Me play with the London Symphamonia? Now? What should I perform?'

Octavia came to confer. 'We're good at busking, so if we don't already know the composition, just hum or sing it and we can improvise. What are you thinking of?'

She thought for a few seconds and then said, 'I'm so joyful at this moment it has to be "I Feel Love".'

Octavia smiled. 'How perfect. We've just recorded an album of classic 1970s dance music and that will be track number one of the running order. The triangle has a starring role in the "falling free" line. For a small instrument, the player makes such an impact!'

'Top tune, She-She. Can you play and sing at the same time?' Cordelia asked.

'I hope so because there are only eighteen words and several oohs, so if I am unable to do both then you might need to remind me how to walk and breathe simultaneously.'

She picked up the full-size 120 bass accordion which was large enough to cover her entire chest when strapped on. It was a vintage instrument in pale blue lacquer and decorated with mother-of-pearl. Air escaping from the bellows as they were pumped carried with it a musty aroma of the 1930s.

'We'll perform the six-minute version with a forty-second orchestral introduction after which you start singing,' Octavia instructed Elodie as she warmed up.

For this arrangement, the double bass underpinned the beat with a kettle drum punctuating it, and the song's repetitive nature lent itself to a dominant string section with the violinists and cellos playing the 'fatter than a caterpillar' bow stroke; a familiar phrase to children who learnt the technique in music lessons. Elodie played with great expression and her fingers moved lightly on the keyboard to a melody that mimicked her vocals, blowing a kiss to Cordelia and Rex as she sang the 'you and me' line.

'Brava!' they shouted after the performance was over, clapping along with the orchestra members who were saluting Elodie.

She applauded back at them. 'I'm buzzing. Thank you, thank you. They were some of the most enjoyable minutes of my life. Standing so close and feeling the power from your instruments is extraordinary.'

'Many thanks, Elodie. Now I know who to call if we need an accordionist in the future,' Octavia said. 'And for our finale...'

It was the Champagne song from the opera *Die Fledermaus* but instead of referring to King Champagne as the original libretto did, naturally with a scion of Bonheur in the house, the title was feminised, and the chorus sang with a smile in their voices:

'Her Majesty is glorious
Won the war over thirst
Bless the reign uproarious
Of Queen Champagne the First!
Long life to Queen Champagne the First!'

'This night just keeps getting better. Blissful,' Elodie exclaimed with the happiest expression on her face.

On cue, fireworks exploded overhead with brocades creating a glittery dandelion effect, girandolas spinning and leaving long trails in their wake, and crossettes scattering coloured shooting stars in all directions, prompting woos and aahs from inside and outside the garden. The lightshow climaxed in a formation of three interlocking circles floating in the air as the initials C, R and E appeared separately in each one.

Elodie beamed and put her arms around Cordelia and Rex's shoulders. 'Could paradise be any better than this?'

To which Cordelia responded, 'Paradise may have the monopoly on manna, celestial beings and pearly gates, but it's certainly not as fabulous, Dr l'Archam-Tanner-beau!'

Blanche, normally upset by pyrotechnics, made an exception this time, and looked at her family, smiled, then lay down by them, tail wagging with contentment.

Author's Note

Thank you for reading my first novel! *Sole Brethren: If the Shoe Fits* is a child of the COVID-19 pandemic because, despite conceiving the idea for Cordelia Tanner and Footloose in 2012, I never had the time to write the story. That was until lockdown started in March 2020 when Cordelia and Rex became my constant companions as I disappeared into the world of House of Tanner and The Weasel Pleasure Gardens.

My previous published writing was non-fiction books with a strict word count so I write concisely and condense a lot of information — no padding allowed! Consequently, I wrote the first draft of this novel in 25,000 words which isn't even long enough to be a novella. I needed a sub-plot and one day on a brisk walk, Elodie l'Archambeau came into my head. The intention was for her to be the most charming, irresistible and engaging individual.

I had read about novelists describing how their characters often decide what is going to happen and never understood what that meant until I met Elodie. She opened up the story and took it in directions I had never anticipated. Elodie also changed the character of Rex, who I had intended to be rather stand-offish, and she turned him into a big, loveable softie.

Cordelia, Rex and Elodie have lived in my head for over two years and as far as I am concerned, they can take up permanent residency. They are such good company and I wish I could have a glass of Bonheur with them. But more than anything, I wish some technological genius would devise Footloose in real life, so I can wear Cordelia's wondrous digital creations over my comfy slippers.

B. A. Summer (aka Jane Peyton), Brighton, England.

Acknowledgements

I'm so fortunate to have ace friends who are clever, accomplished and give me really good advice. And, most importantly, laugh at my jokes.

Here are some people who deserve major thanks (in alphabetical surname order):

Louisa Fitch for being the most creatively brilliant person and creating the fabulous cover artwork.

Vincent Laurentin for advice on French language and grammar and making sure I did not embarrass myself by putting incorrect phrases into Elodie's dialogue.

Clark Massad for top suggestions when I was in book marketing mode and developing customer avatars.

Anne McDonald for her enthusiasm and for making excellent suggestions to improve some lines of dialogue and the back cover blurb.

Annabel Smith for suggestions of who my reader might be and other novelists they might enjoy.

Gail Willumsen for suggesting edits that made the story tighter, and for correcting some of my grammatical howlers.

The lovely people named below are friends and family who so kindly donated to my crowd sourced fundraiser which helped me take time off work in order to complete the manuscript. Grateful thanks, you absolute beauties. Without your generosity, I could not have done it!

Tracy Beighton

Vincent Laurentin

Roisin Rock

Nicole Cantu

Anne McDonald

Ben Wiggan

Louise Darbyshire

Clark Massad

Gail Willumsen

Kate Hempsall

Cassandra Orford

Kate Wiggan

Kate Hyde

Helen Peyton

Lucy Williams

Rachel Howald

JoJo Ripley

Mike Worner

Ruth Harland

Printed in Great Britain
by Amazon

18845901R00140